Griff sighed, longing for the good old days when life had been simple.

He flew, he ate, he slept, and when he had an itch, he scratched it with whatever woman was WA. Willing and Available—a term coined back in flight school, one he hadn't thought of in a while.

Now he did. Was Rose willing and available?

Hell, his life before the crash might not have been perfect, but at least where women were concerned, it had come close.

This thing with Rose Davenport was different. She had a way of making him feel…something like hunger pangs—only, more intense, more focused…

More dangerous.

Some survival instinct encoded on the macho-male chromosome triggered in him, warning him that if he wasn't careful, things with Rose could get *way* out of hand…

Available in August 2003 from Silhouette Special Edition

Tall, Dark and Difficult

PATRICIA COUGHLIN

SILHOUETTE®
SPECIAL EDITION™

*Silhouette, Silhouette Special Edition and Colophon are
registered trademarks of Harlequin Books S.A., used under licence.*

*First published in Great Britain 2003
Silhouette Books, Eton House, 18-24 Paradise Road,
Richmond, Surrey TW9 1SR*

© Patricia Madden Coughlin 2001

ISBN 0 373 24414 2

23-0803

*Printed and bound in Spain
by Litografía Rosés S.A., Barcelona*

PATRICIA COUGHLIN

is a troubling combination of hopeless romantic and dedicated dreamer. Troubling, that is, for anyone hoping to drag her back to the 'real world' when she is in the midst of writing a book. Close family and friends have learned to co-exist peacefully with the latest cast of characters in her head. The author of more than twenty-five novels, she has received special recognition from *Publishers Weekly* and *Romantic Times* magazines. Her work also earned her numerous awards, including the prestigious RITA® Award from Romance Writers of America. Patricia lives in Rhode Island, a place very conducive to daydreaming.

For my parents, Tom and Eileen Madden.
Thanks for always being there.

Chapter One

Summer brought out the best in Wickford, Rhode Island. To be sure, other seasons held their own charms in the pretty little village. But even those die-hard locals who favored winter, when an icy wind blowing off the Atlantic kept tourists at bay, couldn't deny that summer was somehow special.

It was more than simply a season; it was a mood, a scent, an attitude. Wild roses bloomed in the cracks in the sidewalks, time unraveled, and the heat made everything, and everyone, just a little bit looser. It began in late May, around the time the take-out window at Hanley's Ice Cream Parlor opened for the season, and built, steadily and lazily, until peaking just before Labor Day. Then, sometime in mid-September, the inevitable combination of chilly nights and yellow school buses would snap everyone back to their senses.

Well, nearly everyone. There were rumors, legends really, passed down from one generation to the next in the beauty salon and hardware store—and if not everyone who heard believed, almost everyone wanted to.

That's not to say that summer cast a spell over Wickford. Exactly. But facts were facts, and village history held that if an otherwise sensible person was going to swap a thriving medical practice for a fishing boat, or run off with a mysterious and much younger saxophone player, or blow the retirement account on a six-speed, dual-exhaust motorcycle, it would happen on a long, hot day in July.

Watching over all this sun-drenched madness for more years than anyone in the village had been alive, was the grand dame of Wickford, Fairfield House. She was a turn-of-the-century beauty, graceful and charming from her widow's walk to her wraparound porch. From a distance, her pale yellow clapboards seemed to glow against the summer sky and full-leaded windows sparkled like diamonds in the sun.

Sadly, things were not quite so pretty up close. The old lady was showing her age. For two years she had stood empty, and she did not take well to neglect. That was evident in a show of peeling paint and loose balusters, and in the weeds that had taken over the once prizewinning perennial beds.

Inside wasn't much better. A broom, a dust cloth and some elbow grease would help matters, and a decent handyman could restore the oak parquet floor, mottled with dark stains from the time the pipes froze and a radiator valve let go. But it would take something more to bring this particular house back to life.

Outside, it was eighty-five degrees in the shade, but even with the windows open the rooms held a subtle chill that had nothing to do with high ceilings or ocean breezes. It defied logic. As did the feeling of utter and absolute emptiness that clung to the house in spite of a fresh scattering of empty beer bottles and fast-food wrappers, and a trail of dirty clothes. Not even the persistent drone of a television dispelled the air of isolation. It was as if the old house refused to acknowledge the presence of the man who had arrived three days earlier, cleared himself some room in the front parlor, and hardly moved since.

He did occasionally rouse himself to use the bathroom or accept deliveries from Pizza Hut and the liquor store. And once, he made the trip from his chair all the way across the room to the old upright piano to turn a framed photograph so it faced the wall. It was a formal portrait of a handsome young Air Force officer in full dress uniform. His chest was ablaze with medals and his deep blue gaze reflected the unwavering, some might say reckless, brand of self-assurance that was a definite asset in his chosen line of work. Not every man is willing to risk his life in the cockpit of an experimental fighter jet.

It might be his clothes, or the look in his eyes, but a casual observer would never discern that the man in the picture and the man in the parlor were one and the same.

The kindest way to put it would be to say that Major Hollis ''Griff'' Griffin was out of uniform. Way out. Instead of starched linen and polished brass, he was wearing old jeans and an even older T-shirt with faded traces of a tequila logo. He was barefoot and unshaven, and unless someone were handing out medals for bad attitude, he wouldn't be adding to his collection anytime soon. All in all, he looked pretty much like what he was; a man who'd been to hell and back and didn't give a damn about anything. Or anyone.

Least of all himself.

If any of his old friends had happened to walk in and see him at that moment, they would have wasted no time informing the major that what he needed more than the beer in his hand was a haircut and a kick in the butt. However, Griff wasn't expecting company, and if any did show up, he wouldn't let them in. His old friends, like his old life, were thousands of miles away.

From his slouched position in the rocking chair he aimed the remote control, and through a miracle of modern ingenuity froze the image of his late great-aunt Devora on the screen of the massive, state-of-the-art projection television that was the only visible remnant of his home in California. *Former home,* Griff reminded himself, for much the same reason some people can't resist poking at a sore tooth. The hillside condo, located precisely far enough from the airfield for him to drink a medium coffee on his way to work each morning, was gone now, along with everything else that meant anything to him.

Everything but the TV, that is. A man—even a useless, washed-up, broken-down man—had to draw the line somewhere. And so the television—a sleek monument to technology, surrounded by a century's worth of…stuff. And as hopelessly out of place in this godforsaken mausoleum Devora had called home as he was.

"Don't let it get to you, pal," he advised the television, swigging beer as he gazed around the room full of ornate furniture, cluttered tabletops, and overflowing curio cabinets. "Just as soon as we unload all this crap, we'll be moving on."

He'd loved his aunt as much as he'd ever loved anyone, but ever since he'd set foot in this place he'd felt trapped. Which made sense, he reflected without a flicker of amusement. He *was* trapped, and he had sly old Devora to thank.

His gaze wandered from the shelves displaying her collection of egg cups to the tall mahogany breakfront fairly bulging with her wedding china, and her mother's, and her mother's mother's. He'd never bothered to look, but he'd bet there was a set of stone-age bowls with the Fairfield crest tucked away in there somewhere.

His aunt Devora, he had long since concluded, had been certifiable. Sweet, in her own fussy way, but a first-class nutcase nonetheless. What else could account for the fact that she had obviously never, in all her eighty-six years on earth, thrown away so much as a piece of thread or scrap of aluminum foil?

He knew that for a fact, because all of it, nearly a century's worth of string and foil, was crammed into kitchen drawers and wicker baskets and every other nook and cranny in the place. And, just for the record, this three-story, fourteen-room dinosaur had a lot of nooks and crannies.

New England's answer to the catacombs, he thought, mystified that he, who felt as free as the wind in the smallest airplane cockpit, felt so caged in this house. It hadn't always been that way, he mused, recalling a string of long-ago summers, summers he used to wish would never end. Once it had sunk into his eight-year-old head that Devora wasn't nearly as forbidding as she first appeared, they had gotten along just fine. She had taught him to dig for clams and catch fireflies and make ice cream. And on rainy afternoons she turned him loose in her trunk-filled attic, where he would try on several wars' worth of old military uniforms that Devora had saved along with everything else, and pretend he was—

Griff abruptly halted the thought. It, like so many others, led to that large chunk of memory he had shut down and marked permanently off-limits.

Frowning, he returned his attention to the present and his aunt's larger-than-life smile on the screen before him. He still considered it the height of irony that a woman so firmly ensconced in a bygone era that she insisted upon hand-embroidered linen napkins and hand-cranked ice cream, had seen fit to videotape her last will and testament.

He had first viewed the tape in her attorney's office nearly two years ago and had promptly dismissed it with an amused laugh. Good old Aunt Devora, he'd thought, eccentric right to the end. He'd been riding high two years ago and had neither the time nor the inclination to think about his inheritance and the bizarre strings attached.

He wasn't laughing now.

Jaw rigid, eyes narrowed, he jabbed the play button to hear it one more time.

"And so, my dear Hollis," said Aunt Devora, "there you have it. My final request. I am certain you will not fail me, dear boy."

"Perish the thought," he muttered as the tape faded to

black. God forbid he fail at the senseless, totally absurd, utterly *Devora* task that she had set for him. It was still hard for him to believe it was even legal, but all five attorneys he'd consulted had assured him it was.

With the exception of modest bequests to her church and several friends, Devora had left her entire estate to him, with a single caveat. Among the many useless things she'd collected during her lifetime, she most prized the glass birds displayed in a locked curio cabinet in the parlor. Her will explained that it had been her intent to complete the collection and donate it to the state Audubon Society. And now her wish was for him to do it on her behalf.

Strike that. *Wish* was not exactly accurate. It was more like a command, quite literally from on high. And until he accomplished the mission, he was not permitted to sell the house or anything in it.

For a long time after he'd been informed of the conditions, he'd simply put the matter from his mind and hoped that a hurricane swept the place out to sea before he was forced to deal with it. He might have felt differently if he had needed the money, but he hadn't. One thing you could say was that Uncle Sam took care of his own. As long as Griff didn't develop a taste for high-stakes gambling or designer suits, he'd get by just fine. Not that it could hurt to have a nice chunk set aside for security, he thought, his mood turning grimly philosophical. After all, you never knew when life might decide to drop yet another grenade in your lap.

Twists of fate aside, in the end his decision to sell was practical rather than mercenary. As the attorney for Devora's estate had repeatedly pointed out, any vacant property was a liability. An older house of this size, on the waterfront, in an area swarming with kids and tourists, was a lawsuit waiting to happen. And that was a hassle he didn't need.

Selling was the only logical option, he told himself, doing his best to ignore the hot, guilty feeling that kicked up whenever he thought of Devora's reaction to strangers living in her beloved "cottage." Fairfield House had been built by her grandfather, and she had been batty about the place, referring to it as if it were a member of the family. A living, breathing member.

If ignoring the guilt didn't work, he would remind himself just how wily and determined his aunt could be, and how in all likelihood this whole final request business was nothing but a clever posthumous scam to trap him here forever. That thought never failed to snap him back to his senses.

His decision was made. The house had to go. It was just a question of how quickly he could unload it.

Griff reached for his beer, realized he'd finished it, and pondered whether it was worth the effort of hauling himself to the kitchen for another.

Damn Devora, he thought. As if his life wasn't complicated enough these days without this stupid wild-goose chase of hers hanging over his head. He didn't even know where to begin, and she sure hadn't left any clues. At least, not any clues worth a damn. What she'd left was a name: Rose Davenport. Apparently some old friend of hers who might be able to help him. That's assuming the woman was still alive, he thought irritably.

He was fully prepared to loathe Miss Rose Davenport on sight. Her name said it all. *Rose.* What kind of person was named Rose? Griff pictured prissy white gloves and a high lace collar cinched with a hideous brooch like the ones arranged in velvet-lined boxes on Devora's dressing table. It had been one thing to humor Devora. She was blood. And she had given him something solid to hold on to when he needed it badly. However, just the thought of having to sip tea and make conversation with some other eccentric old lady threatened to send him into an even blacker mood than he was already in.

Nonetheless, first thing in the morning, that was what he was going to do. He had no choice. He would visit the old biddy and find out what she knew. And he would be polite. But he'd be damned if he would shave for the occasion. Or dress up. And he definitely would not sip tea out of some stupid cup with a handle too small for his fingers. Not unless it was absolutely the only way to get her to talk.

Suddenly another beer seemed well worth the trouble of maneuvering to his feet. Griff muttered under his breath as he did so. "Brace yourself, Miss Rose Davenport. I've got a hunch you aren't going to like me any better than I'm going to like you."

Rose secured the last of the dried flowers in place and stepped back to view her creation from a better perspective.

She stood with hands on slim hips, head tilted so that her hair tumbled over one bare shoulder. It was hair the color of honey and old gold, thick, and just wavy enough to be a challenge. To gain an edge, and save some time on humid summer mornings, she opted for long layers in back and slightly shorter ones in front and then hoped for the best. It was not the sleek, retro look of the moment, but it had been a while since Rose worried about fashion trends. The casual cut suited both her heart-shaped face and her approach to beauty rituals, which amounted to doing as little as possible.

She would rather fuss with flowers than her hair any day, and as she ran a discerning eye over the nine-foot length of garland on her worktable, she was pleased to see she had achieved exactly what her artist's soul had envisioned; a delicate watercolor blend of the hydrangeas' faded blue and lavender tones, enhanced, but never overpowered, by the deeper violet of the imported, twelve-dollars-and-fifty-cents-a-yard French silk ribbon.

"Magnificent," she pronounced, kissing her fingertips to the air.

But then, she had known it would be from the moment she dived into the Dumpster behind the Wickford Country Club to retrieve the discarded hydrangeas. Her life was nothing if not proof positive of one of the most elemental laws of nature. Human nature, anyway. Namely, that one man's, or woman's, trash is another's treasure. The jettisoned floral arrangements were simply the latest in the long line of rescued castoffs from which she made her living. And a comfortable living at that, she thought, gazing with satisfaction around the five-year-old shop that had been a thirtieth birthday present to herself, and which she had appropriately christened Second Hand Rose.

She loved her work, and even as she'd climbed from the Dumpster and loaded the hydrangeas into the back of her pickup she had been tingling with anticipation, her thoughts spinning with possibilities. Of course, nothing, especially art, is ever really free. After hauling the flowers home, she spent hours cleaning globs of gravy off the petals with Q-Tips and trimming them with manicure scissors. Then for weeks she'd sidestepped through her small cottage, weaving a path around the bunches of fragile blooms hanging everywhere to dry. It was all worth it however, for this one blissful moment of creative triumph.

Perhaps, she mused, the swag itself was not quite worth the astronomical price tag she was affixing to it, but then, that was the point. She regularly overpriced items she couldn't bear to part with right away. Eventually, when she was ready to let go, the piece would be given a steep markdown and find a new home with some lucky customer who appreciated both beauty and a great bargain. Everyone came out a winner, and in Rose's mulishly optimistic view of things, that's the way the whole world ought to work.

All that remained now was to hang the garland in a carelessly romantic swoop above the wide arch separating the two rooms of her shop. No easy feat, considering her aversion to heights.

Luckily, she had one thing going for her that other altophobics might not; an uncompromising case of LETCS. That was her own acronym for Little Engine That Could Syndrome. Given the right motivation, there was nothing she could not accomplish if she put her mind to it, or so she told herself on a daily basis. So far, it was working pretty well, and as she went to fetch the stepladder, a determined refrain of "I think I can, I think I can" was already organizing itself inside her head.

The sound of the bell over the entrance put her plan on hold, drawing her to the front of the shop, as a tall man dressed in jeans and a black T-shirt entered. Rose didn't recognize him, but she sure recognized the breed, and for no better reason than gut instinct, her stomach muscles knotted.

Bright August sunlight pouring through the shop's lace-clad front windows illuminated the man's many defects, and Rose wasted no time taking a complete inventory. His posture was too straight, his shoulders too broad, and his jaw too square. His entire facial structure had the sort of raw, chiseled quality that, when combined with leather and horse-flesh, had been selling cigarettes for generations. Every sharp angle and crease made it plain that the man was a force to be reckoned with, and he damn well knew it. Even the dark stubble on his chin was too blatantly, alarmingly masculine for her liking.

As a rule, Rose wasn't given to snap judgments, or forming impressions based on appearance alone. But there were always exceptions. One look was enough to convince her that the man before her was historically and irreparably flawed, descended from generations of those similarly afflicted, born of a renegade breed. A modern link in a long and all-too-resilient chain of men who conquered nations and broke hearts with equal aplomb.

A winner. A taker. A user.

Chapter Two

All right. So maybe she was a wee bit sensitive—perhaps one might even say a tad irrational—when it came to a certain type of male. The assertive, self-assured, gorgeous-enough-to-arouse-mud type. Which this man definitely was. Even the back of his neck was sexy, she noted when he briefly turned his head. She hated that in a man.

Deranged. That was the word her best friend, Maryann McShane, used to describe Rose's attitude. As the happily married mother of a beautiful six-month-old daughter, Maryann considered it her duty to maneuver Rose into the same blissful state. She was forever finding another "perfectly nice man" for Rose, and Rose was forever refusing to cooperate. Having been married to one driven and demanding man for five years, she figured she had earned the right to be a little deranged on the subject.

She might not have the whole Mars-Venus thing figured out, but she had learned to steer clear of a certain sort of man. The sort who didn't know enough to take off his silly sunglasses when he stepped indoors. Not that it was a chronic problem—men who wore mirrored aviator shades usually only ventured into her shop when led on the invisible leash that some silicone-laden blonde had attached to his libido. Since there was nary a breast implant in sight, she couldn't help wondering what Mr. Mirrors wanted.

As if reading her mind, or her disapproving smirk, he removed the sunglasses and hooked them into the neck of his T-shirt. Rose quickly underscored *too damn handsome* on his growing list of faults, and cursed herself for responding to the genetically programmed urge to suck in her stomach and wonder if she had remembered to put on lipstick.

Not that it mattered. He slid his gaze over her too quickly to notice she *had* lips. Clearly, he found her about as fascinating as the rack of vintage beaded purses by her side. Maybe less so.

For Rose, his utter lack of interest came not as an insult—nor as a surprise, for that matter—but as a relief. She'd have liked to save time by informing him straight off that even though the word *antiques* appeared on the sign out front, she did not deal in rusty bayonets, Civil War memorabilia or vintage auto parts.

She settled for "Good morning," causing his gaze to settle on her directly for the first time.

"Morning," he replied.

"May I help you with something, or are you just browsing?"

The standard query caused one corner of his mouth to quirk. It was a very nice mouth, she noted, adding it to the list.

"Browsing?" His cool gaze took in the shelves of sparkling Depression-era glass, baskets overflowing with freshly laundered vintage linens and, occupying center stage, her current *pièce de résistance,* an old white iron bed, dressed in a faded quilt and generations of loving wear and tear.

"Hardly," he muttered, with a blend of smug superiority and barely concealed disdain.

Obviously, in spite of his attire, this was no common, garden-variety Neanderthal she was dealing with. This was the King of the Heap, Leader of the Pack, the infamous Number One Combo. She knew the type well. Arrogant *and* tactless, and, unless she missed her guess, served with a side order of cynicism. There was only one way to deal with a Number One. Ignore him.

"I'm here to see the proprietor," he announced, before she had the chance. "Miss Rose Davenport."

The way her name rolled off his tongue was the verbal equivalent of the look he'd just given her shop. Rose folded her arms and her chin came up.

"I'm Rose Davenport."

That earned her a closer look—and a frown, something that seemed to come to him quite naturally. And fairly regularly, judging from the pattern of lines around his mouth. The man definitely needed to lighten up.

"Do you have a mother, or maybe a grandmother, by that name?"

"Afraid not. It's me or nothing."

His eyes, a deep and distracting shade of blue, narrowed with impatience.

"I'm looking for the Rose Davenport who was friends with Devora Fairfield," he told her emphatically, as if he could get her to produce another Rose Davenport through sheer force of will. She'd wager the technique worked for him more often than not.

"I heard you the first time, and the answer is the same. If you're looking for Rose Davenport, I'm it."

He eyed her suspiciously. "You were friends with Devora?"

"I sure was. Did you know Devora?"

"She was my aunt," he replied. "Great-aunt, actually."

It was her turn to take a closer look at him. The height...the jaw... Of course. "You're Hollis."

"Griffin," he countered with obvious irritation. "Just

'Griff' will do. Devora was the only one I allowed to call me Hollis.''

"Allowed?" Rose couldn't help arching her tawny brows as she struggled to reconcile the man before her with the spit-and-polished military officer she had encountered only once before, briefly and nearly two years ago.

He shrugged. "Figuratively speaking, that is."

It was a rather terse acknowledgment of the fact that no one had ever "allowed" Devora Fairfield to do anything. The spirited spinster, whom Rose had been honored to call her friend, had invariably done and said precisely as she deemed right and proper and damn well pleased. Rose couldn't decide if it was annoyance or grudging affection that hovered in Hollis Griffin's voice when he spoke of his aunt, and it really didn't matter.

It had been no secret that Devora loved her nephew as if he were a child of her body and not simply her heart, and that was good enough for Rose. She immediately erased the mental list she'd been compiling. For Devora's sake alone, she was prepared to befriend Hollis Griffin in the manner that came most naturally to her—utterly and enthusiastically.

"Okay, 'Griff' it is." Smiling warmly, she stepped closer to offer her right hand, and for the first time noticed the cane in his.

"You probably don't remember me," she went on, concealing her surprise. "We met at Devora's funeral service."

"I'm sorry, I don't remember." He slipped the cane under his arm with an ease that suggested he'd had it a while, and shook her hand.

"That's all right, I didn't recognize you, either, without your uniform."

That seemed to irk him as much as being called Hollis had.

"I'm retired from the Air Force," he explained curtly.

"I see," said Rose, though she didn't.

Devora always sent her nephew a "care package" of goodies on his birthday, and Rose recalled that he was almost exactly five years older than she was, which would make him a few months shy of forty. A bit young for retirement. Especially since, according to his aunt, the man lived to fly; the more high risk the mission, the better. Devora worried about the danger inherent in his work, but she had also sung his praises at every opportunity. Rose's understanding was that Griffin wasn't merely a pilot, but an aviation junkie, as skilled working on a jet's engine as he was at its controls. She added his early retirement to the cane and came up with a half-dozen questions she was smart enough not to ask.

"It would be a wonder if you remember anyone you met that day," she continued in an instinctive attempt to put him at ease. "All of Wickford was there, plus Devora's old friends from as far away as Florida. I hope you know how beloved your aunt was around here, and how very much she is missed."

Especially by me, thought Rose with the same twinge of wistfulness that always accompanied thoughts of the woman who had understood her better than her own family ever had.

"Devora certainly had her good points," he agreed. This time there was no mistaking the affection in his tone, or the look of impatience that quickly followed as he added, "And her quirks."

"Ah, but the quirks were the best thing about Devora," she countered with a chuckle. "Who else do you know who kept a working butter churn in the kitchen?"

"Who, indeed?"

"I'll never forget the first time she invited me for tea. I walked into that beautiful house and felt…" Swept up in the memory, she searched for words to fully capture and share it. "Like…oh, like Alice stepping through the looking glass."

"I can understand that," he countered. "The Mad Hatter would feel right at home there."

"So did I. No, that's wrong. *Home* is too ordinary a word. It was more like wonderland, each room more full of treasure than the last."

"And you like all that ju—treasure?" he enquired in a cautious tone.

"Like it?" She sighed. "I love it. And the furniture…don't get me started."

"Didn't plan to."

"That yellow brocade settee in the hall," she continued, her expression dreamy.

"The low one with the spiky arms? Have you ever tried actually sitting on that thing?"

"Once," she told him, grinning. "I felt like a princess. But my absolute favorite piece is the hand-carved cherrywood cabinet in the sitting room…the one with all the Bavarian china and the ivory figurines. The first time I saw it, I just stared in absolute, dumbstruck wonder."

He nodded. "I've stared that way at a lot of Devora's stuff."

"She had an amazing eye. Did you know the glass sides of that cabinet are a *J*-curve?"

"I had no idea. Is that good?"

"Good and bad. Good because it's so rare and because it's refractive quality is so much greater than a standard curve. Bad because it's so rare and costs a fortune to replace should it be broken."

"Sort of like 'damned if you do, damned if you don't.' Which is something I definitely understand."

"I'm glad."

"You are?"

"Very. When we found out that Devora had left the house to her 'hotshot nephew from California,' as you were sometimes referred to, some folks around here, including me," she confessed with a rueful smile, "were worried you would sell to an outside developer. Do you have any idea how much a house that size, with that much water frontage and a view that would make a sailor weep, is worth on today's market?"

"Some," he murmured.

"What am I saying? Of course you know what it's worth. But much more important, you obviously understand that the true value of a person's home cannot be measured in dollars and cents. Otherwise, you wouldn't have kept it in the family, and Wickford would have one more commercial enterprise to contend with.''

"Pardon me for saying so, but isn't this a commercial enterprise?'' He indicated the shop.

"I suppose it is, if you want to get technical. I prefer to think of it as a labor of love.'' She grinned unabashedly. "Besides, as a New Englander born and bred, I have a geographical obligation to be cantankerous and irrational when it comes to outsiders.''

"Let me guess,'' he said dryly. *"outsiders* would be anyone whose local roots don't stretch back for at least three generations?''

"Exactly. But since your roots are impeccable, things couldn't have worked out better.'' A sudden thought caused her mouth to pucker. "You are planning to live in the house, aren't you? I mean, that is why you're here?''

Those dangerously blue eyes met hers, and Rose got the distinct impression that Hollis Griffin didn't like being asked personal questions. Not that the question struck her as overly personal—but then, she warmed up to strangers quickly enough to turn a chance encounter in a dentist's waiting room into a lifelong friendship. She had a hunch that Griff took a while longer to thaw.

"My long-range plans aren't firm yet,'' he said finally, "but I sold my condo in California and last week I moved everything I own into Devora's place.''

"Last week?'' she echoed, surprised. "I never even noticed.''

"No reason you should have. It wasn't much of a move. Just a couple of suitcases and a TV.'' He shrugged. "I got rid of everything else.''

"That's great,'' she told him.

He gave her a puzzled look. "It is?''

"Sure. There's nothing as exciting as a completely fresh start—new town, new neighbors… Speaking of which, I live in that little cottage just beyond your yard. Weathered gray shingles, white shutters.''

''Pink door?''

''Actually, the color is Sun-Kissed Rose—but yes, that's me. At this time of year the trees and shrubbery provide a buffer, but come fall we'll have a clear view of each other.''

He said nothing.

''Apparently no one else noticed your arrival, either, or the news would have spread like wildfire. You know what they say about small towns.''

''Yes, unfortunately. I tend to keep to myself.''

''You can try, but be warned, Fairfield House is as much a local treasure as Devora was. Folks are bound to be curious about its new owner.'' Her smile was meant to be reassuring. ''Look on the bright side—we're nosy but friendly. If there's anything I can do to help you get settled, just give a shout. I know nearly everyone in Wickford, along with their hidden talents and who has what available to rent or borrow. Whatever you might need—butcher, baker, candlesticks and caviar for twelve,'' she said, ticking the items off on her fingers, ''or just someone to haul away trash—I can hook you up.''

He gave a faint, undecipherable smile. ''Why doesn't that surprise me?''

''Probably because you've seen me in action,'' she countered with the ease of a woman who has taken a good hard look at herself and decided to play the hand she was dealt rather than waste time trying to turn three of a kind into a royal flush. ''After all, I've been standing here talking your ear off without giving you a chance to tell me why you were looking for me in the first place.''

Her expectant silence was met with another of those cool, shuttered stares.

''I…'' He hesitated. ''My aunt mentioned you once, and I thought that as long as I was back in town, it would be…uh, interesting to look up some of her old friends and say hello.''

He was lonely, she realized. Lonely and looking for some

way to connect through the only person he had known in town, Devora. Rose's heart went out to him as if he were a stray kitten, huddled on her doorstep in the middle of a storm. If she could have picked him up in her arms and cuddled him, she would have. However, since practically speaking he resembled a tomcat more than a kitten, she quelled the impulse and instead offered him her brightest, most encouraging smile.

"How sweet of you."

He blushed, which struck her as sweeter still.

"I'm very glad you dropped in," she told him. Then, with laughter in her voice, she added, "Though from your initial reaction, I suspect I wasn't quite the sort of 'old' friend of Devora's you expected to find."

"No," he agreed. "You've been just one surprise after another, Miss Davenport."

"Rose."

"Rose."

"I know what I'm going to do," she said suddenly.

"What?" He looked vaguely uneasy.

"I'm going to throw a party in honor of your arrival."

Now he *really* looked uneasy. Shy, thought Rose, surprised a second time. Shyness didn't fit with his outward appearance. Or with her first impression of him, she realized, ashamed of herself. Maryann was right. She was so gun-shy around certain men that she never gave them a chance. She would work on it, she decided, and she would begin by making up for her rush to judgment by heralding Hollis Griffin's move to town in style.

"A party is…out of the question," he said.

"Nonsense, it's the least I can do for Devora's favorite nephew."

"I was her only nephew."

"All the more reason to make you feel welcome."

"I don't want you to go to any trouble on my account."

"It's no trouble," she assured him. "You're actually doing me a favor by providing me with an excuse to throw a party between the Fourth of July and Labor Day, a period with a notable dearth of occasions to celebrate.''

''I am not an occasion.''

''Of course not, but your arrival in Wickford is. It's also all the excuse I need. Ask anyone—I am a party planner extraordinaire.''

''I'm sure you are. But as luck would have it, I am a lousy guest of honor.''

''Let me worry about that,'' she ordered, thinking he was probably right. For all his professional skills and accomplishments, he was not very good at making friends. Not if his guarded, taciturn demeanor with her was any indication. No wonder he tended to ''keep to himself,'' as he put it. Well, Devora wouldn't have let that happen, and neither would Rose.

She folded her arms and grinned at him. ''It's settled. We'll work out the details later,'' she added as she caught sight of the delivery truck pulling up outside. ''Right now, you'll have to excuse me.''

She moved toward the door.

''No.''

The adamancy in his tone caused Rose to glance over her shoulder as she opened the door.

He smiled stiffly. ''That is, if you don't mind, I think I'll hang around and—'' He cleared his throat. ''Browse a little, after all.''

''Fine. Good morning, Charlie,'' she said to the deliveryman, whose uniform of brown shirt and shorts revealed a pair of great masculine legs. Charlie was young and adorable. Too young and adorable to be seriously interesting to a grown woman, but he had great legs just the same. Rose shipped and received packages daily, and the mild flirtation that enlivened her dealings with Charlie had more to do with keeping skills sharp than real attraction on either side.

''Am I ever glad to see you,'' she said, eyeing his push cart loaded with boxes.

''Me? Or my boxes of chintz?''

"*My* boxes of chintz," she corrected, trailing along like an overeager puppy in her attempt to read the return address labels as he moved past her. "Is it really? Are you sure?"

"Yep." He parked the cart and began lifting the boxes onto the counter for her. "Unless you're expecting another delivery from…" He squinted at the return address. "Biddley-on-Kenn. Hell, no wonder they call it Merry Olde England—they all live in circus towns."

She gave a small whoop of excitement. "It *is* my chintz. Charlie, you're wonderful."

"You don't know *how* wonderful. The schedule had me coming by here late this afternoon, but I switched my entire route around for you."

"Can I help it if I'm irresistible?"

"Actually, I figured since you've been harassing me about this stuff daily—"

"I have not harassed you," she admonished, her fingers itching to tear open the boxes and get at the fine bone china that a British dealer had sworn on the *Magna Carta* would be there three weeks ago. Some pieces were earmarked for specific customers; others were for the shop; a precious two were destined for her personal collection.

"You don't call chasing my truck down the street 'harassment'?"

"Charlie, you *wish* I'd chase you," she retorted absently.

The deliveryman grinned. "You bet I do. I wouldn't be hard to catch, I promise you that, Rosie."

Jerk, thought Griff, surreptitiously monitoring the interplay.

Rose Davenport had thrown him a curve at first, but the longer he spent in her presence, the easier it was to understand why, in spite of the vast difference in age, she and Devora had hit it off. As Devora might have put it, "Water seeks its own level." Beneath those smoldering green eyes and that just-begging-to-be-kissed mouth of hers, Rose Davenport definitely harbored the same streak of insanity that had afflicted his great-aunt.

A flaky, clutter-collecting, overly friendly junk addict if he'd ever seen one. Her shop might not be quite as over-stuffed and smothering as Devora's place, but she hadn't been at it as long. Give her time, and she'd give Devora some real competition.

Peering at the shopkeeper over a vase the color of moldy roses, he tried to imagine her thirty years older, wearing white gloves and a blouse buttoned high at the neck, instead of that pale yellow dress that hung nearly to her ankles. By all rights the dress should have made her appear dowdy, and concealed the fact that she had a slim waist, perfectly rounded hips and very nice, very long legs. It didn't. Taking advantage of her preoccupation with the delivery guy, Griff gave the dress his complete attention and decided it was because of the way the material molded itself to her body. Every distracting inch of it.

A sundress. He was no expert on women's clothing, but he'd removed enough of it over the years to learn the basics, and he was pretty sure that was the name for what she was wearing. Whatever it was called, it was screwing up his attempt to picture Rose Davenport with a brooch at her throat.

The woman had a sexy throat. He'd give her that much. Her shoulders weren't bad, either. Smooth and suntanned, and the crisscrossed straps of her dress presented a clear-cut invitation for a man to slide his fingers underneath and slowly, slowly peel them down. An invitation he'd bet wasn't lost on the deliveryman with the salivating grin any more than it was lost on Griff.

His head ached, his leg was throbbing, and being trapped with so much old stuff was making him feel weird. *Light-headed,* he thought furiously. It was the dust, he told himself, refusing to be dizzy. The fact that he didn't actually see any dust was inconsequential. Everyone knew antiques attracted dust. Salt and pepper, pretzels and beer, antiques and dust. Just one more reason he didn't want to be here, looking at shelf after shelf of useless junk when he didn't even know what the hell he was looking for.

Liar. He knew exactly what he had come looking for, exactly what it was he wanted from Rose Davenport. He wanted her help. The problem was asking for it. He was no good at asking for help. In fact, he flat out hated it. Almost as much as he hated *needing* it in the first place. Being *needy* was even worse.

And he ought to know. In the past year he'd been forced to accept more help from more people than most men do in a lifetime. Doctors. Physical therapists. Even neighbors. And shrinks, don't forget the shrinks. Without their ''help,'' he wouldn't have done such a bang-up job of adapting and adjusting and accepting the fact that life as he knew it was over. *Kaput.* Finished. And the fact that his old life was the only life he had any interest in living? Why, that was just one of those inconvenient, lingering, post-accident *stages* that they insisted he would emerge from. One of these days.

But not today.

Today, this moment, it all added up to one thing; a burning urge to toss the chatty deliveryman out on his behind and get on with it. The other guy might be younger and fitter and faster, but Griff could feel a bigger chip on his shoulder and had been spoiling for a fight longer. That gave him the edge. The only thing holding him back from wiping the grin off Charlie's face was the look on Rose's. Pure ecstasy.

The way her eyes had lit up the second she saw the truck, you'd have thought it was Ed McMahon walking in with the grand prize check in his hand. Griff might not appreciate the appeal of a package jockey in shorts, but clearly Rose did— and he wasn't about to risk ticking her off.

On the contrary, he was going to say and do whatever was necessary to stay in her good graces, until he found out what he needed to know. For starters, that meant keeping his thoughts about almost everything, especially his plans for the house, to himself. It also precluded telling her outright that throwing a party for him was a waste of time since he wouldn't be hanging around long enough to make friends.

And above all, it meant not slipping up and referring to her junk *as* junk.

With that in mind, Griff picked up a battered metal watering can and tried to look fascinated.

The Jerk held out his clipboard. "Care to sign your life away?" he asked Rose in a tone that made it clear it wasn't only her signature he was after.

"For you, Charlie?" She smiled as she scrawled her name. "Anytime. And thanks. I owe you."

"Now we're getting somewhere." He executed a tight circle with the cart and winked at her. "See you tomorrow, Rose. Enjoy your new chintz teapot."

"I plan to…and if you're real good maybe I'll invite you to tea sometime."

Griff managed not to snort.

"I'm at your disposal," said Charlie.

"Don't you mean 'mercy'?"

"That, too," he called over his shoulder, laughing.

"'Bye, Charlie."

Rose carefully slit the tape on the first box and began unpacking the contents. In her excitement, she almost forgot she wasn't alone in the shop. Almost. It was impossible for a woman to actually forget the presence of a man like Griffin. As she carefully unwrapped each piece, checked it off on her order sheet and inspected it for damage, she also tracked his movement around the shop, curious as to what he might find of interest.

Not much, judging from his indifferent expression. She, on the other hand, was just bursting with interest. She wasn't sure how a man using a cane managed to project such an air of invincibility, but somehow Griff succeeded. She had a hunch that it had something to do with world-class shoulders and the way his wash-softened jeans fit his thighs, but she didn't want to dwell on it. His posture didn't hurt, either, she decided. She had never realized it until now, but there was a lot to be said for a man with great posture.

He paused to look at some old wooden bookends with

woodpecker carvings, and he actually picked up one of a pair of ceramic hummingbirds and glanced at the bottom.

Finally, he came to stand across the counter from her, the purposeful glint in his eye a bit unnerving in spite of his reassuring connection to Devora.

"Look…" he began.

Rose flashed him a smile. "Find anything you can't live without?"

"Not quite." The words were hardly out when his forehead creased, intensifying his grim expression. "That is, except for…" His gaze raked across the counter—now covered with plates and teacups named for the brightly flowered fabric that had inspired them—and landed on the hydrangea garland. Looking vaguely relieved, he reached for it. "This—"

Rose was aghast. "That?"

"Right." He glanced at the price tag without flinching, and reached for his wallet.

"Are you sure?" she asked.

"Very sure."

"You don't think it's a bit…pricey?"

"Not at all. It's a bargain, in fact, and exactly what I had in mind."

"For what?"

He looked up from the stack of bills he was thumbing through. "I beg your pardon?"

"I was wondering what you had a nine-foot-long garland of dried hydrangea in mind for? What do you plan to do with it?" she added, when he stared at her in what looked like bewilderment.

"Do?" He looked at the garland with a blank expression.

Please change your mind, Rose pleaded silently.

"I thought I would use it…on the porch."

"The porch?" she gasped, horrified. "Aren't you afraid the dampness will ruin it?"

"Good point."

"I have a wicker plant stand that would be perfect on

Devora's porch," she told him. "Maybe with a gorgeous Boston fern? Ferns love humidity."

He shook his head.

"Geraniums?"

"I'm not much for plants. This thing is fine. I'll figure out what to do with it once I get it home."

"I see." She grabbed a stack of pastel tissue and began wrapping it, doing her best not to look perturbed. As he had pointed out, this *was* a place of business. How was he to know that just because a "thing" had a price tag did not mean it was actually ready to be sold?

With the garland lovingly wrapped and gently arranged in a shopping bag, she wrote out a receipt and calculated the sales tax.

"That will be two hundred and sixty-seven dollars and fifty cents," she said to him.

The creases suddenly reappeared on his forehead, but if he was having second thoughts, he didn't say so. With the same ease he'd shown in handling the cane, he tucked the cash away and produced a credit card. "This okay?"

"Sure."

The transaction complete, Rose handed him the bag, resisting the urge to tell him to take good care of it.

"I'll be in touch," she said. "About your party," she added when he gave her a puzzled look.

"Oh. Well, we'll talk about that. In the meantime, there is something else I'd like to ask you."

A date? Rose braced herself, not sure how she felt about that. It was one thing to be neighborly, another thing entirely to risk thinking of him as anything other than Devora's nephew.

"Shoot," she invited.

"Devora collected some kind of birds. Glass birds, I think, but I'm not quite—"

He broke off, his expression visibly relieved, when she started to nod.

So he wasn't going to ask her out, thought Rose, telling herself she wasn't disappointed.

"Devora collected works by Boris Aureolis, specifically his first nature series. They're not glass, though I can see how you might think so. They have such a wonderful clarity. They're actually hard-paste porcelain from the mid-eighteenth century. Aureolis started out as a colorist for Meissen, but ended up a major creative force. He worked with an alchemist to develop the special glaze that distinguishes his work."

"That's fascinating," he said, looking anything but fascinated. "Do you happen to have any in stock?"

He scowled when she laughed and shook her head.

"Heavens, no. Aureolis is too rich for my blood."

He gave a small grunt. "Really? Just how rich are we talking?"

She nibbled her bottom lip thoughtfully. "I'm no authority, you understand, but they do turn up at auction once in a while, and I was always keeping an eye open for Devora. If I remember correctly, she was missing only four of the series of twenty-five."

"Three."

"Three?" She nodded. "That's right. She snagged the falcon from The Snooty Fox in Burlington."

"Did she mention what she paid?"

"Probably, but my head is always so full of prices, it's hard to remember exactly." She fiddled absently with the sliver of a gold moon that hung on a slender chain around her neck, stopping when she noticed his attention lingering there. Again. "It seems to me it was in the neighborhood of four...maybe high threes."

"Hundred?"

"Thousand."

"Figures," he muttered, then added, "Devora always did have expensive taste."

"Are you thinking of selling the collection?"

"Actually, I'm looking to complete it."

Rose's heart melted a little around the edges. "What a sweet, thoughtful thing to do. Oh, Devora would be so pleased."

"Trust me, it's not thoughtful. It's not even my idea," he insisted, looking uncomfortable with the approval she was beaming his way. "It's what Devora wanted. Her last request, you might say. She wants the completed collection donated to the Audubon Society."

"She always talked about doing that someday. It was her dream. And it's also something a lot of people wouldn't understand, or else would simply write off as the crazy whim of an old lady. No wonder she adored you."

He looked horrified by her praise. "You've got it all wrong. I don't understand anything. I certainly don't understand why anyone would spend their time and money chasing after some old glass...excuse me, *porcelain* birds, just to give them away. I think it's the single wackiest, most senseless thing I ever heard of."

"Maybe so," she allowed with an easy smile. "And yet you're willing to do it, anyway. Sorry, Griffin, that makes you some kind of hero in my book."

"I am not willing," he snapped.

"Then why are you here?"

"Because..." He stopped and clenched his teeth. "Because I have no damn choice."

"I understand...really. And believe me, that kind of devotion is rare." Her smile gentled as she reached out and patted the hand with which he was gripping the cane. "Sometimes it takes a personal setback to make us more sensitive to the hearts of others."

"Sensitive?" His tone was edgy, and a flush darkened his lean face. She could feel the tension in his hand and drew hers back.

"Is that what you think I am?" he demanded, growling now. "Sensitive?"

Oh, yes, most definitely a growl. You'd have thought she'd called him a sissy. Of course, in *his* testosterone-pickled view of reality, she just may have. It was silly, really, when all she had been trying to do was build on the one thing they had in common—a love for Devora. And why? To ease *his* damn loneliness, that's why. After all, it wasn't as if she was the one out hunting for friends. Well, she'd done her part...*and* after he'd had the gall to refer to her garland as this *thing*.

Standing in the pinpoint of his fierce glare, her initial impression of him returned. Conventional wisdom was wrong, she thought. Sometimes you really could judge a book by its cover. She'd have let loose and told him what she really thought of him—but why go out of her way to cheer him up?

She shrugged. "Look, Griffin, I didn't mean—"

He cut her off. "Good. Because if there is one thing I am not, and never will be, it's sensitive. Got it?"

"With a vengeance," she shot back.

"Good."

That said, he clamped the bag containing her fragile masterpiece under his arm and stalked out.

Chapter Three

Two hundred and sixty-seven dollars. And fifty cents.

Griff couldn't decide who was crazier, Rose Davenport for thinking anyone would pay that kind of money for a string of dead flowers, or him for paying it.

Him, he realized with disgust. No doubt about it. She, on the other hand, deserved the P. T. Barnum award for taking him.

He made his way down Main Street, oblivious to the tourists and the historic houses built shoulder to shoulder along brick sidewalks made uneven by time and weather and gnarled tree roots. He was preoccupied with trying to figure out how it had happened. He'd walked into the shop prepared to deal with a sweet and slightly sappy little old lady, and had emerged with his pocket picked. Not to mention his dented pride and the exasperating fact that he was not one damn step closer to doing what he had gone there to do.

Hell, if he'd felt compelled to buy something, why couldn't he have grabbed that beat-up watering can, which now seemed a downright bargain at fifty bucks? Because he hadn't been thinking, that's why. At least, not about what he should have been thinking about. Instead, he'd been checking out the way that gold moon necklace looked against Rose Davenport's skin—skin that was pink and gold and almost luminescent.

And right smack in the middle of that foolishness, it had suddenly occurred to him that he probably ought to buy something. Anything. Sort of as an act of good faith, and to avoid being under obligation to her. Give and get, that was his philosophy. He'd looked around at what was closest to him, and it had come down to the teapot with the violets or the dead flowers. He hated to think what the teapot would have set him back.

Pausing at the corner for traffic to pass, he opened the bag and peered inside. Maybe there was something special about these particular dead flowers that made them more valuable than they appeared. Something he'd missed at first glance. He poked at the tissue paper and shifted the contents around a little, but as far as he could tell there was nothing about the…what had she called the thing? *Garland.* Nothing about this particular garland that ought to make it worth more than two hundred and sixty bucks. Plus tax. Hell, he'd thought it was overpriced when he misread the tag as twenty-five dollars.

The only thing preventing him from tossing it in the nearest trash can was the scent that had wafted up and curled around him when he opened the bag. It was the same scent that filled Rose's shop. The scent of roses. And cinnamon. And wind. All mixed together. At least, that's what it smelled like to him. And to his surprise, he didn't half mind it.

Maybe it wasn't a total loss, after all. He could always hang the damn thing in the can.

He stopped at the library on his way home and wasted several hours at a table strewn with open encyclopedias and books on every aspect of antiques and collectibles. He learned more than anyone should be forced to know about

Meissen, and Boris Aureolis's groundbreaking innovations in porcelain, and birds native to Northern Europe. He finally gave up and went home, tired, grouchy, and still dragging the ball and chain Devora had attached to his life. Not one of the books he'd examined revealed where he could buy the cursed birds.

Worse, at some point it had dawned on him that he wasn't even certain *which* three birds he was looking for. Devora had provided a list of those she owned, but until he could compare that with a complete list, he wasn't even at square one. It was almost as if she'd developed a masochistic streak in her last days and wanted to make the task as difficult for him as possible. Probably because she knew that would only make him more determined to succeed. With or without the help of Rose Davenport, with her smoky green eyes and insider's understanding of the secret world of antiques.

There was no way he could approach her again. Not, he thought wincing inside, after the way he'd stormed out of there like a total jackass.

Not unless he became utterly desperate.

He dragged his fingers through the dark wavy hair that fell across his forehead. His hair was longer than it had been in twenty years and he was still getting used to it. It didn't *feel* like him, and when he looked in the mirror the man who stared back did not look like the man he used to be. Which made sense. That man was gone. He'd had his nose shoved in that nasty little bit of reality dozens of times every day for over a year.

That man, the old Griff, had had everything under control and had never made a mistake when it counted. Well, almost never, he thought bitterly. He certainly would never have overreacted to something as inconsequential as being called "sensitive" by a shopkeeper. Not even a fine-looking one. *Especially* not by one who was fine-looking.

No, that old Griff would have laughed at the very suggestion and let loose on Rose Davenport a grin that never, ever failed. When she touched the back of his hand, he would have flipped it and caught hers before she knew what hit her, and said something clever and flirtatious, and with just enough of an edge to make her blush a little. Make her think.

Then he would have leaned closer, close enough to find out if she, too, smelled like roses and cinnamon and wind, close enough to touch that mesmerizing spot on her throat where the gold moon nestled. His touch would be light, one fingertip only, and quick, no more than a second, so fleeting she might question later if he had actually made contact or if she had only imagined it.

That would have her wondering, and waiting for the next time, which would not come soon. Oh, no. He almost smiled just thinking about it. His timing, as always, would be perfect. And eventually, if she continued to intrigue him, Rose Davenport would end up in his bed.

And it would be great. For her as well as him. The chase and the sex. He'd always relished both. There would be no rushing, and no coercion. No lies, no strings, no promises. The old Griff had a code of honor that demanded it.

What the old Griff had *not* had was a bum leg, loss of peripheral vision in one eye, and no future to speak of.

He rubbed his temple, feeling the ache of a loss so big he couldn't begin to define its dimensions. Some days, it was as if he had his face pressed against the side of a mountain and was struggling to figure out how tall it was, and how the hell he was going to get over it.

Just a few hours ago he'd thought he had the first step figured out, but in what was turning out to be the new story of his life, he had managed to screw that up, too.

Are you calling me sensitive?

He groaned silently. And he'd had the audacity to label the delivery guy a jerk.

No, he decided with grim resolve, there was no possible way he could ask Rose to help him now. That much was definite, as clear to him as the memory of Devora's voice, ringing in his head.

"Really, Hollis, do you think it wise to cut off your nose to spite your face?"

"Two hundred and sixty-seven dollars?" Maryann Pontrelli McShane's lively brown eyes reflected amazement and amusement in about equal parts.

"Plus tax," Rose added.

"Must have been one hell of a garland."

"It was," Rose assured her. "Not that Mr. Hollis Who-are-you-calling-sensitive Griffin appreciated it."

Her friend tossed back long hair the color of expensive mink, glanced at six-month-old Lisa sleeping peacefully in her stroller, and pursed her lips thoughtfully. "Hollis? What kind of name is Hollis?"

"Rare."

"Besides rare. British maybe?"

Rose shrugged. "British, French, Cro-Magnon."

"Easy to see why he prefers Griff."

"I suppose." She climbed onto the stool behind the counter and took a sip of the iced chai tea Maryann had brought. "Mmm."

Iced chai was part of their Thursday ritual.

On Thursdays the shop was open until nine, and Maryann's husband, Ted, worked late at his law office in Providence. Maryann and Lisa stopped by during the early evening lull, and while the baby napped, the two women caught up with whatever was going on in each other's lives. During the busy summer months, the shop *was* Rose's life, and it was Maryann who usually had the more interesting tales to tell. Not so today. Rose had been stewing over her run-in with Griffin for two days and was happy to be able to grouse about it to someone who would understand.

"I'd still like to know what he's going to do with my beautiful hydrangeas."

"*His* beautiful hydrangeas," Maryann corrected with a characteristically realistic expression.

"*I* fished them out of the Dumpster. *I* wiped the gravy off them—one delicate petal at a time, I might add. And *I* was the one who spent hours searching for exactly the right shade of ribbon to embellish them.''

''But he's the one who coughed up more than two hundred and sixty bucks. You do the math.''

''I have,'' Rose informed her triumphantly. She produced a legal pad on which she'd scrawled column after column of figures. ''If you look at all the time I spent—in the Dumpster, cleaning and drying the flowers, and assembling the garland—and then calculate an hourly wage based on average past receipts—'' she glanced up ''—in season, of course. And add it all up, I didn't even come close to breaking even.''

Maryann spoke softly. ''Rose, sweetie, get a grip. I know you're riled, but try not to wake Lisa. Also, I'm not sure you can expect to be compensated for the weeks the flowers spent just hanging around drying.''

Rose's eyes flashed. ''I'd like to know why not. Firemen get paid for the time they spend sitting around waiting for a fire. The crew on a fishing boat—''

''All right, all right, I get the idea. So what's your point?''

''That Griffin *stole* the garland, that's my point. I figure he owes me two thousand, one hundred and seven dollars and thirty-six cents. Plus tax. I'm willing to round it to two thousand even.''

''And just how do you plan to collect?''

''I don't.'' She sighed and tossed the pad aside. ''I admit that legally I probably don't have a leg to stand on.''

''I'm no expert,'' Maryann admitted, ''but I do watch my share of *Judge Judy,* and I am married to a third-generation attorney, and that would be my take on the situation, too. Look at it this way—in spite of the fact that you lost two grand on the deal, it was still nearly one-hundred-percent profit. How many businesses can pull that off?''

''I suppose.'' Rose leaned on the counter and propped her chin on her hand. ''I'd still like to figure out some way to collect. I also wish I hadn't offered to throw a party for him.''

Maryann's eyes widened with fresh interest. ''Do tell? What's this guy like, anyway?''

Rose shrugged. ''Tall.''

''Tall? That's the best you can do? I seem to recall Edie Blanchard saying Devora's nephew is a dead ringer for Pierce Brosnan.''

''When did Edie Blanchard see him?'' she asked, more interested than she cared to be, a fact that would not be lost on Maryann.

''At Devora's memorial service. That was the week we were in Baltimore for Ted's old roommate's wedding,'' she reminded Rose. ''Edie told me all about it when I got back, and I remember how she went on and on about him being the spitting image of Pierce Brosnan. I would have mentioned it to you at the time, but it seemed…trivial, considering the situation and how hard you took the loss.''

Rose nodded. ''Well, trust me, Edie was wrong. He's no Pierce Brosnan.'' She paused and tilted her head to the side, thinking it over before grudgingly adding, ''Pierce Brosnan's bigger, tougher, less charming and not nearly as well-dressed brother…maybe.''

''Hey, that's still not chopped liver.''

''Stop,'' Rose ordered, as a familiar gleam appeared in her friend's dark eyes.

''Stop what?'' Maryann's lashes fluttered with what might be taken for innocence by someone who didn't know her so well and hadn't spent countless evenings on the receiving end of her self-acclaimed gift for matchmaking.

''We had an agreement, remember?''

''Oh, that.'' Maryann waved off the reminder. ''I agreed not to arrange any blind dates for you during your busy season. I never agreed to pretend men don't exist, or that I do not find them—individually and as a species—a source of great interest, potential and amusement.''

"Maryann, I don't want to put a damper on your enthusiasm—"

"Much," her friend interjected.

"But I feel I should point out that you are married."

"Married, not dead. And, at the risk of putting some heat on that wet blanket you insist on hiding under, I would like to point out that you are neither…married or dead, that is."

"And happily so."

"Ha. You just think you're happy." Maryann hoisted herself onto the counter as gracefully as she did everything in life, and zeroed in on Rose with the zeal and determination of a used car salesman on the last day of the month. "You are as textbook a case as the person who insists he does not like *calamari* when he has never even tasted it."

"Squid," Rose corrected. "Call it what it is, Maryann— fried squid."

"My point exactly," Maryann crowed. "*Why* doesn't this otherwise sensible man taste it before ruling out any possibility of liking it? Because even though the menu says, *calamari*, he's thinking, *squid*. Even though everyone else at the table is chomping away and telling him how great it is, telling him, 'Try it, you'll like it,' he's got squid on the brain. Squid, squid, squid. And, I might add, these fellow diners are not strangers.

"Oh, no," she continued, having warmed to the point where her Ivy League education and marriage into a family of hardcore WASPs inevitably gave way to the unbridled animation of her deep Italian roots. She waved her expensively manicured hands, shrugged her shoulders, tossed her head. A one-woman show. "These are the very people he chooses to break bread with, people he knows and trusts. His best friend in the whole, entire world is sitting right next to him, holding out his fork, saying, 'Just a bite, one little bite. Trust me.'"

"All right, Maryann, you win," Rose said. "You've convinced me."

Maryann's beautiful face glowed with amazement. "I have?"

"One hundred percent. The very next time we have dinner together, I swear I will eat the *calamari* right off your plate."

"Very funny." She slid from the counter, straightened her white shorts and replaced the pacifier in Lisa's mouth, just as the baby began to stir.

"As you are well aware," she said to Rose, "the *calamari* was merely an illustration, a device, a metaphor for happy marriage. And just as the man was afraid to try the *calamari* because he couldn't stop thinking, *squid, squid, squid,* you are afraid to give the whole men-love-marriage thing a chance."

"With one small, but critical difference." Rose's tone became emphatic. "I *have* tried marriage."

"Right. To a squid," Maryann retorted, throwing both hands in the air, palms up. "I rest my case."

"Thank you."

"With this one final thought."

Rose groaned.

"If you want to go on living a giant yawning hole of a life, go right ahead."

"Thanks, I will." Rose raised her plastic cup as if to toast the prospect.

"But, as my gramma Viola, God rest her soul, always said, 'God works in mysterious ways.'"

She gave that time to sink into Rose's resistant skull before continuing. "One of these days, that door will open—" She aimed one glossy crimson fingertip at the front door. "And in will walk the one man who can fill all that emptiness inside you."

"Let me guess...his name will be Right. Mr. Richard Right."

"Go ahead and laugh. As my gramma was also fond of saying..." She shifted effortlessly into broken English. "Justa you wait and see, Miss Smarty-Pants."

"I will. But if you don't mind, I won't hold my breath,

because the entire concept of Mr. Right—that is, one specific person out of hundreds of millions who is destined to be the soul mate of another specific person—is a myth.''

Maryann planted her fists on hips that Raquel Welch in her prime would have envied, and rolled her eyes. ''Like you would know?''

''I've read *Cosmo,* too, Maryann. Not to mention having a degree in sociology.''

''Phooey. What does sociology have to do with true love?''

''Plenty.'' It was the best Rose could do on the spur of the moment, especially considering she was a little rusty in both areas. About all she remembered from what she had once thought would be her life's work with the Department of Social Services was the people. She remembered families without homes, babies without mothers, men and women who'd grown old and given up. She remembered those she had struggled to help, and all the ones she couldn't, no matter how hard she fought, how many hours she logged, how many rules she bent.

''Such as?''

Her friend's challenge interrupted her musing. She decided to wing it. ''Such as establishing the fact that a given individual's number of potentially satisfying mates is not limited to one. Studies show there are any number of suitable candidates—a category, in other words—a societal subset of similar Homo sapiens—a particular sort of personality—a character type, if you will.'' She paused to breathe. ''And I assure you, no matter what delusions Edie Blanchard has about the man, Hollis Griffin is most definitely *not* my type.''

The bell over the door sounded.

Lisa whimpered and lost her pacifier.

Griff walked in.

Maryann looked at him, then turned to face Rose and mouthed, *Pierce Brosnan.*

Rose had two silent words of her own. *Why me?*

She was suddenly sorry she had ever mentioned Griff to

Maryann, and seeing the gleam in her friend's eye as he approached, she had a feeling she was about to be even sorrier.

Stopping beside Maryann, he looked directly at Rose. "I need to talk to you."

She eyed him reproachfully. "Forgive my lapse into good manners, but Maryann, this is Hollis Griffin. Hollis," she continued, imbuing the name with just the barest hint of mockery, "this is my friend, Maryann McShane, and her daughter, Lisa."

He turned his head, nodding at Maryann and flicking his gaze over the baby, who was winding up for a good cry. "Pleased to meet you, Maryann. Beautiful baby."

"Hello, Hollis," Maryann replied with a little smile and a nod of her own. "And thank you. I think she's beautiful, too."

"The name's Griff," he told her.

"Griff," she repeated.

Rose observed the brief exchange, as she had observed dozens of other men the first time they laid eyes on Maryann—all five feet, eight gorgeous inches of her. But for once, the instant she was watching for never came, the instant when the man's eyes glazed over and he struggled to keep his jaw from dropping. Instead, Griff turned his attention back to Rose.

"Can we talk now?"

"I'm afraid—" Rose began.

Maryann cut her off. "I'm leaving."

"That's really not necessary," Rose insisted, her look shorthand for *Don't you dare leave me here alone*.

"Oh, but it is," replied Maryann, declining to decipher the code as she wheeled the stroller around to face the door. "I want to get home before Lisa realizes she's hungry for more than that pacifier."

"But we haven't finished our discussion," Rose persisted.

"Oh, we will. Most definitely. For now," she said, doggedly ignoring the silent distress signals Rose was sending, "hold this thought. From my mouth to God's ear, and in record time." She grinned and glanced upward. "Thank you, Gramma Viola."

Then she was gone.

Griff glanced around, frowning. "Who's Gramma Viola?"

Rose shook her head. "It's…complicated."

He nodded.

She stood there.

Alone. With Hollis Griffin. Just where she did not want to be. Devora's nephew or no, the man was insufferable, unfriendly and tasteless. And she hadn't been able to get him off her mind for the past two days, eight hours and sixteen minutes. Give or take a few hours of sleep here and there.

And not, it pained her to admit, simply because he had stolen her hydrangeas. Some inner sense warned that nothing would ever be simple with Griffin, and simple was how she liked things.

So why couldn't she stop thinking about the man?

It was ridiculous. And aggravating.

"So," she said, folding her arms across her chest for much the same reason medieval warriors raised drawbridges: to protect against invaders. He might be wearing khaki slacks and a white shirt, sleeves rolled and neck open, but Rose saw battle armor. "Talk."

Yeah, Griff, talk, he ordered himself. *That's why you finally broke down and came here, isn't it? Isn't it?*

Yes, he assured himself firmly. He was here because he needed the woman's help. Period. Nothing more or less. He was, well, in a word, desperate.

"Look," he began, shoving one hand in his pocket, then taking it out again. "About the other day…the way I left…I'm not usually that…"

"Sensitive?" she suggested, green eyes full of enjoyment.

"Exactly." He presented her with a smile that was both grudging and self-derisive. "I realize I was way out of line, especially after you went out of your way to be friendly and make me feel welcome and all. And I just want to say I'm…''

"Sorry?" she helped out again.

He nodded, relieved. "Right. I'm sorry."

"No problem." Her mouth curved into a teasing smile. "Believe it or not, I wasn't trying to offend you. I just call 'em like I see 'em."

"Yeah. Right," Griff muttered, preferring not to explore it any further.

"Of course, even I can be wrong."

"What does that mean? That now you don't think I'm sensitive?"

"What I think is that I should keep what I think about you to myself from now on."

"Fine with me. So…truce?"

"Truce. Is that what you wanted to talk about?"

"More or less," he hedged. He cleared his throat. "But not exactly. I also came to see you because I…" In spite of the fact that he'd practiced what he had to say all the way there, the word *need* lodged itself in his throat like a chunk of day-old doughnut, refusing to come up or go down. "I…want to hire you."

She looked startled and bewildered by the announcement. Which made two of them, thought Griff.

"Hire me?"

"Your services, I mean."

"I see. And exactly which of my *services* are you interested in hiring me to perform?" she enquired, her tone chilly and mocking.

"Not *that*," he blurted, aghast. Could the woman possibly believe he had to pay women for their company? And that if he did, he'd go about it in such a clumsy fashion?

"That," she repeated, her lips drawing into a soft rosy bow that did not help his concentration at all. "*That* being?"

Her brows arched and her lips twitched.

She was laughing, Griff realized. At him. The sheer humiliation of it bounced around like a pinball inside him, slamming his pride hard enough to trigger some abandoned, deeply buried response system. A sort of Freudian kick in the ass.

As their gazes locked, he felt his grip on the cane relax and his lips settle into a comfortable smile. "That being any service requiring negotiations of a personal nature," he said in a soft, deep voice that was only the slightest bit rusty. "The specific service I have need for at the moment is of a less intriguing, more professional nature."

There was no mistaking the look of heightened awareness in her pretty eyes. It was laced with wariness, and with excitement. It was a look Griff hadn't seen on a woman in quite a while. A look he'd thought he didn't care if he ever saw again. He'd thought wrong, he realized. Suddenly, to his surprise, he felt more at home in his skin than he had in a long time.

"To be specific, I want to hire you to help me complete Devora's collection," he told her. "The birds," he prodded gently, when she continued to stare at him in silence.

"Of course." She ran her fingers through her hair, dislodging an amber-jeweled butterfly clip so that it seemed to be dancing across the sun-kissed waves near her ear. He liked it.

"I'm sorry. I was…thinking of something else for a moment," Rose explained, then wanted to kick herself when Griff's indulgent smile assured her that he knew exactly what that *something else* had been.

She didn't like this, not one bit, and there was no way in heaven that she was going to agree to work for the man. Hire her, indeed.

"I'd really like to help you," she told him, "but as I explained the other day, this really is not my field of expertise."

"Maybe not, but there's no denying you know a hell of a lot more about antiques in general than I do."

She conceded that with a small shrug. "You could learn."

"You could teach me."

"Out of the question. I'm in business to sell stuff, not train potential competitors."

"Understood. You have my word of honor that I will never go into the antiques business for myself. What do you say?"

"I say I really have to get back to work now."

"Does that mean you accept my offer?"

"No, it means I have a business of my own to run."

She began rearranging a display of Limoges boxes, while he looked on.

"I get it," he said, leaning against a mahogany armoire filled with linen. "You want me to beg."

"No, really, I don't—"

"I'm begging you, Rose. I'm a desperate man. A victim of my own ignorance. Take pity on me."

"All right, I'll do this much—I'll make a suggestion." She turned to him holding one of the prized miniature boxes in each hand, one a ripe strawberry, the other a tiny carousel. "If I were you, I would try the Internet."

"I did. Unfortunately my computer skills are limited to flight simulation and engine design."

"You didn't turn up *anything?*"

He shrugged. "Only that one of the three birds I need is a Piping Plover, name derived from the Latin *pluvius,* or rain. The feminine form of rain, to be precise."

"Rain has gender?"

"Evidently the Romans thought so. At any rate, this particular Plover is practically extinct. What does that tell you?"

"That you're in trouble."

"That's what I've been saying." He shifted so he could see her face. "Would it have any influence on your answer if I told you that you have the most amazing eyes?"

"No," she retorted, wishing that were the truth. Just hearing him talk about her eyes in that voice—the sort of deep, dark caress of a voice that every woman hears in her most secret fantasies—had an eroding effect on her resolve. And her concentration.

"Because it's true," he continued. "Just when I'm convinced they couldn't be any greener, you blink, or I do, and they're suddenly full of silver lights."

Rose placed the strawberry Limoges box on the shelf, picked it up and put it back down in the precisely same spot. Maryann was right. God did work in mysterious ways. Right now, he was punishing her for saying that Griff was not charming by making him disarmingly so.

"And you," she said, putting aside both boxes and turning to face him, "are full of baloney."

"You want me to say your eyes aren't green? I will. It goes against my code as an officer and a gentleman, but I'll do it. I'll do whatever it takes to get you to say yes."

"Does this really mean that much to you?"

"Yes. It does."

"Why?"

Griff hesitated. Damn. He'd wanted to play this straight. He didn't consider a little flirting, especially when it came so naturally and she did have incredible eyes, to be dishonest. But now she was digging into his actual motives and intentions, and he was going to have to make a choice. Lie, or tell the truth and make her so angry she'd never agree to help him.

"Bottom line," he said, "it means a lot to me, for no other reason than that it meant so much to Devora. Hell, I'd never be standing here pressing you this way otherwise. She made it clear she wanted the collection completed, and I feel strangely compelled to oblige."

All true, after a fashion, he assured himself. If he was lucky, he might be able to continue to pick his way along a fine line of omissions and insinuations.

"I guess I can understand that," said Rose.

"Good. Because I really need your help. And I'm prepared to be generous," he added, hoping to sway her with the more honest incentive of cold, hard cash.

At first she appeared uninterested in the offer. Then she glanced over her shoulder at the counter behind her and did that distracting, sort of pouty thing with her lips that he'd noticed she did when she was pondering something.

"How generous?" she asked.

Griff considered the price she'd charged for the string of dead flowers and named an hourly rate in keeping with it. He was desperate, he reminded himself as he saw her eyes flash with real interest, and something else—something he couldn't quite name.

"I'll do it," she said. Then, before he could feel triumphant, she added, "But with a few stipulations."

"Name them."

"I'll work for you, but not instead of you. I already have my hands full. I do a lot of business online," she explained, pointing to the computer sitting on a small desk behind the counter, "so I'll handle that part of the search. But you'll have to be available to come along if I decide we should chase down a lead."

"No problem. What else?"

"I'm the boss," she declared. She waited for him to bristle the way he had the other day, and was caught off guard when instead, his eyes crinkled at the corners, and a slow, very appealing grin appeared.

"Well now, I've never had a lady boss. Maybe you ought to go into a little detail about how that works."

"It's not complicated, Griff. Think of me as your commanding officer. I'll think of you as a raw recruit who doesn't know his Waterford from his Wedgwood. Or, to put it more simply, I give the orders and you follow them."

He had a little more difficulty with that one, she could tell, and she relished the moment. Truthfully, if he had asked her nicely, she would have been happy to help and would have refused to accept a penny. But he hadn't asked; he'd waged a campaign. And she felt no qualms about recouping some of her loss on the garland.

"What sort of orders?" he asked finally.

"That's hard to say at this point. Hunting for antiques is more art than science. You have to be constantly on the prowl and you have to have good instincts, good timing and good luck. Since we agree you don't have any instinct for this sort of hunt, we'll both have to rely on mine.''

"In other words, you're the brains and I'm the muscle."

"More or less."

"I can live with that," he agreed.

Rose waited. Neither his tone nor his lazy smile suggested resistance. Still, there was a prickle of apprehension at the back of her neck.

"With one little stipulation of my own," he said.

She folded her arms. "Let's hear it."

"Your conditions apply to work time only. When we're off duty, we're on our own."

"Meaning?"

"Meaning you can forget that rule about officers not fraternizing with enlisted men."

"I guess I can live with that," agreed Rose, wondering what she was getting herself into.

"Good. When do we start?"

"I'll let you know."

Chapter Four

*T*he scent was all around him. Her scent…roses and wind…sweet and fresh, and he was falling into a sea of silvery green, her eyes, Rose Davenport's amazingly beautiful eyes. She was smiling up at him, sighing softly, lost in a cloud of soft, white…ruffles? Pillows, pillows with ruffles. Hell, a motherlode of them, like the pile he'd seen on that old bed in her shop.

He'd had such thoughts about that bed and Rose, and now, like magic, here he was, stretched above her and so hot for her that not even the ruffles bothered him. Griff grinned with pure pleasure. This was like the old days—a beautiful woman tumbling into his arms after minimal effort on his part. Maybe his luck was changing.

He brushed the hair from her cheek and lowered his head to taste her lips.

She touched his mouth with one fingertip—one cool, irresistible fingertip—and screamed in his ear.

He flinched. Why the hell was she screaming at him? It's

not like he'd twisted her arm to get her here. There is no way he would ever become that desperate.

She screamed again. Longer and louder.

Griff opened his eyes to a wall covered with faded pink cabbage roses and realized that the cool fingertip against his lips was merely a damp spot on the pillowcase. He was drooling, for God's sake.

He sat up to flip the pillow over, and whacked his head against the ceiling that slanted above the bed—just one more of Fairfield House's charming period details. It was his own damn fault for opting to sleep in his old room. Considering his reason for being there, it just hadn't seemed right to lay claim to Devora's majestic four-poster. Not to mention the fact that when he'd tried, his first night there, one of the damn bed rails had let go, leaving him sleeping at a sixty-degree angle. Or trying to, anyway.

He realized it was absurd, but sometimes it seemed as if the old house knew what he had planned for it and was responding the same way its mistress would have: with regal disdain.

The earsplitting sound came again. Not a scream, he realized, but a car horn. Who the hell…?

He swung from the bed, wincing as his left leg threatened to buckle under him, and lunged toward the window. With both hands planted on the sill, he checked out the circular drive below.

Directly beneath his window was a white pickup truck. What looked like an old blue-and-white quilt spilled over the rear tailgate and a familiar logo adorned the driver's door.

Somewhere downstairs was a shopping bag full of dead flowers with the same logo: a straw hat with black streamers that seemed to be fluttering in the wind and the words *Second Hand Rose, Specializing in Has-Beens of Distinction.*

So. Has-beens of distinction were Rose Davenport's specialty. How very fitting, he thought, irritable as only a man who's recently been yanked from a sound sleep and slammed his head into a wall can be.

Leaving the engine running, Rose hopped from behind the wheel and grinned up at him. Not, he couldn't help noting, with anything resembling the lustful enthusiasm she had exhibited in his dream.

"Did I wake you?" she called to him.

"No," he retorted, the rasp in his voice something only black coffee, and lots of it, would ease. "I always get up at…" He squinted over his shoulder at the bedside clock. "Six-thirty?" he bellowed. "Woman, do you know what time it is? It's six-freakin'-thirty in the morning."

"Six-freakin'-thirty-five, actually," she corrected. "Which means we're already running late, so move your butt, Griffin."

"Late for what?"

She threw her arms in the air. "Life, Griffin, life. Look at this beautiful morning, the sky, smell the ocean, hear the buzz of the bees. Aren't you just revving to get out and be part of it?"

He yawned. "No."

"I thought you military types were supposed to be early risers."

"Think again," he suggested, turning away.

"I have coffee."

Griff hesitated and turned back to see her reach into the truck for a steel thermos.

As he looked on, she removed the cap and sniffed. "Mmm."

"Black?"

"And strong as sin. There're homemade blueberry muffins, too."

"You made muffins for me?" he asked, surprised.

"Not specifically for you. I made them for a brunch I had a couple of weeks ago and there were some left in the freezer."

"I see."

"I thawed a couple just for you," she added.

"Thanks," he said, feeling considerably less obliged to be

polite than he had a few seconds ago. "Leave 'em with the coffee on the porch. I'll be down in a few hours."

"That's quite an imagination you have there. You can't actually believe I rose at the crack of dawn to fetch you breakfast."

"It sure looks that way."

"Get real, Griffin. This is Saturday. In a few hours we'll have thirty miles and a morning's work under our belts."

"What are you talking about?"

"Yard sales, dozens of them," she added, waving the classified section of the newspaper at him.

"Thanks, I already have more yard than I know what to do with." He yawned again, wondering if he crawled back into bed right then, the dream Rose would pick up where the real Rose had so rudely interrupted.

"Very funny."

He frowned. "I wasn't trying to be."

"Don't tell me you don't know what a yard sale is?"

"I have a vague idea," he admitted, "and no interest in learning more."

"But you do still have an interest in acquiring the pieces to complete Devora's porcelain collection."

"True," he countered, his smile amused, "but I hardly expect to find them amidst piles of used baby clothes and old exercise equipment."

She grinned broadly. "That's the beauty of this business, Griffin—you can always expect the unexpected. You know what the seasoned veterans say…"

"I'll bite. What do seasoned veterans say?"

"They say when it comes to junk, you just never know."

"And on that less than inspiring note…"

"Who do you think coined the phrase 'One man's trash is another man's treasure'?"

"A woman."

"Wrong. A yard sale enthusiast. In case you've forgotten, Griffin, you're the one who asked me for help. You're a desperate man, remember? And desperate men can't afford to overlook a single possibility, no matter how insignificant it may appear to the eye of a raw, still wet-behind-the-ears novice.''

The raw, still wet-behind-the-ears novice resisted the urge to toss something out the window at her.

''So now that you're up to speed on the day's agenda, let's get cracking,'' she ordered, tossing the thermos and newspaper back into the truck. ''Our first stop is an early-bird special in Middletown.''

''I don't even want to think about birds for another five or so hours.''

''I'll give you five minutes.''

''For what?''

''To shower and dress and get down here.''

''That's out of the question.''

''Would it help, from a motivational standpoint, if I pointed out that you are paying me by the hour...and that the meter's been running since I turned into your drive?''

He glared at her, but didn't bother to protest. She didn't seem to be in a capitulating state of mind this morning...if she ever was. Beneath Rose Davenport's soft, pretty facade beat the heart of a cutthroat venture capitalist. Pride alone demanded he not allow her to bamboozle him out of any more money than absolutely necessary.

''I'll be right down.''

''Did you really make these muffins?'' Griff asked, polishing off his second and washing it down with a swig of very fine coffee.

''Sure did,'' replied Rose. ''With frozen blueberries, because that's all I could get. You ought to taste my muffins in August.''

Was that an invitation?

Griff glanced across the small cab at her. Her words held an erotic appeal that he was pretty sure she did not intend, and as tempting as it was to explore the matter further, he was smart enough not to risk it. His belly was pleasantly full, the coffee was just as hot and strong as she'd promised, and a taste of Rose Davenport would top the morning off nicely. Which was just one reason he put the notion firmly from his mind.

He was in a better mood than he'd been in a while, a better mood than he'd have thought possible considering the morning's inauspicious start. It was as close to content as he hoped to get, and he was in no hurry for it to end.

There was also the matter of the damn birds. Because of them, he was more or less at her mercy...as his reluctant presence this morning demonstrated. A smart man knows when to keep his mouth shut and his hands to himself.

For several moments they drove in silence, across the bridge from the mainland to the tiny island of Jamestown. On the other side, another bridge connected Jamestown to Aquidneck Island—home to several towns, of which Newport was the most famous—and yet another, the Mount Hope Bridge, completed the circle. Rhode Islanders were geographically indisposed to driving long distances, and the trio of bridges helped to bring the entire state within their thirty-minute limit.

The water was calm and blue, the fresh air and the hum of tires on pavement was lulling. The view of Rose's long, suntanned legs was a bonus. He couldn't recall when he'd seen someone work a clutch so captivatingly. He also realized that he had a real weakness for faded denim coveralls hacked off above the knee.

He helped himself to another muffin from the napkin-lined basket on the seat between them. "Devora used to make blueberry pancakes for breakfast every Saturday morning," he remarked, surprising himself by voicing the thought even as it drifted through his head.

Rose smiled as she downshifted and changed lanes.

"It's one of the things I remember best about summers here. It was almost a ritual. On Friday we got the berries, either picking them ourselves or walking to that little market down on Haverly. The fruit was piled on round tables out front with big canvas umbrellas for shade— Is that place still there?'' he interrupted himself to ask.

Rose nodded. "Umbrellas and all."

He smiled, oddly pleased. "It was my job to wash the berries and pick off the stems, while she made the batter. I remember she had this special bowl, tan with two blue stripes. And she always wore the same apron," he went on, gazing out at the sailboats on the bay, seeing instead the past as it unfolded inside him, one fragment of memory at a time.

"It was black, with bunches of blueberries and green leaves all over it. It matched the Saturday morning place mats." He gave a short laugh. "I can still see them, with her white everyday china plates on top, and in the center of the table was this special pitcher for the syrup. Damn, I haven't thought of any of this in years."

He wasn't quite sure why he was permitting himself to think about it now, much less share it with someone else. If Rose had spoken or pressed him in even the most innocent way, he would have shut down instantly. But she didn't, and her easy, tranquil silence was difficult to resist.

"It was only as big as my hand," he recalled, "and shaped like a bunch of grapes, with a stem for a handle. But for a kid, grapes looked enough like blueberries to add to the occasion. It was a great little pitcher."

"Majolica," she said quietly.

"Pardon me?"

"I know which pitcher you're talking about. It's Majolica, a type of very colorful ceramic with a special glaze."

"Is it as overpriced as the Meissen stuff?"

"Not quite."

"Good." He turned to look out the window once more before adding, "Because one Saturday morning I dropped it and the handle broke."

They passed meandering stone walls and wild roses and a field of grazing cows.

"I ran," he said. "As soon as I saw that broken handle, I took off and ran all the way down to the water, to a little opening between two rocks where I knew no one else could fit. I didn't wait around to hear her scream at me for being such a klutz.''

"It's hard to imagine Devora screaming," she observed, stopping the truck to toss a token into the toll basket at the head of the Newport Bridge.

"She didn't. She simply followed me and stood at the edge of the rocks, her apron whipping in the breeze, and said, 'Come along, Hollis. All this exercise has made me hungry, and I abhor cold, soggy pancakes.'''

"What did you do?"

"I went along, of course. This was my aunt Devora, remember.''

Rose laughed and nodded.

"When we got back to the house, the broken pitcher was on the counter. I took one look at it and started bawling, so hard I couldn't even tell her I was sorry.'' His mouth curved into a small smile. ''Devora just wiped my face with her apron. 'Oh, that,' she said, waving it off as if it wasn't the special Saturday morning pitcher I had broken. 'I have some glue that will take care of that. Perhaps you can fix it for me after breakfast.'''

"Did you?"

He nodded. "But not very well, I'm afraid. It didn't matter. The next week it was back on the table, and she never said another word about it. It was not the reaction I'd expected.''

They were driving through a neighborhood of large, older homes. Rose stopped at a crossroads to glance at the map she had prepared, then turned left.

"What did you expect?"

"For all hell to break loose. My mother was…" He hesitated. "I guess Devora put it most delicately. She used to say my mother was high-strung. That's why I started coming to Wickford in the first place. To give Mom a break. And because Devora said Manhattan was no place for a rambunctious young boy to spend the summer.''

"Your family lived in the city?"

"Central Park West."

She whistled softly. "Very *Lifestyles of the Rich and Famous,* Griffin."

"Lifestyles of the Ruthless and Neurotic is more like it," he retorted. "And with no fishing, no sand crabs, no blueberry pancakes on Saturday mornings. I liked Devora's place a lot better."

"I know she adored having you. Did you get to come often?"

"I was away at school most of the year," he explained, detecting her surprise. "At first I stayed with Devora for a month, then the whole summer, and eventually I ended up here for just about every school break, as well. I even spent a couple of Christmases with Devora when my mother and stepfather were skiing in the Alps."

"No brothers or sisters?"

He shook his head. "My mother wasn't the type to make the same mistake twice."

"That must have made it even harder for you. Being away from your mother for Christmas, I mean."

"Hard?" Griff laughed. "It was great."

"I take it you're not much of a skier."

"I ski fine. It was more a case of knowing where I was welcome and where I wasn't."

"I'm sorry," she said simply.

"Don't be. I made peace with all that, and with my mother, years ago. She is a brilliant, fascinating and charming woman, whose instincts were more Machiavellian than maternal."

"Ouch."

"I guess you had to be there," he said, shrugging. "Anyway, I was better off than some other kids I knew at boarding school. At least I had someplace to go where I knew I was wanted. I had Devora."

She pulled to the curb and parked in front of a house with yellow shutters and a driveway full of junk.

"I owe you an apology," she told him.

"I accept," Griff countered, nodding magnanimously. "Just don't try it at the crack of dawn again next Saturday."

She made a scoffing sound. "You actually think I would apologize for dragging your lazy butt out of bed?"

"What else?"

"For misjudging you. For doubting, even for an instant, your sincerity in wanting to complete the Aureolis collection on Devora's behalf."

"Oh. That." He shifted uncomfortably, the truck suddenly feeling a lot smaller and warmer than it had previously. "It's no big deal, really. Just something I feel I have to do."

It was the truth, he assured himself. Just the same, he avoided direct eye contact with her as he said it, feigning great interest in the driveway, where several people had already gathered.

Something half hidden behind a sorry-looking vacuum cleaner caught his eye. "Hey, look," he exclaimed. "A bird. Let's check it out before someone grabs it."

She peered in the direction he indicated. "Your enthusiasm is commendable, Griff, but I'm afraid that bird is a little too big to be an Aureolis. Like, say, two feet too big. Besides which, it's a flamingo." She leaned forward to get a better look. "Albeit an interesting one. Besides the Piping Plover, which you already researched, we're looking for a Zebra Finch and a Purple Martin."

"It's an omen," he insisted, reaching for his cane and shoving the door open. "Birds of a feather and all that. Haven't you heard that other old yard sale saying... 'Where there's a Flamingo, a Piping Plover is never far away'?"

"I'll take your word for it," she said, chuckling and shaking her head as she climbed from the truck. "But I'm definitely monitoring your caffeine intake from now on."

Rose worked her way up one side of the drive and down the other. Griff, trailing behind, observed her technique. Thorough but efficient, he decided, watching her pass by rusted tools and racks of clothes. From three boxes stuffed with dishes, she extracted a single teacup. She ran her fingertip around the rim, turned it over and squinted at the bottom, held it up to the sun and peered at it with pursed lips, before returning it to the box and moving on.

He did some rummaging on his own, pretending interest, happy when she reappeared by his side.

"All set?" she asked.

"Looks like you are," he observed, indicating the large brown paper bag she was holding. "Tell me you've got a Piping Plover in there."

She shook her head. "Sorry...but that reminds me..."

Thrusting the bag at him, she dashed across the drive to gently scoop up the flamingo. "I nearly forgot her."

"I thought you said we didn't need a flamingo."

"I said *you* didn't need a flamingo. I, however, am quite captivated by old Gladys here."

"Gladys? You've already named her?"

"She sort of spoke to me while I was checking her out."

"What did she say? 'Hi, my name is Gladys'?"

"Well, not quite that directly, but yes. It was more of a cosmic thing. A psychic connection."

"I see," he lied. "How do you know it isn't a male flamingo? Maybe it was saying its name was Glen. Or Gary."

"Because," she said, shifting the pink bird so he could get a better look. "See this spot on her neck where someone glued her back together?"

"Yeah...looks to me like she has grounds to sue."

"I'm going to try to sand it and touch it up, but if it doesn't work, I'm going to make her a pearl choker to cover it. There's a gold seashell clasp I've had hanging around for ages, just begging for an interesting assignment."

"Well, why didn't you say so in the first place? That explains everything."

"It explains how I know for sure she's a Gladys and not a Glen or a Gary. I don't think I could live with a psychic, cross-dressing flamingo, could you?"

For a split second, Griff actually found himself thinking about it. That could not be a good sign.

"I'll have to get back to you on that one," he muttered, taking his place on the seat beside Gladys and slamming the door behind him.

It was several stops later—Griff had lost count—when he got around to asking about the truck's custom paint job. "At first, I thought it was a real quilt hanging out the back."

"That's the point. You're supposed to think it's real," she told him. "It's *trompe l'oeil*."

"*Trompe l'oeil*," he repeated, his tone sardonic. "The guys at the body shop must have fought for that job."

"Actually, I painted it myself."

"Why?"

She laughed. "I suppose for the same reason I do most things…creative impulse. I thought the truck lacked character, so I added some. It's also something that grabs attention and sticks in folks' minds."

"I'll bet."

"That's an edge in my business. When it comes time to clean out the attic or sell Aunt Fanny's silver, people remember the truck, and I get a call. Of course, the name Second Hand Rose doesn't hurt, either," she added. "Since it's already a part of the vernacular, the visual image of the truck helps cement it in people's minds."

She made a left to take the back roads into Newport. "I had planned to hit a couple of places in Middletown on the way back, but this next stop will have to be the last. I have to be at the shop by noon."

"You plan to work after this?" he asked, surprised because his own afternoon plans called for a nap.

"Of course. Saturday is my busiest day. I have a part-timer, Laurie, who opens for me, but she baby-sits for her mom in the afternoon. Running a business requires stamina."

Rose felt his stare and glanced at him briefly as she turned onto one of the narrow brick streets that characterized Newport's harbor district. "Why are you looking at me that way?"

"I guess I'm still trying to figure you out, Miss Rose Davenport."

"That shouldn't be much of a struggle," she replied with a shrug. "I'm hardly Mata Hari."

"No, you're a woman who communicates with plastic flamingoes and—"

"Gladys is *not* plastic," she interrupted, indignant as she rapped on the bird to prove it.

"All right," he conceded, "you're a woman who communicates with hand-painted wooden flamingoes, looks like a new millennium version of a sixties flower child, and is one hell of an astute entrepreneur."

"Thank you. I think. I'm not sure you meant any of it as a compliment."

"I meant all of it as a compliment," he assured her. "You're not at all what I expected…and I'm not referring simply to age. Frankly, I expected you to be nothing more than a giant pain."

"And I'm not?"

"No, you are, but you're a very intriguing giant pain, and I am…intrigued," he confessed, his tone turning rueful.

"And you don't want to be?"

Griff shrugged. "Let's just say, it comes as a surprise. It's been a while since I've been much interested in anything, much less something as bizarre as a truck painted to look like a quilt."

"What can I say? I took a class in *trompe l'oeil,* started small and worked my way up."

"How small?"

"Let's see…the first thing I painted was a broken egg on the tile floor in front of my refrigerator."

This time he didn't need to ask why.

"I get it…as if someone had dropped it."

"Exactly. Then I painted keys and lace gloves on the table

by my front door and lace swags in the dining room, and then I was ready for the truck.''

"So you're an art major. That explains a lot.''

"Sorry to poke a whole in your theory right off the bat, but I've taken one art class, last year in night school. My degree is in social work.''

"How did you end up dealing in has-beens of distinction?''

"Luck,'' she said brightly. "Long story short? I went into social work because I wanted to work with people that I wanted to help. I graduated with high hopes, lots of energy and absolutely no clue about real life. I did a lot of things in a hurry, made a lot of mistakes and ended up crashing and burning before I was thirty.''

"That was five years ago,'' she went on as she searched for a place to park. "I licked my wounds, whined a lot to anyone who would listen, and then decided that before I tried to work magic on other people's lives, I ought to fix my own.''

"And you did that by going into business for yourself.''

"Well, I wouldn't go so far as to say my life is fixed,'' she hastened to point out. "But I'm working on it, and I've finally figured out that if I want to make other people happy, I have to make me happy first. And this—'' she indicated the truck, now filled with a morning's worth of rescued treasures "—makes me happy.''

She spotted a Volvo wagon pulling away from the curb half a block away. "Perfect timing,'' she said as she took its place. "First Gladys, and now a parking spot on Spring Street. Looks like this is my lucky day.''

They went to the next sale, and ten minutes later were back in the truck and headed for the bridge.

"Not a bad morning's work,'' she remarked. "Can you believe I got that great lace tablecloth for three dollars?''

"Sure. After seeing you pay ten times that for a box of old letters and pictures of strangers, I'd believe anything. What the hell are you going to do with all that cra—stuff?''

Rose gave a noncommittal shrug. "I'm not sure. Maybe use them as filler in a window display."

"I don't even know why I bothered to ask. I'm just about convinced you could sell snow cones to Eskimos."

"The one thing I won't do is sell them," she informed him.

"Doesn't that fly in the face of your whole trash-to-treasure philosophy?"

"No, because they aren't trash. They're mementoes, history, bits and pieces of actual lives. That sort of thing shouldn't be bought and sold."

"What am I missing? Didn't you just…"

"Buy them? Yes, but only so someone else wouldn't. I like to think of it as rescuing them from the insensitive, ungrateful hands they'd fallen into."

"Tell me, is your house full of stray cats and injured birds, or is it only inanimate objects you feel obliged to rescue?"

"I'm not fussy," she admitted. "Though I'm drawn to some castoffs more than others. For instance, I can't stand to see someone tossing out their grandfather's war medals or pillowcases hand-embroidered by a great-aunt. I say if you're lucky enough to have a family heirloom, treasure it."

"I'm sure your ancestors are duly grateful."

"Not likely," she said, just a touch of regret in her tone. "In my family, the only things passed down from one generation to the next were debts and bad habits. Maybe that's why I'm such a zealot on the subject, but it breaks my heart to see the family Bible and scrapbooks tossed into a box along with old paperbacks."

He shrugged. "Maybe they needed the money."

She shook her head vehemently. "No way. When I was with Social Services, I dealt with people who needed money…desperately. More often than not, they kept the family Bible and photo album in a place of honor."

"So what's your conclusion? That the poor are basically noble but that middle-class suburbanites will sell Granny's dentures without missing a heartbeat?"

"I don't think it's a matter of money at all. Like most everything else in life, it's a matter of priorities. Most people are more concerned with tomorrow than with today…much less yesterday."

She continued. "Just think about the pop-psychology expressions constantly being tossed around—moving on, getting on with your life, recreating yourself and, my personal favorite, closure. 'I need to find closure,'" she quoted dramatically and shook her head. "As if the past is something you can put neatly in a box and store in the basement…or sell at a yard sale."

"Time doesn't move backward," he pointed out.

"Yes, but life isn't lived in a straight timeline, either. The past is with us, whether we choose to acknowledge it or not."

"Seems to me there's a lot of room between acknowledging the past and living in it."

"Point taken," she conceded, as they approached Wickford. "I don't expect everyone to share my love of anything and everything vintage." She shot him a grin. "Though it sure would be great for business if they did. The way I see it, if Gramps's old smoking stand turns out to be an original Stickley, worth thousands at auction, it makes sense to sell it and finance the kids' education. Anyone who pays that kind of money for a smoking stand will be sure to give it a good home, and the kids' framed diplomas will be Gramps's legacy. But if instead his legacy is a wooden jewelry box he made for Grams on their first anniversary, I think it should be cherished—broken hinges, peeling paint and all. That goes double when it comes to really personal items, like photos and marriage certificates."

"And if the family doesn't see fit to cherish it, you will?"

"Damn right. Or, in the case of Gramps's jewelry box, I'll find a like-minded buyer who will. Truly personal mementoes are different. I don't feel right profiting from them. It may sound silly, but finding a diary or old letters is like

being a caretaker of someone else's dreams." She glanced
across at him. "You, of all people, should understand that."

He looked startled. "I should?"

"Isn't that exactly what you're doing by completing Devora's collection?"

"Oh. That. Yeah…sure…I—I guess I just never thought
of it in quite that way."

Rose's smile deepened. Her impression of the man was
like an ongoing volleyball game in her head. Just when she
thought she had never encountered anyone less endearing,
she caught a flash of real vulnerability and found herself
softening toward him. It had happened more than once this
morning. He had said he was intrigued by her. Maybe you
could say she was intrigued in return. Devora would have
said she was smitten. All she knew was that the past few
hours had been much more enjoyable than she had anticipated.

She almost felt guilty for charging him. Almost.

He cleared his throat, still looking uncomfortable. Poor
thing. He really had a hard time accepting praise—at least
when it came to anything that smacked of the dreaded *S*
word. *Sensitivity.*

"The thing with Devora and the birds is really more complicated than just me…" He hesitated. "How did you put
it? Pitch-hitting for her dream."

"I said being the caretaker of it, but you've got the idea."

"Yeah, well. There's a little more to it than that."

They turned a corner and caught the red light, with Fairfield House looming before them in all her glory.

"Doesn't she just take your breath away?" Rose asked,
as the truck coasted to a stop.

He sort of grimaced.

"Sorry," she said. "I interrupted. You were saying something about you and Devora's Borealis collection…about it
being complicated."

"Right. Exactly. It is complicated. Too complicated to get
into when I know you're pressed for time."

"I have a few—"

"No. I wouldn't want to make you late. What would Lulu's mother say?"

"Lulu? You mean Laurie?"

"Right, Laurie. I do need to discuss it with you, though. Maybe we could talk about it later. Tonight. Over dinner."

"That would be great," she said. The spur-of-the-moment invitation left her feeling a little surprised, a little nervous and a little disappointed. "Unfortunately, I have plans tonight. It's sort of a standing commitment or I might—"

He waved off her explanation. "No problem. With Charlie?"

"Who?"

"Charlie. Sort of nondescript guy, brown shorts, pushes packages... You called him Charlie the other day at the shop."

"Oh, that Charlie." The suggestion made her chuckle. "Not quite. The thing between Charlie and me is strictly for fun."

"So I take it your regular Saturday night commitment is more serious?"

"You could say that," she returned, not about to reveal where and how she spent her Saturday nights.

"No problem," he said again, his tone jovial. Almost too jovial, as if he was relieved she had other plans. He pointed at the end of the driveway. "You can just drop me there," he said. "No need for you to drive all the way up to the house."

"Sure there is. Door-to-door service is in my job description," she joked, turning into the drive. "Besides, all that climbing in and out of the truck had to be hard on your leg. I couldn't help noticing that you seemed to sag a little as the morning wore on."

"I said stop here," he ordered roughly, and Rose hit the brakes, sending the three of them—Griff, Gladys and her—sliding forward. "I busted my leg. That doesn't make me a damn cripple, or one of those broken-down castoffs you're so good at finding."

He shoved open the door and jumped from the truck without using the cane. The show of agility cost him. Rose could tell from the way his jaw clenched when he hit ground. She winced inwardly, but her expression remained impassive.

The door slammed shut, and he glared at her through the open window. "For your information, not everything or everybody wants to be rescued—not even by Rose Caretaker-of-the-World, Patron Saint of Has-Beens, Davenport."

Any trace of sympathy she'd been tricked into feeling disappeared. She felt her cheeks heat. As if, Rose fumed silently, *she* was the one who had reason to be embarrassed. He was lucky he'd gotten out when he did—if he hadn't, she'd have kicked him in his bad leg without a second thought.

Instead, she yanked the gearshift into reverse and glared back at him. "And then there are those who are too far gone, beyond rescue, lost causes…making the whole thing a moot point."

The truck lurched, forcing him to step away in a hurry and spraying gravel all the way back to the gates. Gears screeching, she shifted and tore into her own driveway next door.

She sat gripping the wheel, temper popping, heart pounding. She had less than a half hour to unload the truck, change clothes and get to the shop in time to relieve Laurie. But first, she had something more important to take care of.

Rummaging in the straw bag on the seat beside her, she found a small notebook and flipped it open to the first page. At the top, in neat even figures, was written $2,107.36. Rose did some quick calculations in her head and, directly beneath it, wrote $137.50, then drew a line and did the subtraction. $1,969.86.

Damn. At this rate she'd be working for Griffin the rest

of the summer to recoup her loss. She would never make it that long. She frowned, then remembered the coffee and blueberry muffins and, with something akin to evil pleasure, subtracted another nine dollars.

Chapter Five

Rose arrived at the Willow Haven Retirement Community shortly before seven that evening. As usual, the others were already gathered in the lounge, eagerly awaiting her arrival.

She'd started the Saturday Night Collectors group for a number of reasons. She enjoyed being around people and helping others. And she missed Devora. Terribly.

At Willow Haven, she'd hoped to recapture some of what she and Devora had shared. And in a small way, she had. But the Saturday night group had grown into something much more than a substitute for a lost friend or a way to keep a bunch of old folks entertained for a few hours once a week. Something more than she and the dozen or so residents who made up the core of the group could have imagined.

It had started simply enough. Devora had shared Rose's pleasure in finding loving homes for her treasures, and in the months before she died she had given Rose a number of things, some of considerable monetary value and some of none, all of which Rose cherished and would never part with. She had also given her over a decade's worth of magazines devoted to antiques and collecting. The boxes they were stored in had literally taken over her small home, and the idea of donating them to the local nursing home had been born of desperation more than anything else.

She had been en route to Willow Haven, the truck piled high with cartons of old magazines, when she happened to remember a club her sixth grade teacher had formed to teach her top math group about the stock market. They would meet one afternoon a week to "buy" and "sell" shares of stock, based on individual research done on their own time. At age eleven she had tracked and charted her way to being the group's first millionaire. That her fortune was only on paper hardly diminished her excitement. More valuable than the math she learned that year was the realization that passion for what you are doing can be its own reward.

It was Newton and the apple all over again. If it worked with kids and stocks, she reasoned, why not seniors and Chippendale? By the time she arrived at the nursing home, she was ready to pitch the idea to the director—and Saturday nights at Willow Haven hadn't been the same since.

The meetings fell on Saturday night more or less by default, but it worked for everyone. Weeknights were reserved for more traditional seniors activities, such as bingo and line-dancing. Saturday nights, when both staff and visitors were scarce, could be long and lonely, with plenty of time for brooding about days gone by and what Devora used to refer to as "the could've, should've, would'ves."

Rose knew all about that. She'd also served enough time in dating bars and on blind dates to know that it was more fun spending Saturday nights with her friends at Willow Haven. It wouldn't do to admit it to Maryann, but the truth was that somewhere along the way she had given up on romance, at least the heart-pounding, head-spinning, happy-ever-after variety that her friend had been blessed with.

Rose was okay with that. She might not be living the life

most single, thirty-something women dream of, but at least she no longer dreaded Saturday nights. From the start, she'd been inspired by the group's enthusiasm and dedication. They quickly outgrew her modest vision of compiling facts and clippings in scrapbooks. They visited schools and church groups, did informal appraisals, and—thanks to a donation of floor samples from a local computer dealer—they also bought and sold through online auctions, earning enough to finance field trips to museums and flea markets.

In the process, they had made new friends and developed a system of international Internet contacts that Rose had no doubt could take over the world if they weren't otherwise engaged. She was counting on those contacts to help her locate the Borealis pieces Griffin needed to complete the collection.

She waited until the end of the meeting to make her request, and received the expected chorus of offers to help.

"I know a fellow in Germany who has a lot of that kind of thing listed on his Web site," said Hal Sanders. "I'll check it out."

"How about that dealer we met at Brimfield last year? Jim…Jack…" Ruth Marshall chewed her bottom lip as she struggled to recall the name.

"Jake," provided a soft voice from the back row. Shelley Rappaport "collected" music boxes, and the scrapbook on her láp was bulging with photographs and advertisements.

Ruth nodded happily. "That's it. *Jake.* Didn't he specialize in Meissen?"

"I think he did," Rose agreed.

"Well, if he can't help you, I'll bet he could put us in touch with someone who can."

"He's on my Wedgewood loop," said Clare, a tall, thin woman with an easy smile. "I could drop him an e-mail and ask."

She was referring to one of the countless online groups that regularly corresponded to share information about a common interest. If a particularly sought-after item appeared in the window of an antique shop in Boston, news of it could quickly be relayed around the globe, triggering an international bidding war that might end with the Boston shopkeeper shipping the item to Iceland or South Africa before the close of business.

"That would be great, Clare," said Rose. "You can let me know what you find out at the auction on Wednesday." Once a month, from March through October, they made the trek to a neighboring town to check out what auctioneer Ben Spencer had to offer.

The meeting ended with the usual punch and cookies. After milling about and chatting for a while, Rose excused herself for what had become another ritual she looked forward to all week.

Willow Haven's sprawling complex offered a variety of living arrangements, from apartments with kitchen facilities for residents who chose to prepare one or all of their own meals, to a separate wing for those requiring full nursing care. Falling in between was the Assisted Living area.

"Hey, Gus," she said, stopping at the open door of the last room before the solarium.

Gus O'Flaherty had cropped white hair, the bluest of eyes and the remnants of a brogue that eighty years away from Killarney hadn't managed to erase. He glanced up from the baseball game he was watching and grinned broadly. "Hey, Rosie. And may I ask what took you so long?"

"The meeting ran late."

Gus snorted. "Little wonder. Can't for the life of me figure out why a pretty thing like you wants to hang out with a bunch of nit-pickin' old blowhards like that lot."

"I don't know," she countered, strolling into the room to check out the clay pots lined up on the window ledge. "I guess I'm just drawn to nit-pickin' old blowhards, especially the grizzly, cantankerous kind whose thumbs are as green as their roots."

This time his snort held an unmistakable note of flustered pleasure. "Women," he muttered.

"Your babies are looking good," she remarked. "I thought this one on the end was a lost cause."

The window ledge was the horticultural equivalent of assisted living. Gus was devoted to raising dahlias, and he lavished attention on each and every plant, but those in his room received even more tender care. Once healthy, a plant rejoined the dozens of others that filled the solarium with color and fragrance year-round.

"Nah," he said, reaching for his cane and coming to stand beside her. "There's no such thing as a lost cause, Rosie. Only tenders who give up."

Tenders. Tending was Gus's word for his work with his plants and in the garden just outside the solarium, and hearing it never failed to touch her heart. There was a rare, peaceful sort of contentment in knowing there were people like Gus in the world, willing to tend to the smallest things in life and never give up.

"Gus, did it bother you when you had to start using a cane to get around?" she asked.

"Not as much as it would have bothered me not to get around at all." He regarded her from beneath a furrowed, sun-browned brow. "Why? Are you worrying about getting older, Rosie?"

"Nope." She flashed him a smile. "I never worry about a sure thing. I was just wondering. I have this...friend, a little older than I am, who needs help getting around, and he's a tad touchy about the whole subject."

"He's using a cane, is he?"

Rose nodded.

"And it's a permanent thing?"

"Who knows?"

"What happened to him?"

"Who knows?" she repeated, her exasperation showing. "He refuses to talk about it."

Gus chuckled and scratched his chin. "A little older than you, you say? And refusing to talk? Well, that explains everything."

"I'm glad you think so."

"It's like this. Women are born knowing what's best for them—and for every other blessed creature on the earth in the bargain, or so they think," he added, "but that's another story. Men, on the other hand, take a bit longer to sort it all out."

"My guess is that your friend was just getting around to the important stuff when a big hand sweeps down from heaven to knock him on his arse—pardon my language—a little reminder that he's not as invincible as he's spent forty-odd years convincing himself he is. Life is full of those little reminders," he added with a rueful smile, "but it's the first one that's hardest for a man to take."

"Men," she muttered, because she knew it would make him laugh.

"Now, about this friend…should I be jealous?"

"Hell, no, Gus. One cranky man with a cane is all I can handle."

He grinned. "Then there's only one thing left to settle. Did you come here to exercise your jawbone all night or did you come to play dominoes?"

She grinned and pulled a polka-dot scrunchie from her pocket. A woman couldn't play dominoes with a shark like Gus O'Flaherty with her hair falling in her eyes.

"You pour the root beer," she told him. "I'll get the tiles."

It was shortly after ten-thirty when she returned home. Not that Griff was waiting for her. It's just that from his chair at the end of the porch closest to the street, all he had to do was lean forward and crane his neck as far as he could to see a sliver of her driveway through an opening in the trees. He listened, heard a car door slam, and then…nothing.

So, Mr. Saturday Night hadn't come home with her. Which meant he wouldn't be spending the night in her bed, he thought with a little lick of satisfaction. Of course, there was always the possibility that Rose was just returning from someone else's bed. Griff's satisfied smile withered as he recalled the casual way she'd been dressed when she left.

Not that he'd been watching—but from the window on the third-floor landing there was a clear view of the back of her cottage, and he happened to have been standing there, gazing out, when she appeared wearing jeans and a pale pink sleeveless T-shirt with darker pink roses all around the V-neckline. She'd looked good. Damn good. But she clearly had not knocked herself out primping for a night of dinner and dancing at the Ritz. And while initially he'd seen that as an indication this date was No Big Deal, he was suddenly having second thoughts.

Maybe this wasn't simply a standing date, but a Relationship. Maybe she went over to his place every Saturday for a cozy evening of dinner and hot sex. Hell, maybe she cooked for him. Prime rib and blueberry muffins, he thought, his jaw clenching at the mere prospect of Rose sharing her muffins with another man. Especially some guy who didn't even know enough to take her someplace nice and treat her to dinner on a Saturday night. He wondered if this jerk knew—or cared—how hard she worked.

In the short time he'd known her, he'd figured out that she was as softhearted as she was wacky—in other words, an easy target. Why else would she be helping him when she clearly had her hands full with her own business? It bothered him that he might not be the only one taking advantage of her generosity, and it bothered him that it bothered him. After all, his interest in Rose Davenport was strictly business...if you could force yourself to refer to poking through boxes of dusty bric-a-brac in search of porcelain birds "business."

He stood and rested one hip against the porch rail, thinking that come winter, when the leaves fell, he'd be able to catch a glimpse of her anytime he chose. Then he reminded himself that with any luck he wouldn't be there come winter. Besides, he didn't want to turn into some creepy peeper, holed up in his old wreck of a house, waiting for the lady next door to take a shower.

He straightened abruptly. Where the hell had that thought come from? He had no interest whatsoever in watching Rose in the shower. All right, maybe he was a little interested. He wasn't dead, after all, just temporarily off his game. But he would never stoop to watching...unless she invited him to do so. That caveat immediately led to all sorts of intriguing possibilities.

He did his best to ignore them. The only reason he remained outside was a lingering...not nosiness, he assured himself...*concern.* That was it. After all his disturbing thoughts of how Rose *may* have spent the evening, he just wanted to reassure himself that she was all right. He was simply being neighborly, he told himself. Knowing it was a lie. Knowing that had it been a sweet dumpy matron living next door, he'd be inside, glued to the Red Sox game—unless he heard sirens.

Keeping watch had been just one more absolutely ridiculous impulse in what was becoming a string of them. So why stop now, he goaded himself. Why, indeed? He had no idea if her actual date had been anything like the erotically domestic version he'd imagined. But, he decided as he headed for the kitchen, he was going to take a shot at finding out.

Armed and determined, he knocked on her back door.

She opened it and peered quizzically at him.

"Hi. Remember me? Griff. I live next door."

"I know who you are," she retorted. "What are you doing here?"

"Returning a favor."

Her eyes narrowed more.

"You brought me breakfast in bed—so to speak," he explained. "So I decided a midnight snack was in order." He handed her what he'd fished out of the freezer.

She examined the colorful cellophane wrapper with that same slightly bewildered, slightly suspicious, utterly adorable expression.

"I didn't have any muffins, so I grabbed the next best thing."

"A bean burrito," she said without much enthusiasm, without much of any expression actually.

"Bean and beef," he corrected.

"Ah. Well, thanks. As luck would have it, I don't have any frozen burritos on hand, so this will…come in handy."

"No problem. I buy them by the twelve-pack."

"Really? I had no idea they came packaged that way."

He nodded. "You can get all the same flavor or a variety pack. Would you have preferred Nacho Chicken?"

"No," she said quickly. "This is…perfect. Thank you again."

He shrugged off her thanks.

She smiled and put her hand on the doorknob.

He rested one shoulder against the pink doorjamb, to discourage any thoughts she might have of getting rid of him.

"So—" he said, and then lost the rest of the thought when she broke into a dazzling smile.

"Look, Griff, if you've come to apologize, there's no need."

"There isn't?" he countered, scrambling to shift focus from her mouth to remembering what he should be apologizing for. Hell, he hadn't seen her since the yard sales that morning, and he'd thought he'd handled them particularly well.

"No. If you wanted to get out at the gate and walk the rest of the way, I should have let you, instead of insisting on driving you to the door."

"Oh, that," he said, still trying to figure out where the apology should come in.

"I don't blame you for snapping…"

Bingo, he thought. He was supposed to be sorry for snapping.

"It was insensitive of me to speculate about how you were feeling," she continued, "when it's clearly a subject you would prefer not to discuss."

He *had* snapped at her, he realized, replaying in his mind the scene in the drive. Hell, of course he had snapped. She had just shot down his dinner invitation and then topped it off by suggesting he was too worn-out to make it to the house on his own. And she'd been right. His leg had been aching by that time. She was wrong about one thing, though; it wasn't pain that had made him snap. It was the sudden image of her being spun around a dance floor every Saturday night by a tall, young and very graceful Fred Astaire...who also just happened to be the world's foremost collector of teapots or some other thing she would consider enthralling.

"You're right," he agreed. "I don't much like to talk about it. The fact is, I don't much like anything about my life lately, but that's no excuse for lashing out at you."

"Maybe not, but it is understandable. And I do understand, though it might not have appeared so when I tore up half the gravel in your drive, spinning out of there."

"It was a pretty scary moment," he teased. "In fact, I think there are a few pebbles imbedded in my back, like shrapnel."

"Really?" Her attempt at concern was foiled by the laughter in her green eyes. "Because I have these really long, really sharp tweezers I could grab and—"

"Thanks, I think I'd rather live with the pebbles...as a reminder not to turn my back on a woman..."

"Scorned?" she suggested, when he hesitated.

"I was going to say 'a woman in a tizzy,' but thought I might come off politically incorrect, or worse, insensitive." He grinned. "Besides, if I remember correctly, I was the one scorned. Speaking of which, how was your date?"

She did that pouty thing with her mouth. "Date?"

"Right...you know, the regular Saturday night thing you have going."

"Oh. That date. It was...great," she said. "As always."

"Good. That's...good. So, did you and Mr. Saturday Night do anything special?"

"No, not really. We just talked and...you know." She waved her hand in the air and gave a small, awkward smile.

Yeah, he knew, all right.

"Later we played dominoes," she offered.

"Dominoes. I hear that can be very...exciting."

"With the right partner," she agreed.

"And you think you've found the right partner?"

"Definitely. He's a master at dominoes, and a number of other things."

"Really? Is he from around here?"

"Not far," she replied. "He's originally from Ireland."

A European. Figured. European men had it all over American guys when it came to pretending they cared what color plate they were eating off or that they were as happy sitting in a French Provençal side chair as a recliner. Rose would be a sitting duck for a guy like that.

"There's something irresistible about a man with a brogue," she remarked, confirming his hunch.

"I'll take your word for it. What does this guy do...besides play dominoes and speak with a brogue?"

"He's a horticulturist, specializing in dahlias."

"Fascinating," he lied.

"He's actually crossbred different plants to create an entirely new variety. He's working on another now."

The more she talked, the more difficulty he had looking into her eyes and not staring at her mouth. Especially when she hesitated and ran the very tip of her tongue over her bottom lip—the way she was doing right now. From out of nowhere came the urge to kiss her. It took hold of him, like a hand at the back of his neck, and he felt himself leaning closer, slowly, slowly closing the distance between them.

She was still talking about the damn dahlias, reciting what sounded like a list of names. Unfortunately, the only words penetrating the warm fog in his head were ones that enflamed him further. *Blazing. Scarlet. Splendor.*

When she eventually ran out of names, they were standing only a few inches apart, so close that it was hard to say where his body heat ended and hers began. In fact, the night around them seemed like one giant, vibrating, overheated mass of expectancy.

"Sounds like one helluva talented guy," he conceded. "Even if he is a little dense."

Her long lashes fluttered. "I beg your pardon?"

Griff shrugged. "Seems to me a man would have to be dense to settle for playing dominoes when he could be painting the town with a woman like you on his arm."

She gazed up at him with eyes that shimmered in the moonlight. "Really?"

"Really."

She was gorgeous, he decided. Not simply pretty, as he'd first thought. Gorgeous. Delicate, almost ethereal, and vibrant all at the same time. And absolutely irresistible...even without a brogue.

"You know, I've never been a big fan of coveralls on women," he said, "but you've changed that."

"Really?" she said again, her voice soft and just a little breathy.

He nodded. "Really. I've been thinking that you look so damn good in just any old thing, you'd be lethal if you really took time to fix yourself up."

"Really?"

As heated as he was, he noted the subtle change in her inflection.

"So you've been thinking, have you?" she drawled.

"I mean—"

She cut him off. "I know exactly what you meant, Griffin, *and* I know what you're thinking, and believe me, you're wasting your time...and your burrito."

Rose slapped the frozen burrito in his hand and slammed the door in his face, then stood staring at it.

The man was impossible...self-centered...conniving... She made several angry, sputtering trips through the small house before returning to the kitchen to reclaim the glass of wine she'd just finished pouring herself when Griff knocked on the door.

So much for a quiet, relaxing hour of reading before bed, she thought, taking a gulp. She wasn't the temperamental type as a rule, but Griffin had a knack for getting under her skin, and disrupting her entire life in the process. And she had been letting him. But no more.

His look of confusion as she'd shut the door on him told her that his comment about her appearance—or more accurately, her *potential*—had been intended as a compliment. As if she should be flattered to hear that if she only worked at it and tried hard enough and turned herself inside out, she had what it took to measure up to his standards.

Well, she was through measuring up to anyone's standards but her own. And Hollis Griffin was about to find that out— and in a way even an aging frat-boy like him could understand.

It took an hour of rummaging through boxes of clothes she had packed away; forty minutes in a scented bubble bath; twenty minutes searching for Velcro rollers; and nearly another hour on hair and makeup; plus two more glasses of wine—then she was ready.

At two a.m. she was picking her way along the path from her house to Griff's, barefoot. She paused at the porch steps to slip on a pair of strappy black sandals with killer four-inch heels, and then rang the doorbell. Twice.

It took a few minutes before she heard him making his way down the stairs, the cadence of his slow, limping footsteps music to her ears.

He swung the door open and stood before her wearing half-zipped jeans and an expression somewhere between unconscious and enraged.

"What the—" He paused and squinted at her, his gaze becoming wider and more alert as it swept from her bare shoulders to her Red Hot Cherry toenails and back.

"Rose?"

He was conscious now, all right. And stunned. Just the way she'd wanted him.

Unfortunately, the combination of bare masculine chest and snug, faded jeans had delivered her a stunning little libido jolt of its own. She hadn't planned on that, and it took a few seconds for her to recall her opening line.

"Hi. Remember me? I live next door."

"I remember, all right," he replied, still staring.

"Did I wake you?"

He nodded. "I think so."

"Good. I just stopped by to tell you that this is for you, Griff."

Slowly, her every nerve fluttering in a way she had also not anticipated, she executed a pirouette exactly as she had rehearsed, giving him plenty of time to take it all in: the short, second-skin black dress that was a relic of her former life, her long, stiletto enhanced bare legs, the neckline that teased in front and plunged several inches below her waist in back.

She even remembered to toss her head full of loose curls, loose, painstakingly created curls, which wouldn't last too much longer in the damp night air. It didn't matter. She wouldn't need them much longer. She could already hear Griff breathing a little harder and feel his heightened interest and was thrilled by the evidence that her plan, fueled by wine and anger, was working.

She had purchased this dress for the express purpose of seduction, one of many desperate attempts to reignite her marriage—but tonight she had something different in mind. She wasn't here to seduce Hollis Griffin, just to let him know that if she wanted to, she damn well could...and without any helpful hints from him.

"All for you," she said again, softly, when they were once more standing face-to-face.

"You smell good," he said, his own voice soft, and rough.

"I know," Rose replied.

"I mean, you always smell good, but you smell even better right now."

"I know." She ought to. She'd soaked, sprayed and dabbed herself with the hideously expensive designer scent that Maryann had given her for Christmas and that she'd been saving for a special occasion. She'd reasoned that bringing Griff down a peg or two was about as special an occasion as she was likely to encounter in the near future.

"So you approve?" she asked, her chest lifting with a deep breath, the dozen slim silver bangles on her right wrist tinkling flirtatiously as she ran her fingers through her hair.

"Yeah, I definitely approve. What's the word for really, head-over-heels approve?"

He reached for her.

Rose backed away with a little laugh. "Oh, no, no touching."

For a few seconds he looked as forlorn as a little boy who just had his lollipop snatched away, then he broke into a slow smile.

"I get it," he said. "This is a dream, right? Just like last night. As soon as I touch you and get you into bed, you're going to scream in my ear again, right?"

Rose had no idea what he was talking about, except that obviously he'd dreamed about her last night, and in that dream they had been in bed together. The image it stirred in her mind was not entirely unpleasant, but it was alarming. The wine must be wearing off, she decided, because it suddenly occurred to her that this might not be as brilliant an idea as it had at first seemed.

Determined to make her point and get out of there, she shook her head. "I'm not going to scream in your ear."

"That's right, you didn't scream. You blew the horn."

"I'm not going to blow any horns, either," she assured him, hoping her growing apprehension didn't show. "And I'm certainly not going to bed with you."

He smiled, his look lazy and hungry and happy, all at the same time. On him, it was a very appealing combination, and if not for the fact that she was there to tell him in no uncertain terms that she was not now and never would be romantically interested in him, she would probably be damn interested.

It irked her to admit it, even to herself, but facts were facts. And the fact was that she was a sucker for the sort of scruffy, wounded rogue, take me home and feed me a good, hot meal and tuck me into bed—preferably *your* bed—persona that he was presenting at that moment.

"Are you sure about that, Rosie?" he asked. "Not the horn, the bed."

"Very sure."

He ran his eyes over her in unhurried appreciation. "But you said that all this…"

"Is for you," she finished for him. "It is. To prove to you beyond a shadow of a doubt that you were right earlier. If I wanted to…how did you put it? Oh, yes, if I wanted to take time to really 'fix myself up,' I could be exactly the kind of woman you like." She took a half step back and made a little swaying motion, arms bent, palms up, her expression flirtatiously quizzical. "Agreed?"

He smiled appreciatively. "Damn straight."

"Good." She dropped her hands and her flirty smile. "That's point one. Point two—and I want you to really pay attention here, Griff—is that I have no interest whatsoever, and absolutely no intention of ever again wasting time, *fixing myself up,* to please you or any other overbearing, self-centered man who thinks I'm just full of potential and has a yen to play Svengali with my life."

She took half a breath, refusing to be unnerved by his placid expression.

"It was just a—"

"To you, maybe," she snapped without letting him finish. "Not to me. I've already wasted too much time trying to mold myself to someone else's vision of what I ought to be. No more. I dress the way I do everything else, as I please. And I really don't care to hear your or anyone else's opinion on the subject…even if comes disguised as a compliment."

"I see."

Rose wasn't sure she liked the nature of his response. It was far too offhand, lending the moment an unsettling, anticlimactic air. "Then we understand each other. I thought it important we do, since we'll be working together."

"Definitely. Hell, with all the sexual harassment going around these days, a man has to think twice before telling a woman she's so pretty just looking at her makes his eyes ache."

Rose nodded, feeling more uneasy by the moment. She wasn't sure, but it was almost as if he was standing there, ostensibly agreeing with her, and doing it all over again. Complimenting her even while claiming to understand why she didn't want him to.

At least it *seemed* he was suggesting that *she* was so pretty she made his eyes ache, but she wasn't about to risk humiliation by making that assumption incorrectly. She also wasn't able to prevent the small ripple of pleasure his words incited. *If* they were meant for her. Of course, there was nothing wrong with feeling flattered, just as there was nothing objectionable about an honest, straightforward compliment, which this seemed to have been. Truthfully, the whole issue was becoming so muddled in her poor, tired head, she wondered if maybe she had overreacted in the first place.

"Is that all you woke me up to tell me?" he asked.

"Yes. Why are you smiling?"

"I was just wondering if, considering how easily we got it all settled between us, maybe there wasn't just a little bit of overkill in your preparation?" He took his sweet time underscoring his point by running his gaze over her. Twice.

"Not at all," she retorted.

"You don't think you could have accomplished the same thing by waiting and giving me a call in the morning to tell me to never again allude to the fact that you're teaching me more about the true nature of beauty than I knew existed?"

"No, I do not."

He *was* doing it again. Rose was certain. She just wasn't sure how to go about calling him on it without appearing ridiculous…especially in the face of his calm, almost indulgently amused demeanor.

Lord, she wished she hadn't drunk so much wine.

And that he didn't seem so damn refreshed on only a couple of hours sleep, while she was finding the cushioned glider behind him increasingly more tempting.

"Moreover," she continued, tossing her head, determined not to let her resolve waver no matter how sleepy she felt, "the fact that you would suggest this could have been handled by phone shows me that you've missed the point entirely."

"What is the point, Rose?"

"To demonstrate to you that I am not the kind of woman you are looking for, and that any overtures in that direction would only jeopardize our working together."

"I get it. You thought the best way to discourage me from wanting you was to show up on my doorstep in the middle of the night looking so good I can't recall ever wanting a woman so much in my whole life."

"Yes," she said, then quickly shook her head. "I mean no. You're twisting it around."

"Why don't you untwist it for me, Rose?" he asked softly, moving closer. She must have moved, too, because somehow one of the porch's solid columns was at her back.

"Cut it out, Griffin. I didn't come here to play games with you."

He grinned, a slow, crooked, knowing grin. "It's good that you pointed that out. Because a less sensitive guy than myself might jump to the conclusion that that's exactly what you came here for."

"Well, it's not—so you can wipe that grin off your face. I simply wanted to lay all my cards on the table…"

"Oh, you succeeded," he assured her, heat replacing the laughter in his eyes. "Admirably."

"…and be honest with you as to where we stand on this matter."

He shrugged. "If you say so."

"I do. It's not my fault that your one-track, overblown

ego causes you to interpret everything with the perceptiveness of an adolescent in a hormonal daze.''

"Ouch. You're a little touchy on the subject, aren't you?''

"Look who's talking," she snapped. "You know how much you hate being called 'sensitive'? Well, that's only half as much as I hate being told I have potential.''

"Make a hell of a pair, don't we," he countered, rubbing his jaw pensively.

His rueful smile was unexpected, and disarming. Rose gave in to a small, grudging smile of her own. "I suppose we do.''

"Hell, there's no suppose about it. Where I grew up, they'd say we're like two hedgehogs in one pocket.''

"You grew up in Manhattan," she reminded him dryly. "I don't usually think of that as hedgehog country.''

"I only grew up in Manhattan in reality," he told her. "That doesn't count for nearly as much as where you grow up in your dreams.''

Rose met his gaze, startled.

"Yeah," he said, nodding with more satisfaction than surprise. "I thought that would hit home with you. Face it, Rosie, you and I are alike in more ways than either of us could have predicted. We've both got sore spots that are like land mines lurking beneath the surface. And we both grew up wishing things were different than they were.''

"You don't know anything about how I grew up.''

"I know enough to know I'm right," he said. "Just like I know that at this minute we're both standing here, wondering what it would feel like to just once defuse the land mines, let go and see what happens.''

"I am not wondering anything of the sort," she insisted, without a shred of conviction.

"That's all right, Rosie," said Griff, his voice soft and rough and very, very close. "I'm wondering enough for both of us.''

Chapter Six

She ought to stop him. She could, despite the fact that he was bigger and stronger and didn't like taking no for an answer. Whatever else he was, Griffin was a product of Devora and the military, and that was enough to assure Rose that all she had to do was say the word and he would back off.

The problem wasn't Griff. It was her. She didn't want to stop him...not now. Not yet.

Instead of pulling her closer, he leaned in to her, his strong hands on her shoulders as he held her against the porch post. It seemed to take forever for his mouth to reach hers, so long that her heart was skittering and her breathing was on hold and the first touch of his lips was like a spark tossed on a field that had been without rain for a long, long time.

His kiss wasn't gentle. Or rough. It was perfect...beyond perfect...beyond any other kiss in her entire life. And like parched earth, she couldn't get enough—of his scent, his touch, his breath...of this singular moment in time.

Pleasure flowed through her as his mouth, warm and sure and appallingly skillful, moved over hers. She grasped his shoulders and was instantly reminded that he was half dressed. There was fresh excitement in the smooth heat of his skin and the play of his muscles. There was nothing between them but the night and this sudden, sweet hunger.

…meant to be…meant to be…

The words flowed from somewhere deep inside her and drummed softly in her head. What had gone before and what might follow ceased to matter, as all of her yearned toward him.

She had to go up on her toes to get closer. She had to taste more of him. She had to moan softly when she did.

He trembled at the sound and yanked her against him, his lips coasting along her throat, his hand sliding down her back and inside the low-cut dress and the barely-there panties that were the only kind that could be worn under it. She'd spent ten minutes hunting for the ridiculous panties, and as his hand curved around her bare bottom, she was very glad she had. When he pressed her close, the contact rocked them both.

He dragged his mouth back to hers, groaning and kissing her in a hard, hot rush. Suddenly Rose understood what it meant to be ravished, and why all those women on glossy paperback covers looked so dazed. She was lost… enthralled…a willing vassal of his tongue and hands and pure, intoxicating strength. Eyes closed, head back, she rode wave after rolling wave of pleasure, as his hands moved over her, claiming and worshipping at once.

Breathless, her senses flooded, she clung to him, as he swung her around and began backing her toward the glider. She felt like a leaf swept up in a hurricane, and the urge to close her mind and just let it take her was powerful.

He lifted his head only enough to meet her gaze. His eyes were black, and there was no mistaking the intent that glittered there. The thought that she should be alarmed drifted through her head and was gone.

"What's your pleasure, Rosie?" he whispered, moving his hands through her hair, caressing her face with his whiskered cheek.

You, she thought, hazily. It was true. He was more pleasure than she'd known existed—maybe more than she could handle. But she was not going to think about that right now.

"Speed or comfort?" he prodded, laughing softly when she gazed bewilderedly at him. "Here or upstairs?"

A side of herself Rose didn't recognize wished he hadn't stopped to ask. But he had, and stopping gave her time to think. She supposed she ought to be grateful. Still, it took every shred of her willpower to press her palms against his chest and ignore the intoxicating scent of desire coming off him.

"Neither."

His hands stilled. He rested his forehead against hers. "Please, please tell me that means you have a yen for the standing position. It might be dicey with my leg, but I'll give it my best shot."

"It means we have to stop. This is happening too fast."

"Sometimes that's the way it happens."

She shook her head. "Not for me. Not this."

"You want this." It was not a question.

"Yes, but I'm not crazy enough to act on every impulse— especially not the ones that take hold of me at two in the morning, when I've had too much wine and a half-naked man has just kissed me senseless."

He lifted his head without letting her go. He did not look amused. "Does this happen to you often?"

"Actually, this is a first."

"Good." He kept his arms around her, but there was no real pressure in his grip, or his tone. "And here I thought acting on impulse was your M.O. Isn't that why you painted your truck—impulse?"

"That's different," she said, reason returning slowly. "If that turned out to be a mistake, I could have painted over it. Once I give myself to someone, it can never be undone."

Her words sank through Griff like lead in quicksand. *Once I give myself to someone…* "I guess I never thought of it quite so profoundly," he told her, knowing it was the understatement of a lifetime.

"I never think of it any other way," she said bluntly. Her expression was direct and unapologetic as she added, "Just for the record, I'm not into one-night stands."

"I guess I should have known that. I think I did, actually," he admitted, running one fingertip across her bare shoulder with a resigned sigh. "The sight of you in this dress must have clouded my judgment."

She offered a rueful smile. "I think the wine clouded mine. Coming here this way was not my finest moment."

"I don't know, it was plenty fine for me. Though I wouldn't recommend it as a way to discourage unwanted male attention in general," he drawled, permitting his hands to slide over her hips and butt, an exquisite form of self-torture now that it was clear he couldn't have her. Not tonight, anyway.

"It certainly doesn't seem to have discouraged you very much," she observed in a wry tone.

"I'm a slow learner. That's no reason for you to give up, though. In fact, you probably ought to come over here wearing this dress every night until I get the message through my thick skull."

"Nice try, Griff. But as soon as I get home, this dress is going back into retirement."

His eyebrows lifted.

"It's from a former life," she added, which only moved him from puzzled to downright intrigued.

"Really?" He traced the edge of the dress where it slashed from her throat to the side of her waist. "What sort of former life?"

"Nothing worthy of that look you're giving me, I assure you."

He remained silent, waiting.

She fidgeted, then rolled her eyes. "You really want to

know what sort of life? Married life. There, now are you satisfied?''

"That's the wrong question to ask me, about now," he countered dryly. "You were married?"

She nodded, clearly irked with herself for allowing the conversation to veer in this direction. He, on the other hand, was downright mesmerized. *Married.* He'd never considered that Rose might have been married, that Mr. Saturday Night might be an ex...or maybe a not-yet ex...maybe simply an estranged husband with every right to—

"Divorced?"

She nodded again, and he felt relieved.

"Kids?"

"No."

"Probably for the best."

She shrugged. "So I've heard."

"How long?"

"How long married or how long divorced?"

He considered. "Both."

"Five years married. Five divorced. Has a nice symmetry, don't you think?"

"What happened?"

Her laugh had a weary edge to it that almost made him sorry he'd asked.

"Lots of things *happened,*" she replied. "Ten years is a long time."

"And you'd rather not talk about it."

"Yes," she said, sighing. "But I also realize it's probably inevitable now that the subject has reared its ugly little head. So, in order to get it behind us, I'll give you the highlights— or, more accurately, the lowlights. I met Jonathan Sheffield at a Brown University fund-raiser. I was a grad student, working part-time in the Alumni Office. He was the pride and joy of the Medical School, an up-and-coming plastic surgeon with the most prestigious firm in the state."

"A match made in Ivy League heaven," he observed.

"More like a mismatch," she countered, her tone sardonic.

"How so?"

"I was full scholarship. The Sheffields have been bleeding blue for generations. Believe me," she said with a small laugh, "they did not think I was heaven-sent."

"Was it his family that broke you up?"

"Oh, no. Jonathan considered their opinions the same as he did everyone else's—when it suited his purposes. That was one of the things that first drew me to him. He was always so certain of who he was and where he was going."

She shrugged, as if to shed the hint of wistfulness that had crept into her voice. "Anyway, we met, fell madly in love— or what we took for love. Turned out to be just plain old madness. But as luck would have it, by the time we realized that, we were married. We worked at it for a while—hence this dress," she added with a self-derisive shake of her head. "But ultimately it was a lost cause. End of story."

Not by a long shot, thought Griff, weighing his wish to know more against her obvious reluctance to rehash it. A reluctance he understood all too well. Still…

"What was it about Sheffield that made you fall in madness with him?" he asked, hoping that by keeping it light, he could lure her into opening up a little more. "Aside from the fact that he didn't give a twit what his family thought about his choice in women. A serious point in the man's favor, I am forced to admit. From where I'm standing, he won that one hands-down."

"Thanks. I think." She yawned. "What was the question…oh, right, what made me fall for Jonathan?" She pursed her lips. Shrugged. "A simple case of mistaken identity," she said at last.

"Mistaken identity?" he countered, his eyes narrowing.

She nodded. "Right. You see, I've always known exactly what I wanted out of life."

"Which is?"

"Everything," she retorted with a self-effacing laugh. "Everything I didn't have growing up."

"Such as..."

Again he heard in her laughter that edge of sadness that tugged at his insides in a peculiar way. He wanted to tell her to forget it, it didn't matter, and at the same time, his desire to know everything about her grew stronger.

"Where do I start?" she said without a trace of her usual spirit. "The basics, I suppose...food, heat, school clothes that fit and were reasonably clean."

She wasn't joking. It took a second or so for Griff to process that fact and catch up with what she was saying.

"So I created a world I did like. You were right about that. You just don't know how right. I would beg folks for their old magazines and I would make scrapbooks of my life. Not the usual kind of scrapbook. Mine weren't filled with mementoes of the life I was leading," she explained. "My scrapbooks told the story of the life I was *going* to lead. Someday.

"I would cut out bits and pieces and use them to build rooms on the pages. Then I'd fill the rooms with the perfect furniture and accessories. When I got a little older, I figured out a way to make closets, with doors that opened, and behind the doors were perfectly arranged shelves of groceries or linens or crystal bottles filled with perfume and bubble bath."

She closed her eyes and rubbed her forehead. "I know what you're thinking."

"Do you?" Griff countered, certain she couldn't possibly know, when he wasn't sure himself what he was thinking...much less what he was feeling. He knew only that the picture she was painting in his mind stirred the brew of rage and helplessness and injustice that was always simmering inside him these days. Except that this time, it wasn't himself he was feeling sorry for.

She moved to lean against the porch rail, and he followed.

"You're thinking it's no wonder I grew up to be the kind of woman who'd paint a truck to look like a quilt."

He grinned. "You did know," he replied, his tone one of mock astonishment.

"Of course. Did you think my psychic connections were limited to flamingoes?"

"Silly me. So what did you do with these scrapbooks?"

From the corner of his eye he caught the look of pain that flickered across her face, before she shrugged and said, "Hid them, so my mother wouldn't rip them up in one of her rampages. She considered them a waste of time...like everything else I did. My mother was one of those people you just can't please, no matter how long or hard you try."

"I'm sorry." He touched the back of her hand, eliciting a quick smile.

"Thanks, but that was a long, long time ago. And besides, the things I wanted most weren't even in the scrapbooks. There weren't any glossy magazine pictures of them for me to clip—only pictures of people who had those things. So I cut the people out and studied their faces and the way they stood and the clothes they wore, so that when the time came, I would get everything right."

"What sort of things?"

"Things you can't see...or buy. Stability—that's what those people in the pictures had, and it was always very high on the list of things I wanted when I grew up. I wanted things to be right. I wanted to be...normal. And safe. And happy."

She hesitated. Griff was stunned. He wanted to say "stop," to spare her from remembering any more...and himself from hearing it. Trouble was, he couldn't think of the right words. The gentlest, most comforting words were called for, and such words were not his strong suit. It was as if his casual curiosity had opened a Pandora's box which he now had no idea how to shut.

"I don't know exactly what to call it," she finally said. "Predictability, I guess. I would have liked to be able to come home from school and just walk into the house the way I saw kids do on television…just toss my books down and grab a glass of milk and some cookies from the cookie jar—they wouldn't even have to be homemade cookies, just Lorna Doones would be fine. It wouldn't matter as long as I could go home without a knot in my stomach, without having to worry whether my mother would be there, and how drunk she would be, and if it would be a happy drunk or a—"

"Rose, you don't have to—"

"I know. I'm rambling. Sorry."

"That's not—"

"None of this answers your question, does it. At least, not in a way you could possibly understand. The point I wanted to make was that I knew exactly what I wanted, and I planned and studied and worked my butt off to reach one goal after another. And then I met Jonathan, and to me, *he* seemed to have been heaven-sent. Handsome and intelligent and self-assured, just like the men in the magazines—from God's drawing board to my private fantasy.

"We married as soon as I finished graduate school. Jonathan was even more successful by then, and I was able to take a job where the pay wasn't great but I really believed I could make a difference. It was very important to me to share the blessings I had been given, with my family, my clients, with others looking for a way out." There was a distance in her gaze that suggested she was talking as much to herself as him.

"By the time I was twenty-six, I had my career on the right track, the right house in the right neighborhood, and the right husband…respected, safe, predictable."

"Only he turned out not to be so safe or predictable?" he guessed, already despising the man for failing to live up to Rose's expectations—for destroying her dreams.

She blinked and met his gaze. "No. I did."

One of these days, he told himself, he was going to stop being surprised every time the woman threw him a curveball.

"What does that mean?"

"It means that in the end, neither one of us got what we bargained for," she returned. "Me, because all that time I was cutting and pasting in my scrapbooks, I left out one very important element. And Jonathan, because while I saw him as the answer to my prayers, he saw me as a blank slate."

"I don't get it."

"Think about it. It's pathetically simple. The man is a plastic surgeon. He deals in perfection. It's his obsession, his life's work—and I was his private playground."

"In what way?" he demanded, prepared to be shocked.

"In every way," she replied. "And much to my surprise. You see, I naively believed in my own fantasy—that through education and determination, I could drag myself up to a social and cultural level where a man like Jonathan would want me. *Me*. Boy, was I wrong." The words were simple, brutal, direct.

"What Jonathan wanted was someone he could mold into *his* image of the perfect wife, perfect hostess and social secretary, perfect career-enhancing ornament. He wanted to play creator, and he was smart enough to know that he could never get away with it with a woman from his own *class*, a woman with social experience and self-assurance and her own ideas of how things ought to be done."

"Me," she continued, bitterness and regret flashing in her eyes. "I was nothing more than a lump of putty. Pretty degrading when you think about it. Some women complain about being seen as a piece of meat, but at least that's an acknowledgment that there is *something* admirable there. I wasn't even that. I was nothing but…*potential*. An opportunity for Jonathan to perform miracles—a scalpel, elocution lessons, a few fashion tips and *voilà*."

Griff felt his muscles tense, his jaw clench. "You're not serious?"

"Quite. You see before you the new and improved version of *moi*."

"What?" he asked, unable to keep from studying her

closely. Her face, her body. "What's different? What did he do to you?" he demanded, squeezing her shoulders too tightly without meaning to.

"He didn't do all of it personally," she explained. "He just suggested and arranged and orchestrated. Laser eye surgery to get rid of my glasses and a peel to get rid of the squint lines at the sides of my eyes. A small implant to enhance my jawline and liposuction to get rid of excess butt and belly."

Griff couldn't explain the heat gathering in his head. It's not that he had any complaints about her butt and belly as they were now. In fact, he considered them top-notch. But the fact that they had been altered, that she had come with another, different butt and belly that he would never get to see or touch, really bothered him.

"New nose," she added, as if struggling to remember it all. "The old one was wider and had a bump here." She touched the bridge of her nose. "That's about it, except…"

"Except?"

"Except for my birthday present," she said with a humorless laugh. "A few weeks after my twenty-ninth birthday, Jonathan announced that he had already decided how we would celebrate my thirtieth—with a romantic getaway to Paris and the French Riviera. I was thrilled…not only was he actually planning something he knew I had always dreamed of doing, but he was going to take ten whole days off work to be with me—a miracle in and of itself. For about a week I was walking on air, and all the niggling little doubts about our marriage vanished."

"And then…" he prompted.

"And then he brought home some pamphlets that he said would help explain the next stage of our trip preparation, the step that would make me worthy of appearing in a bathing suit on the Riviera. They were about breast implants."

Instantly, automatically, Griff's gaze dropped to her chest.

"Too late, Griffin," she snapped. "I had them removed before the ink was dry on the divorce papers."

"I'm sorry," he said, gesturing uselessly. "Not that you...I meant I was sorry about looking. It was...reflex."

"Hmm. I know. That's one of the main reasons I got rid of them. Life is a lot simpler when you don't have to deal with male reflexes on every street corner."

He didn't laugh, didn't even manage a smile. He cupped her face in his hands and gazed at her as if she were a very elaborate work of art.

"I never saw you in glasses, or with a bump on your nose, but I can't even fathom the possibility that any part of you ever needed to be altered in any way. And I can't understand how you could go along with his crap."

"God, I've wondered the same thing. I suppose that back then, I was so accustomed to inventing and reinventing myself according to a magazine photo or what I thought I was supposed to be, that it all seemed...natural."

She turned and faced him squarely. "Does that make sense?" she asked him.

He thought for a moment. "I'm not sure how to answer that. No, it doesn't make any sense at all that a woman like you ever believed you had to change yourself or be something other than what you are. I mean, you're generous and talented and beautiful. But in spite of the fact that it doesn't make sense, I do understand. I'm just glad you finally woke up and got away from that jerk."

"I woke up, all right," she echoed, seeming to shiver. She shrugged. "For a long time after the divorce, I felt like a failure, like I'd thrown away everything I'd every wanted and was right back where I started."

"And now?"

"Now I accept that it was inevitable. The bar kept being raised, and it was harder and harder to reach it and still hold on to some semblance of...me."

She folded her arms across her chest as if hugging herself. Or holding herself together, he thought.

"When I was married, I sometimes looked in the mirror and had the eerie sense that it was a stranger looking back.

I began to think of that woman as *Jonathan's wife.* I began second-guessing everything I did, every thought I had. Even at work or when I was alone, I'd hesitate and ask myself what *Jonathan's wife* should do. More and more it felt as if the part of me deep inside that was still me was getting squeezed out of existence."

If there were words for what he was feeling, he didn't know them. And he sure didn't know what to do about this urge to somehow do something, *anything,* to make up to her for things that were lost forever. Like, for starters, a childhood where the visions dancing in her head at night were of prettier things than survival.

He settled for acting on the far simpler urge to enclose her hand in his and bring it to his lips. "I'm glad that didn't happen," he told her. "I'm glad you're here."

"I'm glad you're here, too," she said, squeezing his hand. "It's like old times. Devora and I logged a lot of hours on this porch, talking things over...though I have to admit, we never pulled an all-nighter."

Griff almost squirmed. The last thing he wanted to get into was a discussion of Devora and his reason for being there.

"One thing's for sure," he said. "This explains why you bit my head off when I came to your door earlier—bearing gifts, I might add."

"You mean when you came to the door with a partially thawed burrito and told me I had great 'potential'?"

"It has a different ring to it when you say it," he acknowledged. "I meant it in the best possible sense. But, I see now how it must have sounded to you. What's that they say about perception and reality?"

"Perception is reality...but now you're getting a little too existential for me. Especially in the wee hours of the morn," she added, the words muffled as she buried a yawn in the palm of her hand.

"Wanna sit and watch the sun come up?" he asked, half

teasing, half hopeful. "I could toss a couple of burritos on the fire."

"A truly tempting offer, but I'll pass this time." She kicked off her high heels and scooped them up by the flimsy straps. "I'm going home."

"Not so fast. There's something I need to know first. I wasn't…misreading you earlier, was I? When I was kissing you?"

"I don't know," she countered with a matter-of-fact shrug. "Was it raw, unbridled lust you were reading?"

He nodded, startled. "Yeah, that about covers it."

"Then, you weren't misreading me." Her smile faded suddenly. "Look, Griffin, if you think I kissed you because I'm still caught up in that people-pleasing mode, then you—"

"That's not it," he interjected.

"Then why did you ask?"

"I wanted to make sure you weren't just…"

She looked perplexed. "Faking it?"

"Something like that." He stuck his hands in his pockets. "I just don't want you kissing me or going to bed with me for some fool reason like you feel sorry for me, or because you were a friend of my aunt's."

"Why should I feel sorry for you?"

He grit his teeth, cursing himself for bringing it up. He had just wanted to be sure, to head off the doubts and second thoughts that were bound to settle in later, when he was alone.

"You *shouldn't*," he assured her. "I was just afraid you might. It's obvious you have a weakness for castoffs and I'm…hell, you must have noticed that I'm not in the greatest shape at present."

"Oh. You mean your leg."

"Yeah. My leg," he shot back, irked by her nonchalance. "And the dizzy spells and the loss of peripheral vision in my left eye and how my balance is off and the inconvenient little fact that more than likely I'll never fly again…which, for your information, is the only damn thing I've ever wanted to do or been any good at.''

"I see. I hadn't really been aware of all that, but it is quite a list, and I guess some people would feel sorry for you. But not me,'' she added before he could respond. "In fact, I can honestly say that from the very first instant I set eyes on you, *sorry* is not among the emotions I've been feeling.'' She broke into a grin. "Hell, Griffin, I slammed the door in your face the first time you tried to kiss me tonight.''

"That's right, you did.'' The reminder cheered him instantaneously.

"Furthermore, even if I were dumb enough to feel sorry for you, I'd be more likely to bring you an ice pack than let you stick your tongue in my mouth.''

"Good. That's good.''

"It is?''

He nodded. "I'm not into mercy sex.''

"Then you can quit worrying,'' she countered, her eyes gleaming darkly. "Because mercy sex is not what I have in mind for you.''

Her candor pleased and amused him. Fascinating, he thought. The woman was absolutely fascinating, like a prism in sunlight. He couldn't wait to see what would be revealed next.

"Then it's settled,'' he said. "There'll be only good, honest straight-up sex between us.''

"Agreed,'' she said, laughter tugging at her lips as she held out her hand to shake his.

"And I understand why you need to take things slowly,'' Griff told her. He slid his hands up her arms and rested them on her shoulders as he idly caressed a stray curl between one thumb and forefinger. "I don't want to press you. You want time, you've got it. How much time?''

"Hell, Griffin, I'd hate to see what it would be like if you *did* want to press me. How do you expect me to answer that?''

"Directly. Twenty-four to forty-eight hours would be the time frame I'd prefer, but, hey, you're in command here."

"You may not look much like a military man at the moment," she muttered, "but you sure think like one. I hate to throw your spit-shined, well-ordered world off-kilter, but I don't have an answer. Because there isn't one. It's just something I'll know when the moment is right."

He frowned. That sounded a little vague for his liking. Not to mention the fact that his world had been off-kilter since he walked into her shop, and he was hoping this might help rectify that. "So what you're saying is that you'll let me know when we're good to go?"

She offered a salute so sloppy that it would have earned push-ups for even the rawest of recruits. "Aye, aye, sir." She giggled and wrinkled her forehead. "Oops, wrong outfit. What's Air Force for 'aye, aye'?"

"That'll do. I'd say 'at ease,' but I'm afraid you'd pass out. You ought to be in bed...your own," he added stoically, as her laughter turned into a yawn, followed by a little swaying motion that had him quickly taking her by the elbow. "Come on. I'll walk you home."

"Right, that officer-and-a-gentleman stuff. Very gallant, Griffin, but now that we've discovered this new hedgehog-in-a-pocket affiliation, I feel comfortable being totally honest with you. It's like this—it's late, I'm tired, and you'd only slow me down."

Surprisingly, the remark didn't bother him at all. The thought of not seeing her safely to her door did, however. Could he trust her to stay put while he went upstairs for his shoes and cane?

No.

"For heaven's sake, Griff, this is *Wickford*," she exclaimed, as he stood vacillating. "And I'm only going next door."

"All right," he conceded reluctantly. "But I'm going to watch from here. Flick your lights when you get inside."

"Okay," she agreed.

He reached for her, bent his head and brushed her mouth with his. The touch was brief and light, but sufficient to reassure him that desire still smoldered just beneath the surface, in both of them.

"I ought to warn you, Rose, I'm a patient man when I have to be, but not nearly as chivalrous as you seem to think. The next time you show up here and drag me out of bed, be prepared to be dragged back in."

He watched her slip into the night, then stood on the porch, grinning for no particular reason, until her kitchen light flashed three times.

He slept soundly until the phone rang a few minutes before nine the next morning. Without opening his eyes, he reached for it and mumbled something into the receiver.

"Griff?" enquired a familiar and welcome voice.

"Rose."

"Did I wake you?"

"Yeah, but I'm getting used to it."

"Sorry."

"Really?"

"Well, a little."

"I'm not getting out of bed to go to yard sales with you."

"This is Sunday. Everyone knows there are no good yard sales on Sunday."

"Hallelujah."

"I'm rushing to get to church on time, then I have to go straight to work. I just called… What's that noise? Are you snoring, Griffin?"

"Mmm."

"Well, stop and pay attention. I called to tell you not to make plans for Wednesday night. I may have a lead on the birds."

"What sort of lead?" he asked.

"It's a little complicated. I'll explain when I see you. If you can be at the shop by five on Wednesday, we can leave from there."

"Sounds like a plan."

"Good." She paused. "Well, then, I guess I'll see you then."

"Wait."

"Yes?"

He hesitated, then said, "I've been thinking…about something you said last night. About the scrapbooks you made when you were a kid."

"God, I really did get into all that," she groaned into the phone. "I was sort of hoping it was only a bad dream." In a brighter tone, she added, "How about if we just forget last night ever happened?"

Forget? "Not a chance," he retorted. "You said that you left out something very important when you were clipping pictures of your fantasy life. What was it?"

"Oh, Griff, I said a lot of things…most of them nonsense."

"I don't think so. You sounded especially serious when you said it, and very…sure. You were telling me how neither you nor your ex got what you bargained for—how he wanted a blank canvas. Remember? What was it you wanted that you didn't put in the scrapbooks?"

It was possible she might not remember, but something about the silence that followed assured him she did. And so he waited.

"It's not so much something I *didn't* put in," she said at last, "as something I *couldn't* have—not when I was nine. Heck, I was still struggling to figure it out when I was twenty-nine."

He recognized the self-directed wryness that crept into her tone, and knew precisely the expression he would see on her face at that moment. What did that mean? he wondered.

"I guess it comes down to what I meant when I said it was a case of mistaken identity. I spent all those years dreaming of the ideal man, a man I could love truly, madly, deeply and all that. The man of dreams," she added, and now there was self-consciousness in her voice. "I had no way of knowing that I'd have been far better off looking for just some ordinary guy on the street who could love me just as I am…a man who believed *I* was the woman of *his* dreams—gosh, will you look at the time?'' she exclaimed without giving him a chance to respond.

A good thing, since he was at a loss for something meaningful to say.

''Gotta run. See you Wednesday,'' she said lightly, and hung up.

Griff rolled to his back and stared at the ceiling that slanted above his head.

Wednesday, he thought, choosing to hold other thoughts at bay for the moment. He needed to think about this whole thing.

Wednesday.

Wednesday was three days away. Four, depending on when you started counting. He wanted to see Rose sooner than that. He wanted to see her now, he realized, his thoughts taking a turn of their own to the previous night and the way her body had felt against his. With a very predictable—and inconvenient—result.

Damn, he thought, shifting restlessly, he really did have to think about this. It had been a long time since he'd woken up with a woman on his mind. Now here he was, hard and hungry, and doomed to frustration. And for how long? Rose needed time. And *time,* coming from a woman, could mean damn near anything.

Once I give myself to a man, it can never be undone.

And what the hell did that mean?

He sighed, longing for the good old days when life had been simple. He flew, he ate, he slept, and when he had an itch he scratched it with whatever woman was WA. Willing and Available. A buddy of his had coined the term back in flight school and it had become an inside joke…one he hadn't thought of in a while.

Now he did. Was Rose willing? She'd been hot for him last night, he had no doubt of that. But when he thought about the word *willing* in connection with Rose, it took on new shades of meaning. And available? He wasn't sure of that, either. Uncertainty, he discovered, took a lot of the humor out of that old joke.

Hell, his life before the crash might not have been perfect, but at least where women were concerned it had come damn close. This thing with Rose was different. She had a way of making him feel...light-headed. And something else. Something like hunger pangs, only more intense, more focused—and more dangerous.

He wasn't sure how he knew that. He just did. It was as if some survival instinct encoded on the male chromosome ages ago had been triggered in him for the first time last night, warning that if he wasn't careful, things could get way out of hand.

Chapter Seven

"How about these napkins?"

Rose glanced across the shop at the faded red-plaid napkins Maryann was holding up, and wrinkled her nose. "Too casual, too…picnic-y," she pronounced.

"I thought that was the point," her friend protested. "This is supposed to be a *picnic* basket, remember?"

"A *romantic* picnic basket," Rose reminded her. "You're bringing this gift to a bridal shower, not a hoedown. Think lace and old silver."

"Here," she exclaimed triumphantly as she found what she was looking for—a pair of creamy napkins with hand-crocheted edging. "These are perfect. Just feel—the cotton is so soft from washing it feels like silk, and this candlewick pattern ties in with the roses on the plates you chose."

"What's candlewick?" Maryann enquired, fingering the napkin. "Ooh, that is soft."

"This—" Rose said and pointed at the rose design that

had been worked in ivory thread on one corner of each napkin.

"These little bumps?"

"Actually, they're French knots, each one worked by hand. These were done by an expert," she added, inspecting the napkins closely. "See? The knots are all the same size and evenly spaced."

"I'm sold," said Maryann, adding the napkins to her growing pile. "This was a great idea for a shower gift, Rose. Thanks for suggesting it…and for offering to put it all together."

"My pleasure. All that's missing now is the food."

"Right. The old 'a loaf of bread, a bottle of wine and thee' routine. I'll run to Maxine's," she said, referring to a local gourmet shop, "and pick up champagne and a bunch of fancy-schmancy tidbits."

"Sounds like a plan."

Instead of leaving, however, Maryann glanced at Lisa asleep in her stroller, adjusted the thin cotton blanket over the infant and made herself comfortable on Rose's stool.

"So, now that all that's out of the way, you can concentrate on answering my question."

Rose groaned.

"You didn't really think I would forget, did you?"

"I hoped you might," admitted Rose.

"Not in this lifetime. And don't look so long-suffering. You'd think I was getting ready to stick pins under your fingernails."

"Is that an option? Because I really think I'd prefer that."

"Too bad…I left all my pins at home."

"I can wait."

"I can't. I have been very patient up until now. You said you couldn't concentrate on the basket and my nosy questions at the same time, and I respected that. But a woman has to know her limitations, and I know mine. I need an answer, Rose. Is Griffin a good kisser or not?"

"What makes you so sure I would be in a position to know?"

"Because I know these things, Rose. Sort of the way you know about old stuff. It's a gift."

"I suppose that's one interpretation."

"So how does he kiss? And don't try that pass-fail crap. I insist on an official Love-o-meter rating."

Rose shook her head, laughing in spite of herself. "Maryann, for pity's sake, we were twelve when we discovered that stupid game at the arcade, and you've been using it as a scale ever since."

"Because it works. It covers the full spectrum of male prowess, clearly and succinctly. You've got your Cold Wet Fish…" she said, raising her left hand. Then, raising her right, she continued. "And your Red Hot Lover. And eight levels in between. So…which is he?"

Rose folded her arms, leaned back against the counter and looked at her friend. "Maryann…"

"Yes?"

"It kills me to have to tell you this, but…he's off the dial."

"You *did* kiss him," she crowed. "I knew it. I knew it."

"You tricked me. You said you already knew it. 'I know these things.' Isn't that what you just said?"

Maryann waved her hand impatiently. "Yes, yes, but this makes it official. I'm so happ—" She broke off and frowned. "What do you mean he's off the dial?"

"The dial. You know, the dial—the wheel with all the little colored wedges that the arrow spins around when you squeeze the Love Handles?"

"Yeah, yeah, I know what the dial is."

"Well, I've actually given this a lot of thought—even before you asked—and Griff doesn't fit into any of the wedges."

Now it was Maryann who groaned. "Please, Rose, don't start. I beg you not to nitpick the poor guy to death without giving him half a chance. I mean, really, Rose, *no one* is off the dial. That's the point of having a dial. Even Leonard…remember Leonard? Skinny? Cow eyes? Labrador ears? Even Leonard, as bad as he was, was not off the dial. Even that awful tuba player with the…''

"Good," said Rose.

"…weird glasses and—what did you say?''

"I said good. Griff isn't off the dial *bad,* Maryann, he's off the dial *good.*''

"Oh. My. God.''

"Exactly.''

"You're in love with him.'' Maryann could not have looked more astonished if Rose had just split an atom with dental floss.

"Don't be ridiculous,'' she retorted. "I barely know the man, and most of what I know I don't like. At least, I didn't think I did, at first, but I've gotten to know him a little more, more than he would like, I suspect, and I don't dislike him nearly as much as I thought I did. I may even like him a little. Maybe more than a little. But that is a long, long way from being in love, for God's sake.''

She could feel her face growing warm and her mouth growing dry and her thoughts tying themselves up in knots the way they had been for days now…ever since that night on the porch.

"It is definitely not love,'' she said again, firmly. "But when he touched me and kissed me, I felt…I felt…''

She looked helplessly at Maryann, who broke into a grin of pure, sweet, long-overdue delight and said, simply, "Oh. My. God.''

She was not in love with Hollis Griffin.

There was simply no way she could be in love with a man like him. For reasons too obvious and too numerous to list. Which is exactly what she'd told Maryann, who'd responded by laughing so hard she gave herself the hiccups.

It was her own damn fault, Rose thought later, as she put the finishing touch of white silk roses on the bridal basket.

She never should have opened her mouth about the fact that Griff was off the dial. Ordinarily, she wouldn't have. Ordinarily, she would have anticipated that Maryann would seize the information and use it as an excuse to jump to exactly this sort of insane conclusion. But all of a sudden, nothing about her life was *ordinary*. Not the smell of the morning or the color of the sky or the sound of the rest of the world going about its business all around her.

Maybe it was some kind of hormonal fluke. Or an allergy. She'd once read that your entire body changes every seven years, making you sensitive to things that never bothered you previously. She hurriedly divided thirty-five by seven and realized she was right on schedule. Her cells were reinventing themselves. Or something. All she knew for sure was that it wasn't love.

She might not have *a gift* for romance, the way some people she knew claimed to, but she knew enough to get by. For instance, she knew...she knew... She heaved a disgruntled sigh. She knew she had never before felt what she felt whenever she thought about Griff. She knew that for certain. She just didn't know what it meant, or what the hell she was going to do about it.

And that was the good news.

The bad news was that it might well be irrelevant. When she thought of Griff and the way he made her feel, she could only compare the erratic, racing sensation inside her to a runaway train.

And it had to stop, she decided, giving the ribbon securing the roses a final tug. Where was her spunk? Her determination? Her confidence that she could conquer anything if she tried hard enough? She was the woman who had surprised everyone by walking away from her marriage, her home and her job, and starting a whole new life from scratch. Certainly she could overcome this silly, adolescent response to a kiss.

She would start by facing it head-on. That meant admitting to herself that it had been more than a kiss. And more than a little groping on a hot summer night. A lot more, actually, in a way that went beyond how long Griff's kisses had lasted or who had touched whom, where. What had happened there on the porch had been intimacy, she realized, her heart skittering at the memory of the way their mouths had mated, their breath becoming one, their bodies molding to each other so easily…so perfectly.

They had connected in a way she didn't understand.

…meant to be…

It had been unplanned and unsought, on both sides, but it had happened. Sort of like spontaneous combustion. And it had been more intimacy than she had permitted in five years.

Five years was a long time, Rose mused. She supposed, if forced to put a name to what she was feeling, she would have to call it lust. She went still in the middle of brushing bits of ribbon and tissue from her worktable into the trash, and stood, turning the word over in her mind.

Lust. Of course. That's what this was…that's *all* it was. How foolish of her to get tied up in knots about something so simple. So natural. So insignificant on the grand scale of life. She laughed out loud, drawing a few curious looks from customers.

What she had was a case of good, old-fashioned lust. Period. Surely that would account for her bizarre behavior since last Saturday night, her mood swings and her tendency to drift off in the middle of totaling a sale, and the embarrassing amount of time she spent gazing out her kitchen window each evening, hoping for a glimpse of Griff.

Lust. Pure and simple. The explanation was strangely comforting. Maybe because the solution was also simple and straightforward.

At least, it could be. If she would only let it.

She glanced at the clock. Nearly five, and it was all she could do not to hustle the sole remaining browser out the door. She was always eager to hang the Closed sign on auction night, but there was an added sense of urgency tonight. One that had nothing to do with arriving in time for the opening bid, and everything to do with a man who, in an absurdly short time, had gone from seeming to be everything she did not want or need in her life, to being the only thing she did.

At one minute before five on Wednesday evening, Rose went to lock up and found Griff sitting on the bench in front of the shop. Something very close to a thrill shot through her. He'd shaved and combed his hair, and there were perfect creases in the sleeves of the white cotton shirt neatly tucked into his faded jeans.

He looked good enough to frame, she thought, wryly recalling the extra time she'd spent getting ready that morning. Since she never knew what she might have to push, lift or crawl under to inspect on auction night, it usually called for her oldest clothes and a no-nonsense ponytail—not her favorite sundress of soft ivory and faded sprigs of roses or upswept hair that required a half-dozen silver butterfly clips to secure.

"Hi. Have you been waiting long?" she asked.

He smiled at the sight of her and shook his head. "I didn't want to rush you."

"Oh." She caught herself staring at his mouth and hurriedly lifted her gaze, only to discover that he was staring at hers. They both looked away and then back—and the next thing Rose knew they were in the truck and, thankfully, driving in the right direction for the auction.

"You want to fill me in on this lead you came up with?" he asked.

"I can't tell you much, because I don't know much," she explained. "Not yet, anyway. A friend of mine, who will be here tonight, has Internet contacts in the area of porcelain collectibles and she's ninety-nine percent certain she's located one of the pieces you're looking for."

"And it's going to be auctioned off tonight? Good thing I brought my checkbook."

"Oh, no, it's not actually here. I'm sorry if I gave you that impression."

"Then where, actually, is it?"

"London."

"That's the lead?" he countered, clearly mystified. "That there's a bird I need in London?"

"Right."

"In that case, at the risk of appearing even more inept at this entire business than I am, why the hell are you dragging me to an auction in a VFW hall in the backwoods of Rhode Island?"

"Because…" She hesitated.

She could hardly say *Because I wanted a reason to see you and this is the best I could come up with.* "Because I wanted you to hear the information firsthand. And because there is always a chance one of the birds could turn up at tonight's auction. One just might be sitting in a box lot with a bunch of worthless old knickknacks—"

"And the odds of that would be?"

"Slim," she conceded. "Very, very slim. All right, I confess, you're here because I wanted to log a few hours and run up the bill."

"I see." He turned slightly in his seat, and Rose could almost feel his gaze on her. It was like velvet being dragged across every nerve ending in her body. Slowly.

"Tell me," he said eventually, "will you be billing me for your time the other night?"

She feigned concern. "Hmm, I'll have to give it some thought. Did we discuss business at all?"

"If we did, I don't remember. But then, I was a little…distracted."

His deep voice wrapped around her, evoking an urge to pull to the side of the road, kill the engine and give him her undivided attention for as long as it took to rid this madness from her system.

"One thing's for sure," he continued. "If you are going to bill for that sort of activity, this project could get mighty expensive before we're through."

She shifted her gaze from the road long enough to flash

him a playful smile. "Perhaps. Just keep telling yourself that it's all for a very good cause."

He gave her an odd look.

"Fulfilling Devora's wishes," she prompted. "That is what this is all about, remember."

"Right," he said.

Straightening, he turned his attention to the scenery on his side of the road. Rose didn't need to see his expression to read his abrupt shift in mood. It was the same vague uneasiness that surfaced whenever the subject arose of this hunt he had undertaken on his aunt's behalf. And another little piece of her melted.

That didn't mean she was in love with the man, she hastened to assure herself. But *if* she had been in love with him, it was moments like this—random flashes of tenderness and vulnerability—that would make her love him even more.

She spotted the dark blue Willow Haven passenger van parked in the front row as soon as she pulled into the VFW's crowded parking lot. After driving up and down each aisle, she finally lucked out and found an empty spot in the corner farthest from the door.

"Don't worry," she told Griff, as they approached the entrance and he observed that it appeared to be standing room only inside. "My friends will have seats saved for us. They're always the first to arrive. Ben jokes that he ought to give them the key and let them open up for him."

"What's their rush?"

"It's the highlight of the day for a lot of them. They like to get here in time to look everything over and stake their claim to the first couple of rows of seats."

He glanced at her, brows raised. "Just how many friends do you expect to be here?"

"Oh, a dozen, give or take a few," she countered, and pointed at the van.

His dark brows lifted another notch. "Willow Haven Retirement Community? First Devora and now a dozen of them? Level me with Rose, you're not some kind of medical marvel, are you? A very well-preserved octogenarian?''

She shook her head, laughing. ''No, though there are days when I feel it…and not the well-preserved part, either.''

''Then why not find friends your own age?''

''I have friends my own age,'' she retorted. ''You've met Maryann, and there are plenty of others—some even younger than I am, believe it or not. But friendship isn't always based on age. I *like* hanging with people who are interested in the same things I am.''

''Then, I guess it makes perfect sense that you would hang out at the seniors center,'' he teased, leaving her no choice but to jab her elbow into his ribs.

''I don't *hang out* at Willow Haven,'' she protested, then shrugged and added, ''except on Saturday nights.''

He stopped in his tracks and spun her to face him. ''What did you say?''

''I said I don't hang out at Willow Haven except on Saturday nights.''

''That's what I thought you said,'' countered Griff, holding on to her arm to keep her there. ''Does that mean that Mr. Saturday Night lives in a retirement home?''

She looked at him in confusion. ''What on earth are you talking about?''

''I'm talking about your regular Saturday night date. Ring a bell?''

''No. Probably because I never said I had a regular Saturday night date.''

''You said—''

She cut him off. ''Commitment. I believe what I said was that I have a regular Saturday night *commitment.* Which I do.''

''You said a *serious* commitment,'' he shot back.

''It is serious,'' insisted Rose. She quickly explained about the Saturday Night Collectors, concluding with ''I never skip a meeting.''

"You also never used the word *meeting*. Naturally, I assumed you were talking about a date."

She fluttered her lashes at him. "You did?"

"You know damn right well, I did," he growled, grinning at the same time. "And I didn't much like the idea. And I have a feeling you know that, too."

She fluttered again.

In a heartbeat, his grin changed, becoming heated and seductive. "You tricked me, and now you're going to have to make it up to me," he told her, drawing her closer with each word.

"How could I possibly do that?"

"Like this—" he whispered, his mouth so close that his breath warmed her cheek and sent her thoughts scattering.

"Yoo-hoo. Rose. Over here."

They both froze.

Griff muttered under his breath. "What the hell...?"

Responding with a small, rueful smile, Rose detached herself from his embrace and glanced toward the hall. Immediately, the slender woman holding the main door open smiled and waved. "I saw you drive in and I just wanted to let you know he's about to get started," she called.

"Thanks, Clare. I'll be right there." She glanced at Griff. "Come on, we better go in."

"If you say so. Just remember," he added as he trailed her inside. "You still owe me."

She simply laughed over her shoulder at him as she led the way to the front row, and, just as she had predicted, two empty folding chairs in the midst of a gathering of bald and silver heads. The seats had been reserved in what seemed to be the accepted fashion, with yellow Post-it notes stuck to the back. On one note someone had printed *Rose,* and on the other, *Rose's Friend.*

Rose's friend. Griff considered that with a degree of wryness. Is that what he was? If so, he wasn't alone. At least, not judging by the number of people who greeted her, giving him a wary once-over at the same time. He had the feeling

Rose didn't ordinarily bring along a *friend,* and that pleased him almost as much as had finding out that Mr. Saturday Night was a figment of his imagination. Inspired by her, of course—and he was looking forward to settling that score later.

Still more people called to Rose and waved from across the room, even after they had reached their seats. Men, women, young and old. Griff looked on with amusement, thinking this must be something akin to arriving at the Oscar ceremony with a rising starlet on your arm. Except, he thought, he'd be willing to bet that starlets didn't share their Saturday evenings with a group of lonely old folks and make it sound like *they* were doing *her* a favor.

The discovery that Rose did so, and with obvious pleasure, brought together the jumble of impressions and insights he'd been accumulating since their very first meeting, when she had offered to throw a party to welcome him—a complete stranger—to town. He'd surmised all along that there was something to her beyond the impulsiveness and completely screwed-up sense of taste that would prompt her to buy a secondhand flamingo. But he couldn't have put a name to that something if he tried.

Until now. It was *goodness.* He nearly cringed, it sounded so corny, but it was true. That's what set Rose apart. It seemed to him at that moment that Rose Davenport ought to be the pinup girl for everything that was good and right and worth fighting for in life. Rose was up there alongside the flag and apple pie, guaranteed to send a man off to battle with a smile on his face.

So what the hell was she doing with him?

Helping him, he reminded himself disgustedly. Helping him fulfill the terms of Devora's will so that—unbeknownst to her—he could sell that creaking headache of a house and get on with his life.

Such as it was.

How the hell could all that have completely slipped his mind?

The chairs had been crammed closely together, and as Rose reached down to retrieve her purse, her bare shoulder pressed against his forearm and the sweet, familiar scent of her filled his head. It was all the answer he needed.

"Do you want chowder?" she asked him.

"I beg your pardon?" Griff countered.

"Chowder. It's either that or a hot dog. The menu is limited, but the food is good. Dessert is homemade apple pie, with or without ice cream."

"You intend to eat dinner here?" He glanced around and noticed some people doing exactly that.

"Sure. There's a little break coming up. We kick in five bucks each, and Bob does the honors."

She nodded toward the elderly gentleman wearing saddle shoes and holding a coffee can, who was working his way along the row in their direction. When he reached Rose, she dropped a five-dollar bill in the can and made a check mark on the small notepad he provided.

Glancing at Griff, she asked, "Have you decided?"

"Just make it two of whatever you're having." As he pulled a bill from his wallet, she made another mark beside the first.

"You won't be sorry," she told him. "The chowder here is the best."

Griff rested his arm across the back of her chair, wondering if it would be out of line for him to touch her shoulder. Yes, it would be, he decided as he happened to glance to his right. Most definitely. The Yoo-Hoo Lady—Clare, he seemed to recall Rose calling her—was giving him the same look Devora used to give him whenever she so much as suspected he had been gulping directly from the water bottle in the refrigerator.

Privately, he used to think of it as the Evil Eye, and the message was as clear to him at forty as it had been at fourteen. *I know what you're up to* the look said.

Bloody hell, he thought, expecting his palms to start sweating any second. It was like being a kid again, and on a first date with a girl who brought her parents along…the entire, eagle-eyed dozen of them.

The feeling of being under a microscope persisted through the dinner break. The chowder was as good as Rose had promised, and the apple pie even better. But hungry as he was, he had to keep reminding himself to take small bites, timing them around the questions that came at him from all directions. By the time he managed to escape, by volunteering to collect the trash and carry it outside, he'd decided he was wrong. It was a lot less like a first date than an appearance before a Grand Jury.

"Sorry," Rose said, smiling ruefully at him as he rejoined her. He'd stalled outside until the action resumed. "They mean well, but they can be a little overprotective."

"Really? I hadn't noticed."

She laughed at his dry tone and disgruntled expression.

"So? Did I pass inspection?" he asked, surprised that he cared.

"With flying colors." Before his head had time to swell, she added, "Except…"

He regarded her with narrowed eyes. "Except what?"

"Some of them are a little concerned that you're… unemployed."

"I am not unemployed," he retorted, teeth clenched. "I'm retired. Surely that's a concept this group can understand."

"Oh, they understand it. It just doesn't…I think 'doesn't sit right' is the phrase I heard most often. It doesn't sit right for a young man like yourself to be idle all day. What can I tell you?" she said, shrugging as he shook his head in disgust. "Some people are just hung up on age."

Griff could swear she was biting the inside of her cheek as she shifted her attention to the pine armoire going up for bid and said, "Surely *you* can understand *that* concept."

He soon learned that things picked up speed toward the end of the night. Rose explained that the most highly sought items are always put up early, when the crowd is at its peak and pockets are still full. The best bargains, however, come later, when the auctioneer is eager to unload things rather than have to move them and store them another month.

Griff had started the evening with every intention of remaining a silent, detached and slightly bemused observer of the entire spectacle, but it didn't quite work out that way. An auction—at least this auction—swallowed you whole, he discovered. Before he knew it, he was discussing toy trains with an old guy two seats away, and he actually coached another who was bidding on a box full of old bottles.

"You must have quite a collection if you buy them in bulk like that," Griff commented when "their" bid topped all others.

"Collection? Nah. Personally, I wouldn't give you two cents for any dirty old hunk of glass," the older man retorted, his lined face scrunched up with disdain.

"Then why…?"

"eBay," the man shot back, before Griff finished the question. He pulled a business card from the chest pocket of his green plain shirt. "Online I'm known as BottleMeister— look me up sometime."

Griff just nodded, then turned to find Rose regarding him with amusement.

Rose watched him for a moment, then chuckled and held up her card to bid on a white metal candelabra. She was high bidder on that and an assortment of other small items, as well as a pine bureau, a vanity with a three-panel hinged mirror and a wicker settee. All of which she planned to paint white for some reason that completely escaped him, but evidently made perfect sense to everyone else in what he had at some point come to think of as "their group."

When the time came to load it all into the truck, he groaned silently. In spite of the cane, he was by far the youngest and fittest male in "their group." But as he hauled and lifted and wedged things into the van and truck, he began to take grudging pleasure in the sense that his stock was rising with each item he loaded. By the time he closed the van's rear doors, even the Yoo-Hoo Lady had warmed up to him.

"I sure wish our Rosie had gotten that bed," she said to him, looking wistfully at the narrow bed being lifted into the truck parked beside them. On the side of the oversize cab, Chubby's Treasures was written in block letters on the door. Pretty mundane, he found himself thinking, wondering what else would appear there if Chubby turned Rose loose with her paint box.

"It's the perfect bed," Clare continued.

"Perfect for a prison inmate, maybe," he suggested, drawing a withering glance from his companion. "Sorry, that's what it looked like to me, a prison bed—and a pretty dirty one at that." He suddenly thought to add "Though I suppose a little white paint would fix that in no time."

"Now, that's using your head the way God intended," she said, looking at him a little less like he was a fish she was fixing to throw back. "By 'perfect' I mean it's exactly the style of bed she's been wanting for her Bed of Roses project." Clare sighed heavily. "I tried to tell her they were starting without her. Of course, even I had no way of knowing Ben was starting with that particular bed."

He shoved his hands in his pocket, feeling guilty. He knew that Clare knew he was the reason Rose had dallied in the parking lot and missed out on the prison bed.

"What Bed of Roses project?" he asked in spite of himself.

"It's something special she has planned for her garden. She's going to use an old iron bed as the focal point and plant rosebushes all in where the mattress would be, so it will look like…"

"A bed of roses," he finished for her, needing no further explanation of an idea that he knew would have struck him as the epitome of bizarre only a few days ago, but now made a strange kind of sense.

He was leaning against the van to take the weight off his left leg. Clare sidled over to join him, her tone turning conspiratorial as they stood shoulder to shoulder in the shadows, waiting for the others to settle up inside.

"The bed idea is what Rose calls 'thinking outside the box,'" she informed him. "That's when you forget everything you thought you knew about a thing and look at it with new eyes. There are some who don't understand that sort of thinking at all," she told him, the curl of her lip expressing contempt for those unfortunate souls. "But not Rose. Our Rose is very good at thinking outside the box."

She cocked her head and cast a frankly probing eye on him. "How about you, young man? You any good at thinking outside the box when you need to?"

"Well, Clare," he said, "it's like this. I'm still learning."

It took a second, but the glint in her sharpshooter, blue eyes turned from suspicion to approval. "That's an honest enough answer. I like that in a fellow."

Feeling as if he'd just made it into the next round of the championship spelling bee, he relaxed his shoulders and took a deep breath, savoring what had turned out to be a surprisingly good night. Aside from Rose, there had been good food, interesting company, and it was entirely possible that in coming up with that answer, he'd just done some genuine outside-the-box thinking.

Rose would know, he thought. He'd have to remember to run it by her later.

Chapter Eight

"If you're not in a hurry to get home, I'd like to swing by Willow Haven and drop this stuff off tonight. I won't have time before work tomorrow," Rose explained, as they pulled onto the highway, "and I know how eager they always are to inspect new acquisitions."

"I've got the whole night," he replied. "Not that it will take long to unload. Most of their stuff fit in the van. I could probably have gotten all of it in there, but it would have been a tight squeeze. And frankly, a few of the passengers look like their bones are on the brittle side."

"Very prudent of you," she said, remembering to avoid all the *S* words, such as sweet and sensitive, but not because she was fooled by his dry tone or indifferent attitude. Bringing him along tonight had not been a test, at least not one she'd consciously planned, but if it had been, Griff had passed with ease.

Elderly folks could be difficult to get along with. They didn't want to be patronized and they didn't want to be treated as if they were already dead, and each had his or her own notion as to where the line ought to be drawn between the two. A lot of younger people couldn't be bothered to figure it out. Or else they could not get past the age spots and cataracts and connect with the person inside enough to see that being seventy is a lot like being forty, only with worse vision and more wrinkles.

Gradually, throughout the night, Griff had managed to strike the right balance, and he had done it with a grace and a respect that reinforced all the good things she surmised about the man, and made his rough spots seem insignificant by comparison.

"It's true they're not as limber as they used to be," she agreed, "but they're a surprisingly lively group just the same."

"You got that right." He cleared his throat. "Maybe a little too lively for their own good in some cases. At the risk of being…indiscreet, I think I should tell you that the little lady with the pink cat's-eye glasses…Minnie? She goosed me when I was helping her friend into the van."

Rose swung her gaze from the road long enough to see if he was serious.

He held up a few fingers. "Scouts' honor."

Her laughter bubbled uncontrollably. "Why, that sly devil Minnie."

"It's not funny."

"Yes, it is."

"Well, it won't be if she tries it with the wrong guy," he insisted, sounding disgruntled.

"You mean someone who's not an officer and a gentleman?"

"Something like that."

"She won't. Minnie has exquisite taste in men."

"That's a relief." His tone was dry. "I was afraid she zeroed in on me because I looked easy."

"Not at all. I'm sure she just found you…irresistible."

"Thanks."

"Would you like her phone number?"

"No thanks." He paused, then added, "It so happens I have my eye on someone else at the moment. Someone *I* find pretty irresistible."

"Is that so?"

"It sure is." Reaching across the seat, he put his hand on her shoulder, sliding it beneath the tendrils of hair that had loosened during the evening, and curling his fingers around the back of her neck. The touch was slow and gentle, and Rose felt it in every fiber of her body.

"This someone else—the one you have your eye on—is she a younger woman?"

"She *claims* to be. Not that it matters," he added, his voice pitched low and threaded with amusement. "I'm not one of those people hung up on age."

"How very open-minded of you," she countered.

"I do my best." He began kneading her neck with the same slow and easy touch. Considering that they were in the high-speed lane of I-95, the effect he was having on her concentration was dangerous. "But young or old, what she is, this woman I have my eye on, is…unique."

"Unique? In what way?"

"Every way."

"That tells me a lot," she retorted, exasperated by his reply and struggling to keep her speed constant and the truck in its own lane, as his caress continued to send pleasure sliding through her. She'd had no idea that the back of her neck was so sensitive.

"She's unique because she does things to me that no other woman ever has. Things I'm beginning to think no other woman ever could. She can make me think and make me laugh and make me crazy…sometimes all within a matter of minutes."

"Maybe she's mentally ambidextrous. Or something."

She could feel his smile, feel it as surely and sweetly as she could feel his fingers on her neck. It wasn't possible, of course—you couldn't *feel* a smile—but that didn't make it any less true. A lot of things she'd considered impossible were happening to her lately.

"Maybe she is," he agreed, his deep voice stroking her in a different way. "I'm sure looking forward to finding out."

The turn for Willow Haven was just ahead. "Well," she ventured, hitting the turn signal lever, "you know what they say."

"No. What do they say?"

"They say…" Rose pursed her lips, trying to reorganize the thought that had been so clear and simple just a second ago. "Hold on, I remember…they say anything worth having, is worth waiting for."

"Sounds reasonable. The problem is that *they* only say that *some* of the time." He smiled and squeezed her neck, as she pulled the truck under the canopied entrance and stopped. "Other times, they say if you get tired of waiting for your ship to come in, you ought to swim out to meet it."

"I've heard that one, too. So how the heck is a person supposed to know the right thing to do?" she grumbled.

"I suppose it comes down to how good a swimmer you are."

His kiss caught her off guard. It was quick and hard and smack on the mouth, and he was out of the truck before she had her door open.

Bum leg or not, something warned her that Griffin was a very good swimmer.

The van had arrived just ahead of them, and some of the night shift appeared suddenly to help with the unloading, making quick work of it. There followed a chorus of good-nights, and Rose was about to climb back behind the wheel, when she remembered the news clipping she had tucked into her purse earlier.

She hurried to catch the aide who was holding the door for the stragglers. "Linda, would you do me a big favor and give this to Gus O'Flaherty in room 121? It's a little late for visitors."

"I'd be glad to, Rose."

Rose handed her the clipping. "Thanks. Just tell him it's the article about slow-release fertilizer that I mentioned last week."

The other woman chuckled. "Knowing Gus, I'm sure he'll be tickled."

She glanced at her watch as they drove away, surprised it was as late as it was. Usually by this hour she was exhausted and eager to get home. Instead, she felt wide-awake—restless even.

"As long as you're not in a hurry, how about stopping by the shop and checking up on this lead from Clare?"

"Now? It's the middle of the night in London."

"True, but that's the beauty of the World Wide Web— twenty-four-hour access."

"*Virtual* access," he corrected.

She shrugged. "Works for me. In fact, I had some time this morning, and I thought I would get a head start by seeing what I could find out about this British dealer whom Clare was referred to by the friend of a friend."

"And?"

"He's strictly first-class. Has a shop on Portobello Road and a very impressive online site." She hesitated, then added, "So impressive, in fact, that I took the liberty of making an offer on your behalf."

He winced when she named the amount.

"It's a lot of money, I know, but considering the quality and scarcity of what you're buying, it's to be expected." She paused, deciding on the best approach, then said, "You know, Griff, you don't have to follow through on this. The thought and effort you've shown is itself a tribute to Devora, and I am sure she would not expect—"

"You're wrong," he interrupted. "This *is* something I have to see through to the end. There's no other way, believe me."

"Then you're not upset I made an offer without checking first?"

"Hell, no. If you say it's reasonable, that's good enough for me."

His confidence pleased her. "Good. I could have withdrawn it, but it's not considered good etiquette."

"I'm glad you got the ball rolling on this. The sooner we strike a deal, the sooner we can cross one of the damn things off the list. And that's what this is all about, after all."

"I'm hoping Shippington—that's the dealer's name—has responded to my e-mail by now. Usually I bring my laptop home with me, but it must have slipped my mind this afternoon."

She spoke offhandedly, as if she didn't know exactly why the computer, along with assorted other bits and pieces of her usual routine, had developed this tendency to *slip* her mind lately. There was no *slipped* about it. There simply wasn't enough room there since Griff had moved in and started staking claim to every crack and crevice of her thoughts.

"Ideally, I would have liked to simply visit the site several times and see if we could tempt him to make the first move by enquiring if we were interested in the Borealis piece."

"Does it really matter who makes the first move?"

"Does it *matter?* Does the sun rise in the morning?"

"Well, if you want a technical answer…"

"Wrong analogy," she interrupted. "The point is that it matters very much when you're dealing with rare collectibles, which don't have a fixed, generally accepted price—the way, say, a loaf of bread or a cup of coffee has. There is no such thing as comparison shopping if a buyer can't go around the corner—or even around the world—and purchase the same thing. That means the item's value is determined by how badly the buyer wants it. If two or more buyers want it badly, all the better for the seller. And so it becomes a game of strategy, high-stakes tic-tac-toe, if you will. And who makes the first move can be critical."

"Sounds like tic-tac-toe meets virtual haggling," he observed wryly. "I sure hope *you* know what you're doing."

"I do," she assured him with a confident smile. "That's why you're paying me the big bucks, remember?"

"It's tough to forget when you're constantly scribbling in that logbook of yours."

"That's because I don't trust my memory. You don't want to be billed twice, do you?"

"No, ma'am. Speaking of memory, you said something back there that jogged mine."

"What was it?"

"A name. Gus O'Flaherty. I couldn't help overhearing you mention it to that nurse by the door."

"That's right, I did. Do you know Gus?"

"I know a man named Gus O'Flaherty," he told her. "At least, I used to. I'm not sure he's the same one."

"What are the odds of there being another Augustus Finnegan O'Flaherty?"

"You have a point," he said, chuckling. "Augustus Finnegan O'Flaherty."

Something different in his tone drew Rose's attention from the road briefly. Something she hadn't heard there before. *Wonder,* she decided, growing even more curious about how he knew Gus.

"You're right. It has to be the same guy," he declared.

"Do you know him from around here?"

He nodded. "He used to do some work for my aunt."

"Really? Devora never mentioned it."

"No reason she should. It was a long time ago."

"I always assumed she knew Gus from doing business with the nursery."

"Nursery?"

"You know, the kind with shrubs and garden supplies. Before his stroke, Gus ran that big place out on Route 4."

"That's news to me."

"I know Devora would stop in and say hi to Gus whenever she drove out to Willow Haven to visit her—"

"Whoa. Hold on. Devora didn't drive."

She shot him a dubious look. "Of course she drove. Why else would there be a big old Buick parked in her garage?"

"I'm telling you, my aunt never learned to drive," he insisted. "It was one of that long list of things she didn't consider ladylike. And she certainly didn't drive a big old Buick."

"And I'm telling you that I've been in that Buick with Devora at the wheel, and we were moving." She shrugged. "I call that driving. What do you call it?"

Ignoring the question, he said, "I know someone who did drive a Buick, though. Dark blue with white interior."

"That's the one. Who…?"

"Gus O'Flaherty, that's who. The damn thing must be nearly forty years old. Hell, I couldn't have been more than ten the first time I sat for hours on the hood of that car."

"Really?" she said, both confused and fascinated. "Just what sort of work did Gus do for your aunt Devora?"

His brow creased as he tried to remember. "All kinds of stuff. He trimmed the shrubs and hung the shutters. I think he used to cut the grass, before that became my job."

"No surprise there. I mean, that Devora made you earn your keep," she explained, the affection in her voice reflected in Griff's smile.

"I couldn't complain. Every dozen or so passes with the mower, she'd appear with a cool washcloth for me to wipe my face and a big glass of cold lemonade. Real lemonade," he informed her.

"But of course," she agreed with exaggerated formality. "We are talking about Devora, after all. And it had to be made in that stainless steel pitcher with the red handle…"

"And the dent on the side," he finished for her as their gazes touched in one of those rare instants of total affinity.

He exhaled deeply. "This really is bringing back some memories. First Gus, then mowing the lawn and Devora's lemonade."

"Do you suppose she bought the car from Gus?"

"Beats me. I know I didn't keep in touch the way I should

have in recent years," he acknowledged, regret a rough edge in his voice. "But Devora always seemed so…self-sufficient, so sensible."

"She was."

"You call it 'sensible' for a woman to suddenly decide to learn to drive at the ripe old age of—"

"Sorry, can't help you there," she replied. "She was already getting around like a wild woman when I moved to town five years ago. And just for the record, I do consider it sensible *and* self-sufficient on her part."

"She was plenty self-sufficient *without* wheels," he argued. "I can't for the life of me imagine what made her change her mind after all those years."

"I can," Rose said, a sudden insight bringing a smile of astonishment to her face. "Love. Don't you see? Devora and Gus were secret lovers."

"Lovers?" He sounded more than astonished. "That's ridiculous."

"Is that so? Then, what's your explanation? I say Gus gave her the car after his stroke, when he moved to Willow Haven and could no longer drive it himself, and Devora learned to drive so she could visit him there whenever she pleased, without anyone knowing about it."

"That's so far off base, it doesn't even bear discussing."

"Why?"

"Because…because…we're talking about Aunt Devora, and she wasn't the type to take a 'secret lover,' especially not Gus O'Flaherty."

"And why not?" demanded Rose. "Gus is a wonderful man. He's witty and intelligent and kind and—"

"I'm not denying that. The Gus I remember was all those things, but he was also…"

"The hired help?" she suggested, when he hesitated.

"More or less, and as great as she was, Devora had that uppity streak about her at times. I just don't see it."

She couldn't hold back. "I do. It makes perfect sense, all of it—the car, their friendship, the interests they had in common. Devora was devoted to her gardens, and Gus knows everything there is to know in that regard. Even now he keeps his hand in.'' She told him about Gus and his beloved dahlias.

"Did you say dahlias?'' he enquired, and she nodded. "Didn't you also tell me that Mr. Saturday Night grew dahlias?''

"Uh-huh.'' She tried to suppress a grin and failed. "Did you know that Gus is also a whiz at dominoes? Taught me everything I know.''

"So you're telling me that Gus O'Flaherty is Mr. Saturday Night?'' Now he sounded astonished, and a little bit indignant.

"You idiot,'' she said, laughing. "There *is* no Mr. Saturday Night and there never was…except in your imagination. I'm telling you that you now know all there is to know about how I spend Saturday nights.''

"You sure reeled me in,'' he acknowledged, his smile grudging.

"Only after you baited the hook yourself,'' Rose reminded him.

"Yeah, I guess maybe I did. Damn, I don't know whether to feel relieved or annoyed as hell.'' He said it without rancor.

Just the idea that relief was among the things he felt upon learning she wasn't seriously involved with another man pleased her more than it should have. She was still savoring the remark, when he spoke.

"If the Gus O'Flaherty I knew played dominoes, I don't recall it,'' he said. "I do know that he also did inside work for Devora. He was the one who built those glass-front cabinets in the pantry. I remember standing right beside him with the nail bucket and handing them to him, one at a time. And I remember her calling him the time she was poking around the fireplace in her bedroom and dislodged a bee's nest the size of a watermelon.''

"Good heavens, that must have been awful.''

"It was pretty scary," he acknowledged.

"All those bees." She shuddered.

"The bees were bad, too," Griff countered, deadpan. "I was scared because it was the first time I ever saw Aunt Devora all…'atwitter,' as she would have put it. First time I ever heard her scream, or saw her sweat, for that matter. Or cry. Then Gus showed up, charging up the stairs like a one-man cavalry brigade. He got rid of the nest and got Devora to stop crying, and the world resumed normal operations."

"And you don't think he was her lover? Her knight in shining armor?"

"No, I don't. I think she was a woman accustomed to having someone handle the messy details of life, and Gus was the logical one to call on to handle that one. Period."

"Clueless," she muttered.

"Delusional," he muttered in return. He laughed then and shook his head. "Man, that was a long time ago. Almost thirty years." He whistled softly. "Damn, thirty years."

"Better watch out, Griff," she teased. "It's a sure sign you're getting old when you start saying things like *Where did the time go?* and *It seems like only yesterday.*"

"It *does* seem like only yesterday. Sometimes anyway," he added, his tone taking on an edge of cynicism. "Other times it feels like…another lifetime. Someone else's lifetime."

She knew better than to push or pry. So she simply drove.

"It was Gus who got me hooked on flying," he revealed out of the blue. "He would take me up to Quonset…you know the old Army airfield at Quonset Point?"

She nodded, familiar with the former military base about fifteen miles up the coast.

"The guard at the gate was an old war buddy of his. Gus would tell me stories about when they'd been stationed in Italy together. Great stories. His friend would wave us through, and we'd park at the edge of the field and spend hours watching planes take off and land."

''That explains the hours sitting on the hood,'' she guessed.

Griff nodded. ''Today you'd probably think twice about letting a kid that age go off with a stranger, but there was nothing like that about it.''

''I don't know. I think even then Devora would have been wary, *unless* she knew the man in question very, very well. Intimately, even.''

He sent her a quick, quelling look. ''And we'd eat,'' he added, grinning at the recollection. ''Gus brought the food, and it was always the same—meat loaf sandwiches. And sarsaparilla, the real thing, and we swigged it right from the brown-glass bottles. Something Devora would never have approved of.''

He spoke slowly, as if the process of remembering were a private archeological dig, with pieces having to be unearthed and brought to the surface painstakingly and one at a time, to be examined.

''You know, I never really thought much about it back then,'' he went on. ''Maybe because Gus always had the food waiting on the back seat when I got into the car. But it was definitely Devora's meat loaf in those sandwiches.''

''Ah, a meat loaf connoisseur from way back.''

''Hey, don't knock meat loaf. It's right up there with franks and beans on my list of specialties.''

''Would it come before or after frozen burritos?''

He shot her a look of indignation. ''Ingrate.''

''I'll work on broadening my horizons, I promise.''

''I'll help by making dinner for you tomorrow night.''

Rose glanced his way, positive the invitation was not serious.

''I mean it,'' he said, reading her mind.

''Gee, that would be…great.'' Suspicion furrowed her brow. ''What's on the menu?''

''I think I'll let that be a surprise.''

''Do you have to smile at me like Hannibal Lecter when you say that?'' she griped.

"You have my word of honor—no fava beans."

"I'll count that among my blessings." She brushed her hair back from her face. "How did we end up talking about food, anyway? That's right, Devora's meat loaf sandwiches—which I will refrain from pointing out are one more argument for my side."

"Your restraint is admirable," he offered, his tone droll.

"I work at it. So how did Gus know you wanted to be a pilot when you grew up?"

"He didn't. Back then, I didn't know myself. I think the first time we drove out there was because Gus wanted to catch up with his friend. Looking back, I think maybe he was killing time, looking for some way to entertain this poor kid who'd been shuttled off to Devora's for the summer. Who knows? Maybe at first he did it more for her sake than mine, to give her a break."

She peered at him, letting her silence make the point this time.

"Whatever his reason," he said firmly, "everything changed for me after that. *I* changed. From the very first time I watched a plane go up, and felt the vibration of the engines and that swelling feeling in my chest and my head, I was hooked. It was like my heart went up with it, and I made up my mind then and there that someday I would, too."

"And you did...spectacularly, I might add." Her admiration was sincere. "It's not many people who figure out what they want so early and stick with it."

"I guess I ought to consider myself one of the lucky ones," he countered, cynicism creeping back into his voice. "I definitely stuck with it. I never wanted to do anything but fly. As soon as I was old enough, I bugged my mother until she let me take lessons and get my pilot's license. Then the only thing that mattered to me was getting better, getting good enough to fly solo, then to fly for the military and then to fly the best they had to offer.

"For a while, I thought nothing could even come close to matching the rush I got flying combat missions, but I lucked out again. Something did. I found out that the only thing that could get me more pumped than flying the best combat craft, was flying it first... 'while the ink was still wet on the design' was how we put it.''

"Devora sometimes mentioned your work as a test pilot. She worried, of course, but she was also very proud of you, and rightfully so,'' Rose added, aware of the increase of tension in the air. "It always sounded to me like a very dangerous, high-risk way to earn a living.''

"That's the point,'' he retorted. "Risk. It's a test pilot's job to reduce the level of danger and risk for the pilots who'll be flying the plane when it really counts...in combat. And just for the record, it's not about earning a living at all.''

"I figured that out just listening to you. It's obvious that it's much more. More like a passion. A labor of love.''

He nodded, facing straight ahead. "A labor of love. Yeah, I guess you could call it that. Only it's not just that I loved flying. It's...''

His hesitation prompted her to glance his way, taking in his balled fist and the rigid set of his jaw.

"It's that I loved being a flyer,'' he said finally, the stark words underscored with regret in a way that turned Rose's heart inside out. "Hell, I didn't just love it. It's what I *was*.'' He gave a short, harsh laugh. "Are you ready for the punch line? It turns out that's *all* I was. *Was* being the operative word. But then, you've probably already figured that out, too.'' He shoved the cane against the door with a bitterness that was unmistakable and heart-wrenching.

She hesitated, knowing how important it was to choose her words, even her inflection, with care. Anything that smacked of pity would make him recoil for sure. She had a hunch that false cheer and false hope would also be met with contempt.

"Look,'' she said finally, "I'm going to be honest with you. I don't have much experience in the high-risk department. None, actually, unless you count climbing a ladder, which is sort of my own personal Mount Everest. When I see troubled waters, my first instinct is to smooth them, not dive in."

"I'd say that makes you a whole lot smarter than me."

"But this isn't about intelligence, is it. It's about passion. And that happens to be something I do understand, how something can be a true labor of love. And because I do, I think I can also understand, at least a little, how it must feel to have to give that up."

He still didn't look at her, but at least she didn't sense that he was throwing up the barbwire barricades.

Heartened, she asked, "Is that what happened, Griff? Were you injured somehow and forced to retire because of it?"

"More *G*s than I could handle, that's what happened." His voice nearly shook with disgust—most of it directed toward himself, would be her guess.

"I *never* had a problem with *G* force before. Not in all the hours of lab tests, not in training, not in combat." He slammed his fist against his left thigh.

These memories were not being excavated with care, but with contempt.

"I was flying an F-15 Eagle—"

"Is that like a jet?" she risked interrupting to ask.

He looked indignant. "It's not *like* a jet. It *is* a jet. The F-15 is *the* fighter jet, as far as the military is concerned. It's the perfect mix of power and grace, moving faster than the speed of sound."

"I see."

His look suggested he doubted that, but he continued, anyway. "It was a routine test flight, BFMs—that's Basic Fight Maneuvers, the kind of moves I could make in my sleep. The flight plan called for me to make a sharp turn over the ocean. I received an in-flight modification so that the turn came sooner and was even sharper—but even that wasn't unusual. The turn should have maxed-out around six *G*s. Instead it went over seven."

"Is that bad?"

"It was that day," he retorted. "I'd handled more than that before without *G*-lock. I guess my luck just ran out."

"What's *G*-lock?"

"The technical term is Gravity-Induced Loss of Consciousness. The extreme pressure changes at high speeds force blood away from your heart and brain. There are techniques and equipment a pilot can use to counter the effect. Most of the time they work."

"And when they don't?"

"You black out. *G*-lock."

"And that's what happened to you? You blacked out? All alone up there, going who knows how fast? How could they take a chance like that with—?"

"Taking chances is the whole point of test flights. I knew the risk going in."

"So you crashed? Into the water? Was it awful? What am I saying? Of course it was awful."

Her sputtering caused a small, indulgent smile to form on his lips. "Actually, I don't remember. The one nice part of *G*-lock, my brain never recorded the worst of it. I do know the plane was a total loss, to the tune of fifteen million."

Rose realized she was clenching the steering wheel, the same way she would clench the theater seat armrests during the climax of an action movie. But there was no confusing what she was feeling with excitement or entertainment. The pain in the man beside her was too raw, too all-encompassing *not* to share.

"Did you...how could..." She tripped over her own words, wanting to know it all, and right away.

He laughed, but without any real amusement. "Lots of questions, right? Unfortunately, I don't have any definite answers for you...or for myself. The official report by the crash analysts purports that as improbable as it is, I somehow regained consciousness in the seconds before contact with the water and automatically pulled the ejection handle."

"It sounds like your guardian angel was working overtime that day," she told him.

"That was more or less the *unofficial* consensus of the experts. All I know is I woke up in the hospital." He pounded his left thigh. "And in more pain than I knew was in me. My leg got the worst of it, broken in eight places, a shattered kneecap and damage to every major tendon. There were also some broken ribs, a collapsed lung and a bruised spinal cord. You come out of a plane at 730 miles per hour, and you take some hits."

"I can't believe you made it…that you're sitting here…or walking at all."

"Early on, the doctors warned me I might not walk again. They wouldn't even discuss flying, which is the only thing I wanted to hear about, so I just filled in the blanks my way. I made up my own recovery plan and spent eighteen lousy months at their mercy, learning to breathe and crawl and roll over…all the way to walking again." He grimaced. "With a damn cane—temporarily, I told myself. At first, I was just glad to be walking under my own power."

"And now you're not?"

He shrugged. "Now I figure that as far as it counts, the plane wasn't the only thing wasted that day."

"I'm not going to say that's ridiculous, even though it is. Griff, I really don't know *what* to say. I can't even imagine what it was like for you. The physical pain alone must have been horrible, but to have the threat of never walking again *and* the end of your career hanging over your head at the same time…"

She had the most intense urge to stop the truck in the middle of the road and take him in her arms. She settled for taking one hand off the wheel long enough to squeeze his shoulder. "You're pretty remarkable, you know."

"So I've been told," he returned, his voice too smooth, too even. "A testament to what hard work and being stubborn as a mule can accomplish. Too bad it was all for nothing."

"Nothing?" exclaimed Rose. "Look at you. You look…wonderful. I meant to say…healthy. Strong. You can walk, and you may prove to be right about the cane being a temporary thing. God knows there's plenty of proof that when you make up your mind to do a thing—''

''I can't fly,'' he snapped, loudly enough that the words reverberated in the small confines of the truck and hung in the air between them. ''I don't get to make up my mind about that. Someone else does.''

''And the decision not to let you fly is based on your leg?''

''My leg…and the loss of peripheral vision in my left eye, and problems with my equilibrium that cause these freakin' dizzy spells to come on me out of nowhere.'' There was a weary edge to the sigh that followed, suggesting what it cost him to even acknowledge those ''failings'' aloud.

''I'm sorry,'' she said, frustrated by the inadequacy of the words. ''I understand that there have to be strict standards for pilots, but my God, did they have to force you to retire? Surely there must be something that a man with your experience and knowledge, not to mention courage—''

''Nobody forced me,'' he interjected, cutting short her impassioned tirade against the military hierarchy. ''They wanted me to head the unit developing test flight plans and procedures for a plane that's still on the drawing board—the one slated to bring air warfare into the new millennium. Code name Skywalker.''

''Griff, that sounds so exciting. I should think you'd love—''

He cut her off harshly. ''Don't you get it? I love *flying*. Not sitting on my ass watching others fly. And it's over for me. For good. That's what matters. That's *all* that matters.''

''You're right,'' agreed Rose. ''It does matter. Given what you've told me tonight, and the way you've chosen to live your whole life, it's obvious it's what matters most—and anybody who tries to convince you otherwise is lying.''

He eyed her warily.

''It seems to me that whether it's some*thing,* like flying, or some*one,* or simply a private dream that you build your life around, when it's taken away, it leaves the same size hole. That's size extra-large-to-the-nth, in case you're wondering," she added, causing his mouth to quirk ever so slightly.

"To the nth, huh? That's sounds about as large as this hole feels."

"I wish I had some words of wisdom to offer about how to go about filling it, but I don't."

"Good. If you do happen to come up with any, do us both a favor and keep them to yourself. I've had enough advice and words of wisdom dumped on me to last me several lifetimes."

"Anything help?"

"Not a bit."

"No surprise there."

"What's that supposed to mean?"

"It means you can't advise someone how to do something that can't be done."

"Please, spare me," he groaned. "I've been down the reverse psychology path before...with professionals."

"That wasn't reverse psychology, you big dope. It was the truth."

"What is? That my life is nothing but a big hole, so I might as well throw in the towel now? Is that your idea of cheering up a cripple?"

"I've got news for you, Griffin, it's not my job to cheer you up, and the only thing seriously *crippled* about you is your lousy attitude." Now he was lucky her hands were clenched on the steering wheel. As long as she was driving, she couldn't devote her full attention to telling him off. "If it's anyone's job, it's yours...if you want it. If not, you can just go on being miserable."

"That's the plan."

"Forgive me for speaking from personal experience."

"You flew?" he countered, reeking with disbelief.

"You really are self-absorbed, aren't you. Look around, Griff. There are several hundred million people sharing the planet with you, and a fair number of them don't give a rat's ass if their feet never leave the ground.''

"Their loss," he muttered.

"Wrong," she shot back. "That's the point I was making—or trying to, anyway. That it's not their loss, it's yours. There are as many different losses as there are…dreams to lose."

She was wasting her breath, she thought. Far from "cheering him up," as he'd accused, all she'd done was poke at what she should have realized was an open wound. She knew for a fact that when your own heart is still festering, you couldn't care less that you were not alone in your suffering, much less be comforted by the knowledge. Misery may love company, as held forth by another old saying, but only when it was damn good and ready.

It looked to her as if it would be a while before Griff reached that stage, and so it threw her when, after several moments of brooding silence, he turned and said, "So what's yours?"

"My what?"

"Your loss. You said everyone has one, and you were willing enough to share your personal experience a minute ago, so, what's yours?"

"Oh. I guess…mine is sort of complicated. I suppose the short answer is my divorce was my biggest loss. At the time, I felt as if I had lost everything—everything I had and everything I ever wanted."

From the corner of her eye, Rose saw him nod.

"That's the feeling, all right," he said.

"I remember waking up the next morning and deciding to take stock. So I took a good, long, hard look at my future, and saw more hole than life. Does that sound familiar, too?"

"I'd say you've nailed it."

"Your circumstances are very different, of course. I didn't wake up in pain in a hospital bed. But I have to believe that it doesn't matter who you are or what you've been through, the hole that looks the biggest is always the one that's sitting on the path straight dead ahead of you.''

"Okay. Your point being?"

"The point is that you can either sit and stare into the hole for the rest of your life, or find a way to get around it.''

"Damn if I don't hear the unmistakable pitter-patter of words of wisdom on the way,'' he said, striking a note between ridicule and sarcasm.

"Then be damned,'' she retorted. "I'm simply saying that if you try to get over that hole by finding something else to fill it, you're wasting your time. Because even if you did find something as big as what used to be there—that thing you loved and nurtured for years and years, the thing that made that particular hole in the first place—the replacement wouldn't be the right shape, or color or something. And don't snicker as if this is some half-baked theory I'm making up on the spur of the moment, because it's not.''

"You had me fooled,'' he said dryly.

"You're entitled to your opinion, as misguided and illogical as it might be. But I've given this matter a great deal of thought and that's just not the way it works.''

"Really?'' He folded his arms across his chest, his tone a mocking drawl. "Then why don't you tell me how it does work?''

Rose shrugged nonchalantly, smiled smugly, and executed a flawless three-point turn to back the truck into the narrow drive beside the shop.

"It's simple, really,'' she said as she killed the engine. "If you want to fill that hole, you have to chip away at it. You have to try to find lots of little things, or let them find you, and then let them fall into place on their own. In the hole, I mean. Sort of like a box of cereal,'' she added with a flourish.

"A box of cereal?''

"Right, you know how they always have that line on the label about it being packed by weight, not volume, and the contents settling during shipping?''

"As much as I hate to admit it, I actually see where you're going with this."

He did not sound impressed with what seemed to Rose to be the perfect analogy for one of life's great challenges.

"Anyway, you have to just keep adding to it, and one day you'll look and see that the hole is full, or nearly full, or maybe just half full. The important thing is, it won't be empty."

Rose turned in the seat and leaned back, unfazed by the fact that he continued to appear underwhelmed and was also beginning to show signs his patience was wearing thin.

"So what? Now all you have is a big hole that's half full of…who the hell knows what? All shoved in there like crushed cereal, for God's sake? It's still a damn hole."

"Exactly, and it always will be a hole—just not an empty one. It can never be the same as it was, as perfect as it was, or at least as perfect as you wanted to believe it was."

He stared at her in silence, in a way that made her think he wasn't catching on as well as she'd first thought.

"Maybe you could try thinking of it in terms of dentures versus your own teeth," she suggested.

"No." He shook his head firmly and grabbed the cane. "I've heard enough for one night…more than enough. You can just save the denture part for another session."

"All right. I do think you've grasped the basic idea very well."

"Oh, I have. Definitely. Completely."

"And what do you think?"

"What do I think of this…black hole theory of yours? You want an honest answer?"

She nodded.

He sighed, deeply, then in a rush said, "I think it's the most bizarre take on the whole loss and grieving process that I've ever heard."

"You *do* get it," she said, smiling brightly at him.

"And," he went on, after having again stared at her in what she was beginning to suspect was closer to speechlessness than mere silence, "I think you have the most amazingly beautiful shoulders, and eyes, and smile ever created."

As he spoke, he drew closer. That's all it took to make Rose lean toward him in turn. She closed her eyes, felt his mouth barely brush against hers, and everything inside her started to hum.

"And," he whispered, breathing into her, breathing her into himself, "I think I'm going to have to kiss you again, real soon, as soon as possible, and keep on kissing you, soft and deep and slow, for, say, an hour...or two...or..."

He paused, teasing her with his heat, his tongue, the sweet ache of her own anticipation.

And she let him.

Thanks mostly to Maryann, she was a blind-date veteran and highly skilled at fending off unwanted male advances. She hadn't given much thought to how to handle a *wanted* advance in years, however. And it was probably just as well that she hadn't wasted her time. Because regardless of the strategy, it wasn't in her at that moment to resist anything about him.

"Or?" she prompted, curling her fingers around his shoulders. The single word encompassed a subtle but complicated blend of feminine teasing, invitation and surrender.

The reply was quick, less complicated, and gloriously, unmistakably masculine.

"Or longer," he said, at last covering her mouth with his and pulling her with him into a kiss that started recklessly and quickly spun out of control.

Just the way she wanted it.

Chapter Nine

Later, Rose would muse that had it not been for the diligence of the local police, the odds were overwhelming that she would have had sex in a truck for the first time in her life that night. She wasn't sure if that made Officer Lyle Rancourt's rap on the window a cause for gratitude or regret, but as she climbed from behind the wheel and slammed the door, she was definitely leaning toward regret.

She and Griff had reacted to the intrusion as smoothly as two kids caught groping in the back seat at a drive-in movie. They lurched apart, lips puffy, clothes disheveled, and their eyes squinting against the brightness of the high-wattage, police-issue flashlight aimed at them through the steam coated window. Griff proceeded to mutter something appropriately adolescent and obscene, while she fumbled to lower the window far enough to reassure the officer that she was experiencing no trouble, engine or otherwise.

The blushing patrolman's hasty, apologetic retreat did not mollify Griff, who was still muttering, as she unlocked the rear door of the shop and keyed in the code to deactivate the alarm. Turning on only the table lamp near her computer desk, she headed for the bathroom. She needed a moment alone. Not to come to her senses; she knew she was way beyond that. But she would feel better if she had a chance to straighten her clothes and gather her thoughts. Hopefully, it would also allow enough time for Griff to cool off and quit referring to poor Lyle as that "meddling pervert getting paid to harass people."

It didn't, but as soon as she logged on and it was announced she had e-mail from Mr. Shippington, his grousing ceased.

"What did he say?" he prodded, impatiently tapping the back of her chair, as she read the London dealer's response to her offer, twice, wanting to be certain it was merited before she let loose a whoop of excitement.

"He says it's a deal," she exclaimed, grinning as she quickly scanned the screen and read important bits aloud. "He says our offer is "fair and reasonable," and that while he had hoped for a "spot more profit," he's done some checking of his own with the friend of a friend..."

"Right, right, go on."

"In other words, the someone who gave Clare the lead. And he wants you to know he is honored to assist you in your most commendable quest on your aunt's behalf. Isn't that sweet?"

"What's his angle?"

"His angle? Offhand, I would say it appears to be ordinary human decency."

He hooked his fingers into his front pockets and nodded noncommittally. "I suppose that's always a possibility. Go on."

"That's it. The rest is more or less the fine print about payment and shipment—which I will read and respond to first thing tomorrow," she promised, logging off. "That's assuming you're still interested, of course."

When he failed to respond to her teasing, she glanced

askew at him. "Laugh, Griff—that was a joke." Then, puzzled, she asked, "This *is* what you want, isn't it?"

"Of course, it's what I want. And of course, I'm still interested...very interested. I'm just surprised it's happening so fast."

"Sometimes," she deadpanned, "that's the way it happens."

He tipped his head, acknowledging her appropriation of his own words from the other night. "Touché. Seriously, this is great news. And it's all thanks to you."

"And Clare," she reminded him, "and a whole lot of luck. Believe me, I'm as shocked as you are that our first attempt went this well." She grinned up at him. "This is so cool. Why aren't you as excited as I am?"

"I am."

"Then show it. Smile. That's an order," she growled, laughing and coming out of her seat in a playful attempt to tickle his ribs, which somehow detoured into a less playful attempt to hug him. Instantly, the air around them ignited and any hint of playfulness disappeared.

His arms were around her, pulling her hard against him, and it was as if the rap on the window and the time since had never existed. Their bodies remembered precisely where they had been when they were made to stop, and brought them there again, quickly. Their mouths collided in an explosion of heat and longing that left Rose breathless and wanting more...wanting all of him. She clung to his broad shoulders, beseeching without words, and Griff responded with a fervor that made clear his intention to indulge her.

He held her, touched her, his hands everywhere, sliding, memorizing, massaging her shoulders, her breasts, her thighs and the small of her back, and always pressing her closer, until there didn't seem to be a part of her that was not under his domain.

She welcomed the possession, gloried in the assault of his tongue, parrying and submitting and exploring him in turn. A fresh quickening of desire rocked her, and she felt his strong, hard body tremble in response to the urgency she couldn't conceal, much less control. This was a reckless brand of passion she had never known. If there was a way to curb it, she had no knowledge of that, either. And no interest in learning. There was too much pleasure raining on her, drenching her senses, overriding old taboos and boundaries.

His amazing hands moved through her hair and down her back, as his warm mouth painted kisses along her throat. Rose was reeling, swept by a strange and wonderful lightness…a sense of pure and utter freedom that engulfed her, body and soul. She felt outside herself, and at the same time, more aware of herself than ever before…of each and every awakening cell and pleasure point.

In yet another triumph of the impossible, time had warped, leaving her outside its constraints, safely cocooned in the sweetness of the moment…a moment of absolute clarity about who she was and what she wanted.

She wanted *this*. She understood that with all that was in her. She wanted *him*. Right there, right now.

If she had ever felt anything close to this before, the memory was lost to her. This was all new, all glorious. She was unfettered, flowing, from someplace deep inside where the only laws to be heeded were as old as the stars and the sea and the miracle that had first set everything in motion. It was not the law of civilization guiding her, but the law of nature and of spirit, and every movement, every response, was as easy and as spontaneous as breathing.

Rose was content to let this fiery desire lead the way, following without qualms or reservation, without a thought for anything beyond the spiral of arousal building within. Griff nibbled on the side of her throat and strummed his thumb across the tip of her breast, and it was like a million silvery strands of pleasure were strung inside, winding tighter, cutting deeper.

His other hand came to rest on her belly, one fingertip slowly tracing the zipper on her jeans, sliding ever lower.

When he reached bottom, there was a wild fluttering at her core that radiated outward, racing through her veins in currents so strong that she was certain her knees would buckle if he let her go.

But he did not let her go, and when he tipped her head back and sought out her gaze, the dark and reckless gleam in his eyes made it plain he had no intention of doing so.

Black mirrors, she thought, staring into his eyes for what seemed to be forever. Black magic mirrors, reflecting outward, reflecting his soul and a thousand questions hidden there.

He gave voice to only one. "Tonight?"

It was more texture than sound—gritty, ragged, hopeful.

Rose didn't think, didn't need to. She nodded. "Tonight."

His mouth softened, curved, not so much with pleasure, she thought, as with the same unguarded wonder she had glimpsed in him earlier. It was the look of a man who couldn't quite believe his own luck.

His hand inched lower still, his touch light—a whisper, a promise.

"Now?" he asked, as the warm, sweet ache beneath his fingertips grew stronger.

"Now." She lifted into him, her lips parted, wanting.

"Not here."

Not here? Rose was pretty sure she whimpered aloud as her mind filled with thoughts of hauling herself back into the truck, of driving the short distance home, of leaving the shelter of his arms for even a few minutes. It was out of the question, far beyond the ability of a woman whose legs had turned to jelly and muscles to mush, and she was about to tell him so—when he astonished her by scooping her up in his arms and heading toward the front of the shop.

"Griff! Where...?"

"Shh."

"But your leg. You can't—"

"Apparently I can. Chalk it up to adrenaline," he grunted.

"Don't you mean testosterone?"

"Got plenty of that bottled up, too."

She lifted her hand to his cheek, aware of the undercurrent of pain in his humor, and felt both concerned and very happy.

He bent, depositing her on the old white iron bed in the center of the shop, and heaved what was unmistakably a sigh of relief.

"That was pretty dumb," she told him.

"Not from where I'm standing." He was gazing down at her, his look so tender, so nearly worshipful, that a sudden lump formed in her throat.

"From here, it's looking like the smartest move I've made in years. You have no idea," he went on, reaching out to loop a lock of her hair around his finger, "of the dreams I've been having about this damn bed."

"You've dreamed about the bed?"

"The bed with you in it."

She had goose bumps. "You've dreamt about me?"

He nodded, grinned and lowered himself next to her, sinking with her into the artfully arranged feather mattress and multiple layers of embroidered sheets and heirloom quilts intended to inspire in her customers visions of romantic liaisons. Never, in her wildest imaginings, had Rose envisioned herself in this lovely old bed. In the middle of the night. In the middle of the shop. With Hollis Griffin.

But here she was. And what she thought, as Griff rolled to half cover her, looking hungry enough to devour whatever she was willing to offer him…what she thought for as long as she was able to think, was that she was very, very glad she had decided to position the bed facing *away* from the windows, *and* discreetly tucked behind a hand-painted screen made of solid old folding doors.

…*meant to be, meant to be*…

As soon as he had settled in, she found herself on the receiving end of so many things that made her glad, and grateful and astonished, that she lost count. And still they came, delivered by Griff's big hands, as they roamed over her, unbuttoning, unsnapping and removing everything in his path that wasn't part of her; bestowed on her by his sweetly stubbled jaw, the scrape of it in tender places making her shiver and squirm; and by his very adventurous mouth, which seemed dedicated to tasting every square inch of her.

It was pleasure so pure it almost hurt. When she could no longer hold it all inside, it seeped from between her lips in soft, broken murmurs of delight and demand.

"Your hands," she whispered, unable to keep from arching so that her breasts filled his palms, pressing, wanting. "I love your hands...I love the way they feel on me."

"Glad to hear it. I've been wanting to get my hands on you for so long, I don't plan on taking them off you in a hurry." His words rasped against the side of her throat as his palms moved in lazy circles around her breasts.

"Forever," she breathed. "I want this to last forever."

"I'll do my best," he promised, nipping her, rubbing his face against her tender flesh.

She tilted her head back into the pillows, her thighs shifting restlessly, as he slid lower, the unhurried exploration of his hands clouding her mind, igniting her body. Until—

In the same way sudden lightning can rip through a lazy summer night, a fleeting image of the scars beneath her breasts flashed into Rose's mind, threatening to yank her from whatever spell she was under. How could she have forgotten about them, she fretted as her stomach muscles clenched, starting a chain effect all through her.

The scars were small, like hairline cracks in fine porcelain, barely discernable even in full light—but they were there. Would Griff notice? Would he mind?

Her rush to panic was interrupted by his deep voice.

"I ought to warn you, Rose, my hands aren't the only thing I've been wanting to get on you. These past few days I've also given a great deal of thought to how your skin was going to feel on my tongue." Even before he finished speaking, he was stroking her with it, following the downward curve of her breasts, and lower, paying that part of her no more, or less, attention than he had any other.

"Just thinking about doing this made me crazy, but my fantasy didn't even come close to the real thing. Your body is so much sweeter…and riper…and more fascinating…than anything even my imagination could conjure up."

She had no way of knowing if he had read her mind, and chosen words to soothe her, but that was the result. His praise was powerful magic, shielding her safely within the spell.

"I dreamed of tasting you here," he went on with a lavish caress of her ribs. "And here…" His hands framed her waist as he traced the swell of her hip. "And…what the—?"

He raised his head to get a look at what his fingers had encountered.

Rose went still. "It's a belly button ring," she explained casually, as if body piercing was nothing unusual in a thirty-five-year-old divorced woman who frequented rest homes and adhered to a moral code rooted in Sister Mary Raphael's fifth-grade catechism class.

Despite the lack of light, Rose could tell he was frowning. Boy, that was irony for you. She'd been so focused on the scars, she'd forgotten all about the ring in her navel.

"You had your belly button pierced?" He sounded stunned.

"Sort of." She gave herself a mental shake. "I mean, yes, I did. I probably should have mentioned it beforehand, to avoid this big, awkward moment of surprise."

"I like surprises."

She could feel his warm breath on her belly, as he studied her closely.

She felt an overwhelming urge to fill the silence. "I probably would have mentioned it, but this is the first ti—that is, I don't make a habit of jumping into b—this sort of thing, and it just…slipped my mind."

"Does it hurt?"

"Not at all."

"Did it hurt when you had it done?"

She shook her head, cleared her throat. "Not much. But then, I was a little…tipsy."

"You're not tipsy now. How does…this feel?"

She shivered at his touch. "Good."

"How good?"

"Too good."

"No such thing."

"Then I guess it doesn't…you know, turn you off?"

He laughed and moved so he was on top of her, his thighs outside hers, leaning so that most of his weight was on his right leg.

"Sweetheart, I don't think there's anything known to man that could turn me off now. I've got the woman I want right where I want her, just the way I want her…" He ran his hand over her naked body. "I'm as close to knocking on heaven's door as I'm likely to get."

The tension in her muscles eased. She almost laughed.

"Besides, the damn thing is flat-out erotic…you have to know that. I've always had this secret fascination for women with pierced belly buttons."

"Have you known many?" she enquired, not sure the revelation pleased her.

"You're my first," he assured her, his grin fading into something raw and ravenous. "Damn, Rose, I wanted you like hell already. Now I want you so bad it hurts."

"I want you, too, but…" She saw him jumping to the wrong conclusion and continued in a rush. "First I just want you to know, I did not have it done to be erotic. At least, that wasn't the main reason. There's a very simple exp—"

He stopped her mouth with his. "Later," he said when he finally lifted his head and let her breathe. "I want to hear every fascinating detail about it—later. Right now, I only want this…"

He moved so he could kiss her belly, touching the tiny— very tiny, very tasteful, she reassured herself—gold ring, lightly, then catching it with his teeth and tugging gently.

There was something sexy, in an exotic, harem-girl sort

of way, about lying in bed, naked, while a fully clothed man played with the ring in your belly button. Rose vaguely recalled that it was a very similar notion, encouraged by Maryann, which had led to her inebriated decision to cap off her *après* divorce liberation celebration by having it pierced in the first place. But until tonight, that particular fantasy had never come close to being fulfilled.

She closed her eyes, wanting to lose herself in the fantasy. It was not difficult. What would be difficult for her, probably even impossible, would be to *not* feel sexy and sultry, when Griff was touching her the way he was touching her now. Everything that made her a woman found its match in him. Her uneasiness waned, giving way to a mysterious feeling of power flowing from deep within.

He straightened and took her face in his hands, his touch still gentle, and completely at odds with the unleashed heat and hunger that burned in his eyes.

For Rose, the combination was lethal, irresistible.

Lust, she reminded herself. That's really what all this shimmering and tingling and throbbing was about. Lust. No big deal. She'd figured it all out hours ago, and she could handle it.

She wanted this. A good thing, because despite an awareness of her own feminine power, she was rapidly moving from being simply willing, to being defenseless, to being his for the taking. She was ready even before he rocked his hips against hers, pressing her deeper into the mattress, grinding into her in a way that was brazen and wildly arousing. Rose met his thrusts, gloried in them, demanded more.

When his rough hands closed over her breasts, she clutched the front of his shirt, her shaking fingers clawing at the buttons. She managed to free one, swore at the second and ripped off the third. She wanted hot, slick, skin-to-skin contact, and she wanted it now. To get it, she dragged the half-buttoned shirt over his shoulders and shoved it to his waist.

She urged him closer, writhed under him, rubbing against

the damp heat and hair-roughened splendor of his chest. Excitement coursed through her. She was on fire, her senses running over, and greedy for more. She touched him, again and again, everywhere, her hands skating along his ribs, around and up his back, all of him new and uncharted and wondrous to her.

The powerful yearning at her core drew her hand lower, her fingers sliding beneath his belted waistband, trailing the enticing line of dark hair that went from rough to silky to coarse and dense. He was hard, and the brush of her fingers made him shudder and fall still. He sucked in air and didn't let it go.

Wedged against the back of her hand, his shaft felt steely and smooth and scorchingly hot. The intimacy of it made her tremble, made her bold. With her heart pounding wildly, she turned her hand and curled her fingers around him.

Griff threw his head back, his mouth open, his eyes tightly shut. His voice was hoarse, coming from deep in his throat. "Oh, my."

Instantly her hands were on his belt buckle and his were on hers. Together they fumbled and yanked, tore and shoved. He rolled to his back with her on top of him, locked in a tangle of tongues and murmurs and jagged, open-mouth kisses. Somehow they dealt with buckle and zipper, and his clothes came off, revealing flesh and muscle and scars. When they were both naked, he rolled back, urging her legs apart, positioning himself between them.

He stroked the inside of her thighs, first one, then the other, as he made his way with maddening slowness to the slick, heated cove at their apex, the place that most ached for his touch. He made her wait, made her shiver, made her squirm.

And when his fingers at last found and opened and possessed that waiting portal, Rose had only one thought. *Hurry, hurry, hurry.*

Slow down, slow down, slow down, Griff ordered himself when he could no longer resist letting his fingers breach her nest of silky curls to claim the treasure beyond. The warning did little good. Not surprising, when one considered how long it had been since he'd been with a woman. It had been just as long since he'd wanted one, much less wanted one as badly as he wanted Rose. Understanding why he was so desperate for release, however, was not the same as liking it.

Hard and fast would serve his needs at the moment, but it wouldn't take care of Rose's—not really, despite the increasingly insistent rise and fall of her hips beneath his that suggested otherwise. He'd resolved that if this happened, he would see to it that it was long and slow and sweet, that he would spin it out until she surrendered control, until she surrendered everything and went crazy in his arms the way she had in his dream. He wanted it that way for himself, sure, but mostly he wanted it for Rose. After hearing about her marriage, he wanted to burn clean any place inside her where a doubt or second thought might hide.

Unfortunately, he was rapidly being forced to accept the fact that all the resolve he could ever muster would not be sufficient to override the clawing, twisting need that was inside him and growing stronger. He couldn't slow down, couldn't hold back, couldn't stop himself from taking what he needed.

He pushed against her, seeking entry, then drove into her. She was tight and hot and wet. Heat and honey. He struggled to show some restraint, but she felt so good that it was impossible not to be greedy. With each stroke he was in deeper…and wanted more.

Beneath him, Rose shuddered and quaked, lifting one arm to grasp the iron bedpost above her head. Her expression told him all he needed to know. She was already right there, at the edge. The awareness that she was about to go over drove him closer, as well. His thrusts became even harder and faster, the frantic pace echoed by his tongue as it mated with hers until they were both panting for air.

His mind shut down, leaving something more primitive to drive him. His sense of touch intensified, others dimmed. It was from inside a darkening haze that he felt her hips buck, saw her head arch back, heard her crying his name.

Her explosion triggered his own. He was hurtling toward oblivion, and in the final instant before he went under, he knew with all certainty that his plan had failed, big time. The realization only made his fall faster, the rush of pleasure stronger, the slow drift back to reality sweeter.

Rolling to his side with her still in his arms, Griff savored the aftershocks, letting them carry him along aimlessly. Just as satisfying to him as those lingering waves of pleasure was the knowledge that he had not succeeded in getting Rose to surrender. Not even close.

Instead, he'd gotten what he'd really wanted without realizing it, something that was both a hairbreadth and a universe away from surrender. It was something you could never force the way you could a surrender. Something that could only be given, willingly and under the right circumstances. That something was abandonment.

He had seen it for himself. In those final few seconds, with fulfillment hovering ever closer, Rose hadn't simply given in to the pleasure he wanted to give her—she had thrown herself in the air to meet it. She had abandoned herself, utterly and completely. Not to *him,* though he would like to believe he'd played an integral role in the whole thing. What she had really abandoned herself to was passion…she had given herself up to the unrestrained quest for pleasure and fulfillment. And for the first time ever—if he was any judge of the slightly unfocused, very bedazzled way she was looking at him.

When his breathing was steady, he brushed the hair from her cheek and smiled at her. "Whatever your asking price is for this bed, it's not enough."

Her lips curved. "Granted I'm no expert, but I'm pretty sure that what just happened had more to do with you than this bed. Still, why risk a good thing? First thing tomorrow, I'll reprice it high enough to keep it around a while."

"That still sounds too risky to me."

"Trust me. I do it all the time," she assured him, her hand moving across his chest in slow, random exploration.

"And it actually works?"

"Like a charm." Her hand fell still and her lips formed a rueful slant. "Except…"

"Except?" he prodded.

"Except one time—one time in five years." Sighing, she explained. "It was when you bought my garland of dried hydrangeas that no one was supposed to buy."

"Then why was there a price tag on?" asked Griff, slightly bewildered, but very, very content.

"Because things in a shop are supposed to have a price tag."

"So it had to have a tag, but it wasn't actually for sale. Is that what you're saying?"

"It was for sale," she corrected. "Just not yet."

"Then when…no, wait, don't tell me…you would have just known when the time was right to sell it?"

"Exactly."

"I have to admit, I was skeptical the first time you ran that one by me, but after tonight, I'm a believer." He stroked his hand along her arm, trailing off to follow the curve of her hip and lingering there. "Tonight was right for this. Our planets must have been ascending, or whatever the astrological arrangement is for perfect timing."

She smiled but said nothing.

"At least," he went on, fishing, "that's how it felt to me. Perfect." For some reason, tonight he wanted reassurance from her that she felt the same way he did about tonight.

"That's how it felt to me, too," she said softly.

"No regrets?"

"Just one."

Damn, he thought, frowning. Why couldn't he have left it alone? "What's that?" he asked.

"I regret that at some point in the not-too-distant future, we have to leave this bed and drive home."

Groaning, with relief as much as dread, he pulled her close

and rubbed his cheek against her hair. "I suppose it wouldn't be too good for business if we're still here when customers start showing up."

"On the contrary," she maintained in a dry tone. "Since most of my customers are female, I'd venture to say the sight of you sprawled in bed, just as you are, would attract all kinds of traffic." Nodding thoughtfully, she added, "Probably sell a lot of bed linen, too."

"What's my cut?"

"Nothing…because it's not going to happen. Some things I don't share."

"Stingy with profits, are you?"

"Profits are negotiable. It's lovers I don't share."

He nodded, conscious of her shift in tone from teasing to somber. "Got it—no one-night stands and no musical beds. That works for me."

"Good."

"Now all we have to decide is where we're going to spend the rest of the night." With great reluctance, he retrieved her T-shirt and tossed it to her. "My bed or yours?"

"Both," she replied, pulling the shirt over her head. She caught the look of lecherous intent he shot her and laughed. "Before you get carried away, let me clarify that answer. Both beds, one of us in each. Something tells me it's the only way we'll get any sleep, and I have to work in the morning."

Unfazed, he reached for his pants and pulled them on. He had no intention of spending the rest of the night alone, and he had the whole ride home to change her mind.

"Griff?"

"Yeah?"

"Why *did* you buy the garland?"

"Truth?" He glanced over his shoulder and saw her nod. "Because it suddenly occurred to me I ought to buy something before I asked you to do me a favor. To even things out, I mean." He shrugged. "The garland just happened to be sitting there.'' He hesitated, then somewhat sheepishly admitted the rest.

''You actually thought the price was twenty-five dollars?'' she exclaimed, evidently incredulous.

''I thought even that was a little on the high side, actually, but figured it was worth it if you agreed to help with the birds.''

She shook her head with acute disdain. ''Okay, that settles it. Bring back my garland, and I'll refund your money.''

''Why?''

''For starters, because you don't deserve it.''

''Don't deserve it? What are you running here? A shop or an adoption agency?''

''A little of both, actually. And you are not my idea of a fit guardian for my garland.''

''That's ridiculous.''

''Really? I'll bet you anything the poor thing is still in the bag.''

''Anything?''

She met his glittering gaze head-on. ''Anything.''

He shrugged.

''I'm right,'' she exclaimed. ''You haven't even opened the bag.''

''That doesn't prove anything,'' he argued.

''Of course it does. It proves you have no use for it and never did.''

''Not so fast. It so happens I do have a use for it. A very good use. One even you will approve of. I'm going to start a collection with it.''

''What sort of collection?'' she enquired, her arms folded, eyes narrowed with suspicion.

''A collection of useless, overpriced objects bought from beautiful women who show up in my dreams and do all sorts of incredible things.''

''What sort of things?''

"You sure you want to know?"

"I'm sure," she countered, not looking it.

He grinned. "Then come home with me and I'll show you."

Chapter Ten

She had missed the chance to make love in a truck, but Rose did manage another first…her first all-nighter. At least, that was her take on it. Griff argued that since she'd cat-napped once or twice, it did not qualify as an authentic all-nighter.

Something in his tone had suggested he spoke from experience, and plenty of it. Which would account for how appallingly accomplished the man was at the sorts of things folks did to pass the time in bed when they weren't sleeping or watching the *Tonight Show*. He did not elaborate, how-ever. Clearly, if she was foolish enough to want to know more, she would have to ask.

All morning she had been going through the motions of an ordinary day, chatting with customers, tallying sales, ap-pearing perfectly normal on the outside. While inside, she wasn't even on the same planet as everyone else. She was somewhere far away, someplace new and wonderful…and dangerous. For as long as she could, Rose wanted to hold on to the wonderful part without worrying about the rest.

Not that she was the type to go building castles in the air based on one night of great sex. Not even earth-shatteringly great sex—sex that was soft and slow, and sex that was hard and raw, and hit more notes in between than she had dreamed existed. Well, she might have conjured just one very modest castle.

Nosing around in Griff's past could rob her of even that.

It was one thing to understand in theory that he was not the kind of man to want for female companionship, and quite another to know the precise number of women who had carved notches in his bedpost. Knowing would bring into focus the all-too-real possibility that she was simply one more. Therein was the danger, and Rose was in no hurry to confront it.

She did her best to ignore a little undercurrent of uneasiness. The ostrich-with-its-head-in-the-sand approach was not her usual style. But then, neither was falling into bed with a man *before* the first date. And not just any man at that, but a man she'd been certain was everything she did not want in a friend, much less in a lover. Suddenly, Griff was both. Could one woman be so wrong about so much?

There was only one explanation she could think of, and it sounded crazy even to her. However, that in no way detracted from her willingness to believe. A woman with her head in the clouds will grasp any straw handy to keep from falling—even the notion that there had been other forces at work last night aside from the obvious…that is, an uncontrollable, mutual torrent of lust.

Fate. Nature. Spirit. She didn't know what to call it, only that the entire time she was in Griff's arms, she'd felt a connection too profound to be merely physical, a heady sense that everything was, at long last, right with her world. Knowing the conventional wisdom about things that appear too good to be true, she had been prepared to wake up as Dorothy had, back in familiar surroundings that were colorless in comparison to where she had been in her dreams. But the dream hadn't ended when she opened her eyes. She was more than a little amazed that the feeling of rightness was still with her. Amazed and joyful.

Admittedly, she was no authority on passionate escapades or the feelings they could inspire, but she did happen to be the world's foremost authority on her own heart. She knew what she felt and she knew when something felt right. Being with Griff had felt as right to her as breathing.

She'd wasted years trying to make herself "right," and worse, pretending things felt right when they didn't. When her marriage vows failed, she'd made a new one, to herself this time—a vow always to be honest about herself and with herself. It had not been easy or quick, but she had managed to make peace with reality and accept herself—flaws, quirks, insecurities and all. Along the way she had also learned to trust her own instincts, no matter what.

Where men were concerned, her instincts invariably told her the same thing. They warned her to play it safe, not to get too involved, and above all, not to do anything that would put her heart at risk. She was proud of how much she had come to rely on her own inner voice. Only now did it occur to her that it's not difficult to heed a voice that's telling you exactly what you want to hear. The question was, did she have the courage to listen now, when her instincts—and her heart—were saying something very different?

She had a chance to find out, when Griff dropped by to see her later that afternoon. Unfortunately, instead of providing answers, the mere sight of him complicated things even more, making her feel both hot and cold, restless and content.

He paused just inside the door and ran his gaze over the shop, where a half-dozen or so shoppers were browsing and soaking up the cool, rose-scented air before venturing back out into the summer heat. When he spotted her sitting on the stool behind the counter, logging in a shipment of baskets from Nantucket, he stopped looking. His dark eyes warmed, and he broke into a smile that was light-years away from the arrogant expression he'd worn the first time he crossed her threshold.

He started toward her, moving easily with the cane. She'd been concerned about his leg, but when she broached the subject during the night, he'd simply kissed her until she shut up. Still, as the hours passed, it was impossible not to sense those instants when the pain gripped him.

Knowing he wouldn't respond to sympathy or reason, she'd done the only thing she could do—seized control. The first time she had playfully but firmly rolled him onto his back and straddled him, pinning his hands on the pillow above his head, he'd looked surprised, but he hadn't protested. After that first time, he hadn't even look surprised.

She smiled to herself as he moved closer, already familiar enough with his habits to know it was not by chance that his path through the shop was along the widest aisles with the fewest people. The single exception was the slight detour he took at the end. Her puzzled expression quickly evolved into one of amusement when she realized the reason he'd gone out of his way was to check the price tag on the old bed.

As he glanced at it, his own smile deepened, and when he reached the counter he greeted her with a conspiratorial nod.

"Smart lady," he said, obviously approving the Not For Sale tag she had attached to the headboard first thing that morning.

"I decided you were right, after all," she explained. "Any price would be too risky."

He didn't offer a response right away, and Rose knew why. He was staring at her mouth, wanting to kiss her, and it was taking all his concentration not to. She understood because it was taking damn near all of hers to do the same. Between the memories evoked by the bed and fresh yearning that stretched between them like a magnetic field, the temperature felt as if it had shot up twenty degrees.

"You can say that again," he said finally.

When her lashes fluttered with the effort of trying to recall what it was she had said that she could say again, he smiled and helped out.

"About the bed, I mean…and any price being too risky."

"Right. At first I intended to simply triple the price I had on it, but then I thought of you and the hydrangea garland and how, for all I knew, a retired sea captain could wander in here at any moment and want to butter me up so I'd help him in his search for whale blubber bowls or old rudders or whatever else retired sea captains collect, and—" she waved her hand "—there would go our bed…I mean, *the* bed. That bed."

"I think 'our' bed covered it just fine," he informed her in a husky tone that prevented her from forming a coherent response. "You wouldn't do that, would you?"

"Do what?"

"Help him look for whale blubber. Or anything else. I don't know as I like the idea of you running off to yard sales and auctions with other men. Especially not when you're still on my payroll until you come up with those other two birds."

"You do realize what an absurd conversation this is?"

He shrugged noncommittally. "I suppose…but absurd isn't what it feels like when I think about you getting mixed up with some lecherous old seaman."

"Don't scowl," she urged, patting his arm. "It will cause wrinkles and bad karma, and besides, I'm only interested in working for lecherous old *airmen*."

"How comforting," he said dryly.

"Which reminds me, I took care of all the details and the Purple Martin is on its way to you even as we speak. Here's your credit card," she continued, returning the card she'd used to make the purchase on his behalf.

"Thanks. I really do appreciate your help."

"I know."

As he slipped the card in his wallet, she flipped open her notebook and paused, pen in hand, nibbling her bottom lip, as she calculated the time she'd spent on the phone with Mr. Shippington.

"While you're at it," said Griff, "put me down for a few extra hours this afternoon—starting as soon as we can boot these folks out of here and lock the door behind them."

"I beg your pardon?"

"What can I say?" His shrug was more matter-of-fact than apologetic. "I want you all to myself again, and soon."

"Are you talking about what I think you're talking about?" she asked, shocked, tempted, praying she didn't blush, or worse, surrender what restraint she had left and go along with what he was suggesting.

"I'm talking about taking you for a nice, long ride," he drawled, grinning unabashedly.

"You've got to be kidding."

He dropped the grin and looked offended. "I'm dead serious. I'll have you know I've been getting ready for it all morning...since the minute you deserted me."

Rose folded her arms and bestowed on him a look somewhere between chiding and amused. "I'll consider your wish to 'take me for a nice, long ride' a compliment, albeit a slightly adolescent one. But if you think I'm going to close shop in the middle of the day and climb into that bed with you, then—"

"Who said anything about bed?"

"You did. You said you wanted to take me for a ride—"

"In a car," he interrupted again. His lips curved suggestively. "But hey, I'm more than willing to swap my idea for yours. Just say the word."

Now she was blushing.

"You don't have a car," she pointed out.

He replied by pointing to the dark blue Buick Roadmaster parked directly outside her front window. The sun gleaming off its big shiny chrome bumpers produced a halo effect.

"That's Devora's old car," exclaimed Rose, her embarrassment slightly diluted by a wave of nostalgia.

"You mean *Gus's* old car."

"How about if we compromise and call it *their* old car?"

"Deal. And it may be old, but it's still got a lot of spunk. Now that I've cleared the mouse nests from the engine and changed the oil, that is."

"My, my, you have been busy."

"Damn right. Now, do you want to announce that it's closing time or shall I?"

"Don't you dare."

"Why not? I can tell from the way your eyes are sparkling that you're itching to come with me."

"You're right, I am. But I can't just lock up and take off during business hours. I won't."

He scowled.

"I really am sorry, Griff. And I don't blame you for being disappointed. You went to a lot of trouble to surprise me."

"It's not that," he responded. "We can go for a ride another time. It's just that I had the rest of the day planned and I..." He glanced around awkwardly. "I miss you."

Rose smiled, pleased. "That's very sweet."

He scowled. Oh, no...another one of those damn *S* words, she thought, cringing inwardly.

"It is not sweet," he retorted, keeping his voice low. "It's...weird, that's what it is. At least, that's how it feels to me. Damn it, Rose, I've never missed anyone before."

"Never?"

"Never. Not like this. Not in a matter of hours, for God's sake. And..."

His obvious uneasiness with his own feelings touched her deeply. It was almost painful to watch him struggling for words. Her heart was close to complete meltdown when the unexpected flash of naked vulnerability passed, chased away by his irritable, and much more familiar, expression.

"And I don't like it," he concluded, glaring at Rose as if the whole thing was entirely her fault.

She waited for him to turn and stalk out. She hoped he would, in fact. It would give her time to mull all this over. It might even provide a reality check.

He did not walk out, however, at least not immediately. Instead, still scowling at her, he said, "So, what time do you want to have dinner tonight?"

Now what?

He was behind the wheel of the Buick, somewhere just outside town, headed west to nowhere in particular. Everything was going according to plan except for one detail—Rose wasn't with him.

It irked him that he'd shaved for nothing. Not to mention going to the trouble of tossing in a load of laundry so he'd have a clean shirt to wear. *And* he had polished his shoes—something that had once been as routine as saluting and brushing his teeth, but which he'd been boycotting for months. Just one more meaningless little way of thumbing his nose at fate. So here he was—clean shaven, clean shirt, shiny loafers, and alone.

"All dressed up and nowhere to go," he muttered.

Nowhere to go and—he glanced at his watch—five hours to get there. It was just after two, and he wasn't meeting Rose until seven.

Five hours. He tried telling himself that shouldn't be such a challenge when you considered all the empty hours and days and weeks he'd filled since the crash. He thought he'd known all there was to know about staring down the tunnel of another endless day. He figured he'd had a handle on boredom and being alone. Instead, he was discovering that "alone" came in a size and flavor he hadn't known existed until that morning, when Rose dropped a totally unsatisfactory kiss on his cheek and slipped from his bed to go home and get ready for work. Ever since, all he could think about was seeing her again.

When he'd killed all the time he could by showering and shaving and puttering around the house, he'd wandered outside. That's when he remembered the Buick, and his grand plan was born. It had been more work than he anticipated to get the old buggy running, but he'd whistled the entire time he was lying on his back beneath it, years' worth of black sludge dripping on his face and spiders crawling up his legs. Would Cinderella gripe about changing the oil if that's what it took to turn the pumpkin into a magic coach? Maybe, Griff decided. Women were very unpredictable. He only knew he would put up with worse than spiders and sludge if it meant seeing Rose a few hours sooner.

He'd been so caught up in his increasingly elaborate preparations, he hadn't stopped to consider that she might have other plans for the day. And responsibilities she couldn't walk away from. A life, in other words. Unlike him, whose focus at the moment consisted of a house he didn't want, a woman he wanted more than he should, and a picnic lunch for two with no one to share it.

Cars had been steadily passing him on the right. The latest, full of teenage boys, slowed as it drew alongside, and the sneering kid in the passenger seat stuck his middle finger out the window and shouted, "Try getting out and pushing—it'd be faster."

Ordinarily, Griff would have returned the gesture. Of course, ordinarily he wouldn't have invited it by doing twenty in a forty-mile-an-hour zone, in a car that had rolled off the assembly line before he was born.

Instead, he heard himself calling back, "Where's the fire, laddie?"

He yelled it with a smile, just the way Gus O'Flaherty used to whenever someone passed them as they chugged along with all the windows rolled down, enjoying the ride and the moment and the breeze that smelled of gravel and summer. Content to be in no particular hurry.

He glanced in the rearview mirror, at the reflection of the old picnic basket on the back seat. Just ahead was a clearing on the right. Griff braked and swung in to it, cutting the wheel back hard to the left. He'd forgotten how much muscle it took to make a U-turn without power steering.

Now *this* was driving, he told himself as he pulled back onto the road, heading in the opposite direction. None of that automatic transmission, cruise control stuff. Just the horses under the hood and him at the controls. Almost like flying.

The notion drifted through his mind, and instinctively he braced for the recoil he'd come to expect whenever he lowered his guard and thought about flying. The inevitable downdraft that resulted could suck him into a pit of bitterness and self-pity faster than he could say "Life is what I make it" or "Decision is destiny" or one of the other countless, pithy little sayings clueless, well-meaning people had advised him to use to get through bad moments.

Only, this time it didn't come. No recoil. No downdraft. There was a twinge deep inside, and a cynical voice from the same place pointed out that *driving,* of any sort, resembled *flying,* about as much as the current Madonna resembled the original. But that was it. Griff gave the Buick a little more gas and went to work trying to figure out the fastest route to where he was going.

When he drove through the front gates of Willow Haven a while later, he was still not sure exactly what his next move should be. He could go through the proper channels and risk being told no, or he could simply skip all the red tape and handle it in the way that felt most natural to him. His way. It took him all of two seconds to settle on the second option. Only a fool went looking to get shot down twice in one day.

When he reached the fork in the drive, he veered right and drove around back, noting all doors and windows. It was rudimentary reconnaissance, and if anyone had told him back in basic training that he would someday be using it to scout out a retirement home, he would have laughed in the guy's face.

He spotted the greenhouse as soon as he turned the corner. *The solarium,* Rose had called it. Whatever the proper term for it, he couldn't miss the flowers blooming in every window. Dahlias, he decided, not knowing a dahlia from a doorstop. They had to be dahlias. Whatever they were, there were more of them in planters and urns on the patio just outside.

And connecting the sunroom and patio was the answer to his prayer: a door propped open with a plastic chair.

Parking as close as he felt was safe, Griff sauntered—as much as it was possible to saunter with a cane—through the open door. Rose had mentioned that Gus's room was next to the solarium.

There were two rooms directly adjacent to the solarium. Griff got lucky and found Gus in the one with its door ajar. The man seated by the window, reading, was older and grayer and thinner, but he was definitely the same Gus O'Flaherty whom Griff remembered. In a matter of seconds, it all came flooding back to Griff, not the details of the times they'd shared, but the feelings, the friendship, the encouragement from which he'd drawn the first tentative threads of the dream that would come to dominate his life. And with them came a new, long-overdue feeling—gratitude.

Griff gave a perfunctory rap on the door and said, "Hello, Gus."

The old man by the window looked up from his book. His face was weathered from years of working outdoors, but his eyes were as blue and his smile just as big as Griff remembered.

"Well, well," said Gus. "Look what the cat dragged in, will you? The Griffin lad, as I live and breathe."

"I wasn't sure you'd remember me."

His snowy brows shot up. "Not remember the rascal who wrapped a rug around my drive shaft?" He snorted. "Not bloody likely to forget you."

"I'd forgotten all about that," Griff countered, the memory making him both smile and wince.

"And why wouldn't you?" Gus retorted, trying to look stern, just as Griff recalled him doing the day it happened. "It wasn't you who had to stand under the car lift for hours, picking bits of wool and twine from the poor gears until your back was bowed."

"What the hell were you thinking to let a twelve-year-old drive, anyway?"

The older man shrugged. "You asked. How was I to know we'd come upon a mound of rug in the road and you'd charge straight over instead of going around like I shouted for you to do?"

"As I recall, what you shouted was 'Look sharp, laddie.'"

"'Look sharp, go around.'" Another shrug, then a smile. "As I recall, when I said it, you straightened up in the seat…just as you hit the rug dead-on."

"You're right, I did," Griff recalled, chuckling. "Hell, I was so used to Devora telling me to throw my shoulders back and stand up straight, I figured 'Look sharp' was just your odd way of saying the same thing."

"Ah, yes: Your aunt Devora was a stickler for that kind of thing, for sure. Posture and manners and the rest." He sighed, still smiling, but his eyes were misty. "She taught me a thing or two, I can tell you that."

"She taught me a thing or two, too," said Griff.

Gus moved toward him, his right hand extended.

"And it's better off—we both are because of her," he said, grasping Griff's hand in what became a clumsy masculine mix of handshake and embrace.

They pulled apart and immediately looked in opposite directions. Griff cleared his throat. He thought Gus might have dragged the back of his hand across his eyes, but he didn't want to know for sure. So he took his time looking over the simple room.

"Still got a green thumb, I see."

Gus brushed off the compliment, but Griff could tell he was pleased. "I do as I always did—stick seeds in the dirt and let God do the rest."

"Then I'd say you two make a good team. Yep," he went on, deciding it was probably safe to look Gus in the eye again, "all in all you have a pretty nice setup here."

"Is that why you came? To check out the accommodations? I notice you've already got yourself a cane."

"Very funny," retorted Griff, wondering if the fact that it had come from Gus was the only reason the remark didn't bother him. "I did hear they have a waiting list at this joint. I might consider adding my name to it, if I could be guaranteed this room."

Gus snorted. "Then I wouldn't be wasting any ink signing up, if I were you. I've just planted a whole two dozen third-generation Lady Violets that I'll be crossing with the Midnight Ruffles over there." He nodded at a row of pots to his right. "I've a mind to see how well they turn out and won't be taking a final curtain call before I do—not even to accommodate you, Major."

His gaze narrowed and scoured Griff from head to toe. "Speaking of which, you're out of uniform."

"This *is* my uniform these days," he replied. As Gus looked disparagingly at his faded jeans, white shirt and loafers worn without socks, Griff explained the circumstances surrounding his retirement as succinctly as possible.

"Tough break, laddie," said Gus, when he was done. "So, what kind of work are you doing now?"

"None. I'm retired," he said again, a little louder this time.

"No need to shout," Gus told him. "I'm not deaf. Or dumb, either. I know what *retired* means. *I'm* retired. In case you haven't noticed, I'm also an old man."

"You look pretty go—"

Gus stopped him with a raised hand and a puckered, impatient expression. "Save your breath. I know I'm old, just like I know you're not. Seems to me a fellow your age who doesn't work and doesn't plan to, is just marking time." He shrugged one rounded shoulder. "Or else wasting it."

"If that's so," he continued, making Griff wish he wasn't too polite to tell him to mind his own business, "then maybe you ought to sign up for a room here, after all. There's plenty of your kind here."

"No offense, Gus, but I'm beginning to regret coming to visit, never mind moving in."

"Any particular reason you did come?"

"Yeah, there's a reason," he retorted, not about to admit

to anything that might prompt Gus to tell him that in addition to being lazy, he was also suffering from self-pity and sentimentality. "You once let me take that old tank of yours for a spin when I wasn't supposed to be driving. Since I'm just marking time, anyway, I figured I'd stop by and return the favor."

"You don't say?" The wrinkles in his brow deepened as he pondered the explanation. "How'd you know where to find me?"

"We have a friend in common," Griff told him. "Rose Davenport."

Gus's mouth immediately curved into an affectionate smile. "Ah, Rosie. She plays a mean game of dominoes, my Rosie."

"She says the same about you."

"I like that girl," he said, fixing his piercing blue gaze directly on Griff. "I like that girl a lot."

Griff understood that the statement was also a warning, and nodded. "I do, too."

"So. Back to business. Just what old tank were you speaking of a moment ago?"

"How many did you have? I'm talking about the Buick, of course."

"The Buick?" repeated Gus, his eyes wide but still skeptical. "*My* Buick?"

"The very one," Griff assured him, and watched his disbelief give way to excitement. "If you don't believe me, take a look. She's parked right outside there."

"But how...? Where...?"

He trailed off, as if not knowing what to ask first.

"It was still parked in Devora's garage. It didn't take much to get the old girl up and running. I've done enough tinkering with airplane engines to handle the basics."

"Well, I'll be..." Gus was beaming, speechless. Griff could almost feel fresh energy simmering beneath the older man's wrinkled skin. "Does that mean you're game?" he asked.

"Game?" Gus looked around excitedly. "Just let me grab my hat and—"

He stopped. His shoulders sagged. "Who am I kidding? They'll never go for it up at the desk. You have to give them a day's notice and then fill out a stack of forms and sign your life away before they let you out the door."

"That's the *front* door," Griff said.

Gus frowned impatiently until the comment settled in his head. Then he peered quizzically at his visitor.

"It just so happens I'm parked outside the *back* door," Griff informed him. "If you catch my drift."

Gus caught it, and his smile lit up the room. It lit up something inside Griff, too. In that second, he knew that even if the old man did nothing the entire time they were together but nag him about being a lazy, good-for-nothing bum, he would still never be sorry he had come.

"The hell with the hat," Gus chirped, heading straight for the door, his gait slow but steady. He paused to stick his head out and take a look along the corridor before continuing. "Coast is clear," he whispered. Then, glancing over his shoulder at Griff, he added, "If you can't keep up, laddie, just toss me the keys."

Griff kept up, thinking the entire time that the two of them must be quite a sight.

When they drew close to the car, Gus stopped in his tracks and just stood still, staring at it. "She's as pretty as the day I got her," he pronounced.

"That's great, Gus, but do you think you could finish admiring her while we're moving?" Griff held open the passenger door expectantly. When Gus hesitated, he said, "I thought I should drive getaway. You know, just in case you're a little rusty."

"Good thinking," Gus agreed, and climbed in.

Griff wasted no time taking off, resisting the urge to floor it or glance over his shoulder to see if a posse of nurses was after them. Belatedly, it occurred to him that what he was doing might well be illegal. Not kidnapping, exactly. Seniornapping, perhaps? Even if it wasn't an actual crime, it was a hell of a lot more nerve-racking than he'd anticipated.

"You're not on any medication, are you?" he asked abruptly.

"No more than any man my age," Gus replied.

"What kind of an answer is that?"

"Stupid…same as the question."

"I was just wondering if this is going to mess up your schedule. It might not be good if you miss a dose."

"Having second thoughts already?" Gus asked, smiling and caressing the velvety upholstery of the armrest.

"No," he lied.

The older man chuckled. "Good. Because I haven't had this much fun in I don't know how long." He sighed and looked around, sighed again. "Just so I don't have to look at that nervous twitch in your jaw the whole time, I'll tell you that I take my blood pressure pill in the morning and my cholesterol pill at night, and in between I get everything I need for my heart trouble from a patch they stick on my chest."

Cholesterol, blood pressure *and* heart problems. Griff supposed that was pretty typical for a man in his eighties, just as Gus had claimed. It still carried a sobering awareness of the ebb and flow of life.

"Glad to hear it," he said. "A side trip to the ER isn't part of my plan."

"What is your plan?" Gus enquired, leaning to catch the breeze on his face.

Griff grinned with anticipation. "Wouldn't you rather be surprised?"

"With *my* heart?" Gus retorted, thumping his chest as he shot Griff a look of exasperation. "A surprise could kill me. Course, then my room would be available."

"Very funny. All right, we'll do it your way and skip the element of surprise. I thought we'd swing by Quonset Point like we used to." Motioning with his head, he added, "Check out the back seat."

Gus twisted stiffly to look over his shoulder. At the sight of the familiar old picnic basket, he broke into a grin that made Griff doubly glad he hadn't mentioned the fact that this was actually Plan B for the day.

"I didn't have time to make meat loaf for sandwiches," he confessed—as if he would have known where to begin. "So we'll have to make do with what I picked up at the deli. But I did chase down some bottles of sarsaparilla."

"Sarsaparilla." He shook his head. "That brings back a few memories, all right."

"I figured it would," said Griff, quite pleased with how his backup plan was progressing.

"So, we're headed for Quonset. That should be a fine time." A couple of seconds passed before the old man added, "If you don't mind sitting around watching the grass grow."

Griff's brows drew together. "What are you talking about? I thought we'd eat lunch and watch planes take off and land, the way we used to."

Gus responded with a snort. "That was a long time ago, laddie. Things change—you have to keep up. Nowadays they use Quonset to build submarines." He shrugged. "I suppose we could always sit and watch 'em do that."

His lack of enthusiasm was obvious.

"All right," Griff said, ignoring his own disappointment as he scrambled to formulate Plan C. "Maybe we could take a drive along the coast. You know, look at the scenery."

"Sure, old folks are supposed to like that kind of thing."

Griff eyed him suspiciously. "Do you have a better idea?"

"Since you're asking," he said, sitting forward, "it just so happens I do. Let's head for Foxwoods."

"Foxwoods? You mean the casino?"

"I sure do."

"That's in Connecticut, for Pete's sake."

"Connecticut," mimicked Gus. "You say it like it's as far away as Alaska instead of only a hop, skip and jump down the highway from where we are right now."

"An hour-long hop, skip and jump," argued Griff.

"Forty minutes," Gus corrected. "If you're tired of driving, I can—"

"I'm not tired of driving," he broke in. "It's just that…a casino? Hell, Gus, it's one thing to break you out for an afternoon, but then to take you gambling…somehow it doesn't feel right."

"That's the stupidest thing I ever heard, and I've been around long enough to hear plenty. Foxwoods is a beautiful place. Clean, classy, first-rate. Think about it, laddie. If there was anything the least bit disreputable about it, would your aunt Devora have gone?"

"Devora went to Foxwoods?" Griff was astounded.

"Once a week," Gus told him. "As regular as church."

"I don't believe it."

"Suit yourself."

"How do you know?"

"Who do you think drove her?"

"Don't kid around, Gus. Is it true?"

"Sure, it's true."

"It's funny, I don't ever remember her going."

"That's because there was no casino way back then," Gus pointed out. "The Pequot Tribe didn't get the go-ahead until the eighties. You must remember your aunt going off to bingo on Thursday nights."

"I do now," answered Griff. "But playing bingo in the church basement is a long way from going to a casino. I just can't imagine Devora shoving quarters into a slot machine."

"I should say not. Devora had no use for the slots. 'Slots are for sissies,' she always used to say."

He had to know. "Then, what did she go there to play?"

"Craps. And she was a crackerjack at it, too, let me tell you. She knew when to quit and when to let it all ride…to shoot for the moon. 'I can feel it in my bones, Gus,' she would tell me. 'Tonight,' she'd say, 'we shoot for the moon.'"

He turned to gaze out the window, looking not at the road but up at the sky.

They rode in silence for a moment or two. Then Griff spoke, mostly to avoid thinking about how many other things he didn't know about Devora. The question he posed was purely rhetorical; his fate had been sealed the moment he walked into Gus O'Flaherty's room, and he knew it.

"Are you sure we can make it in forty minutes?" he asked.

"Sure, I'm sure," replied Gus, perking up. "I know a shortcut."

Gus's shortcut required leaving the highway and traveling along winding, narrow country roads that Griff was certain did not exist on any map. While he concentrated on driving, Gus talked, and much of what he talked about involved Devora.

Gus told Griff things about his aunt that made him smile, and things that made him proud. It occurred to him that he had known her in the limited way a child can know an adult. He'd stayed in touch, true, but his visits had become shorter and less frequent as his career became more demanding, until there were only letters and phone calls connecting them. And memories. But he hadn't had much time even for the memories. He'd been too driven, too focused on his own agenda.

When he'd received news of her death, he had felt guilty—guilty that he hadn't made time for her…guilty for short-changing her, for failing her in some way.

Now, listening to Gus, wishing the drive were longer so he could hear more, it wasn't guilt he felt, but regret—not for Devora, but himself.

"I thought I knew everything there was to know about my aunt," he said to Gus. They were nearing the outskirts of the Pequot Reservation, where Foxwoods offered the only legal casino gambling north of Atlantic City.

Gus chuckled knowingly. "I made that same mistake myself once. I learned better as the years went on."

"One thing I definitely didn't realize was that you and Aunt Devora were such good friends."

"Oh, the best of friends, to be sure."

Griff tried again. "I knew you worked for her..."

"In a manner of speaking," agreed Gus.

"But from the sounds of it you two were...close. Very close."

Gus offered nothing.

Griff gave a short laugh and shook his head. "Rose said the craziest thing the other night. She said maybe you and Devora were, you know...lovers."

"Did she, now? She's a smart cookie, that Rose— You want to watch for that sharp right I spoke of—it comes up on you fast."

"I'm watching," Griff assured him. "So are you saying she's right? You and Devora *were* lovers?"

"I'm saying a gentleman doesn't kiss and tell—and if you need it spelled out for you better than that, you're dumber than dirt."

"I'm not dumber than dirt," Griff told him, not nearly as shocked or puzzled as he'd expected to be, to learn that Rose was right, after all. "How long?"

"Nearly forty years," said Gus. In a softer, almost reverential tone, he added, "A lifetime, it was. *My* lifetime."

"You loved her." He wasn't asking, didn't need to ask. Just needed to say it, to hear the words out loud, to make them real.

"Aye. I loved her."

"She had to have loved you, too. Otherwise, she never...Why didn't you two just get married?"

There was a weariness to Gus's short laugh. "Why, indeed? I suppose because it never seemed like a question of *just* getting married. It was always more complicated than that."

"Complicated how?"

"She was Devora Fairfield, you see—a lady, and a woman of means. And I was Gus O'Flaherty, who mowed lawns and hauled trash and always had to scrub the dirt from under my nails before I dared to touch so much as her cheek."

"That's bull," Griff retorted. "I may not have known all

there was to know about Devora, but I sure as hell knew her well enough to know she wasn't like that. She may have been proud, and maybe even a little fussy, but she wasn't a snob. She never looked down on anybody, and if she loved you as much as you say, she would never have refused to marry you because of the size of your bank account or what you did for a living.''

"You're right about that. She would never have refused me. That's why I could never ask, you see. It was *me* who wouldn't marry *her,* laddie, not the other way 'round. I knew from the first time I looked her way and she looked back that I wasn't good enough for her. For years I lived in dread of the day when *she* would figure it out, as well.''

Griff was struck by the bleak honesty of Gus's words, so full of sorrow and acceptance, as simple and as wrenching as the final, lingering note of a bluesy sax solo.

"I couldn't bear to lose her, you see," Gus went on. "So I settled for what I had…what I could be sure of, rather than risk losing everything. I'm not sure if that makes me more a fool or a coward.''

"Neither," Griff said, his own voice firm. "Your way worked…for a lifetime, just like you said. That's what counts.''

"It did work in its own way," Gus agreed, forcing a grateful smile. "I've a lot to be thankful for, to be sure. Look sharp, laddie, there's that turn I—''

"I see it," Griff said, taking the turn that brought the sprawling casino complex into view in front of them.

Grinning, Gus patted his back pocket. "Let's hope I've a speck of good fortune left in me.''

"I can't believe I'm doing this," Griff muttered, following Gus's directions to the valet parking area closest to his favorite table.

They were the third car in line *and* the one drawing the most stares and grins. Gus was loving it. Griff hated intruding with one last question, but he had to know. "Gus, if you could go back and do it over, still not knowing how it would turn out…"

"Would I do things differently?" Gus finished for him. "Now, there's a question I've asked myself a million times or so. The answer is, I don't know. I only know what I *hope* I would do if I had the chance. I hope I'd be quicker to learn what Devora always knew—that any love worth having is worth trusting.

"Next time," he said, an almost cocky gleam in his blue eyes, "I'll do it her way and shoot for the moon."

Chapter Eleven

Hours after their furtive departure, Griff and a happy but worn-out Gus returned to Willow Haven. Conscience and common sense had ganged up on Griff and demanded he phone from the casino—if only to prevent the rest home from launching an all-out search for Gus. He explained to the woman who took his call that he had been so eager to fulfill his "Uncle Gus's" wish to visit the Maritime Museum that he had completely forgotten to stop by the nurse's desk on the way out. The combination of charm and profuse apology succeeded in smoothing things over.

He parked outside the front entrance this time, opened the passenger door and waited as Gus took a long, final look around the interior of the car before swinging his feet to the curb.

"So what do you say, Gus?" asked Griff as he helped him out. "Same time next week?"

"Maybe. At my age, it's best not to go making long-range plans." The older man took a couple of steps and stopped.

"But if we do go next week, don't forget it's my turn to drive getaway."

"I'm sure you'll remind me."

Gus was weary enough to permit Griff to help him up the steps, as well. The woman seated at the front desk noticed their slow approach and moved to open the door. Before she got there, Gus gave Griff's arm a gentle pat.

"Thanks, laddie," he said. "This was a day of days, to be sure."

"For me, too, Gus. I…"

Gus waved him to silence. "Don't go getting sloppy on me. And don't go running over any rugs with my car, either."

"No rugs, I promise."

"See to it." He glanced once over his shoulder as the door opened. "You did a pretty good job of getting her running again—the engine sounds as smooth as ever." He didn't allow time for the compliment to settle before adding, "You might try looking for work at the filling station down on Main Street. Tell 'em I sent you."

Griff just nodded amicably. He didn't have time to explain all over again that it was not because he couldn't find a job that he was out of work. The fact was, he could pick up the phone any time he wanted and claim the job he'd been offered as a technical advisor for the Air Force. He just plain didn't want to. And to a man like Gus, who'd had to work hard every day of his life until he was no longer able to, that was just plain inconceivable.

A day of days. Gus had always had a way with words. Griff had to agree that it had been a good day. A great day, actually, in spite of the fact that it had not gone according to his plan. Any of them. It felt good being with Gus again. It felt real good to be able to pay the man back in even a small way. It also felt good to have a purpose that meant something to someone other than himself.

There had also been some sadness, to be sure, mostly at seeing the physical changes a couple of decades could make

in a man. But once he'd gotten past that, Gus was…Gus.
The same Gus he'd always been, still with his own take on
life and still knowing more about more things than many
people with a string of letters after their names. History and
baseball and honor—in the course of this one day Gus had
managed to teach him a little about each of them.

Griff just wished he'd thought to ask if Gus knew any
shortcuts back to Wickford. Ironic, thought Griff, pushing
the old car as hard as he dared. After all his griping about
having to wait so long to see Rose again, he might end up
being late.

He wanted to take her somewhere really nice for dinner,
and that meant stopping home to shower and shave and iron
another shirt. He wouldn't change one minute of last night,
but he wanted tonight to be special in a more traditional way.

Even before he stepped inside, he sensed something different about the old house. No loose planks popped up to
trip him as he crossed the porch; the old screen door didn't
scratch him or rip any of his clothes in passing. Plus, the
place looked a lot better than it had since he'd arrived and
set up camp. But that was because before leaving that morning he'd washed and put away the dishes that had overflowed
the sink and covered the counter; then he'd swept the floor
and hauled all the empty beer bottles out to the recycling
bin.

He'd done it partly to kill time, but also because all those
years in the military had left him with a low tolerance for
clutter and disorganization. When he'd come downstairs this
morning and realized there was not a single clean cup or
mug left for his coffee, he knew he had to do something.
Either buy more cups or wash the ones in the sink. This time
he decided to wash the ones he had.

It might have made more sense to clean up his act *before*
bringing Rose home with him. They hadn't bothered with
lights as they hurried through last night, trying to climb the
stairs and undress each other at the same time. But Rose had
surely gotten an eyeful in the morning light.

Just as well, Griff told himself. No sense pretending to be something he wasn't. There was a certain comfort in knowing Rose had seen his worst and was still interested.

He glanced around the kitchen once again, wishing he could figure out why it seemed even neater than he'd left it. Then he saw the shopping bag folded on the counter—the same bag the hydrangea garland had been in since he'd brought it home from Rose's shop—and he knew why the house felt different.

Smiling slightly, he picked up the bag and held it close to his face, knowing the scent alone would stir him, wanting it to. He put the bag aside, but the scent persisted, and he followed it upstairs. Rose's scent. Rose's presence. That was the reason the house felt different to him. He couldn't explain it, not even to himself, but that didn't make the feeling any less real. It was as if the old house was as happy as he was that she was here. There was a feeling of rightness, of contentment, around him and inside him.

His heart was pounding frantically, but his steps were slow. His entire life had been about speed, being the first and the fastest, getting in and getting out. Now he found himself caught in something so good, he wanted it to last forever.

He found Rose exactly where he'd expected—in his room. She was sitting in the old rocker in the corner. Just sitting, waiting. Waiting for him. Something about that nearly brought him to his knees in front of her.

When he walked in, she smiled and stood. "Hi," she said.

"Hi."

He was lucky he managed that much. She was wearing something pale and flimsy and totally unsuitable for having dinner anywhere but bed. The silvery fabric clung everywhere it touched her, and where it didn't her skin looked dewy and golden. He wanted to look at her that way forever, and he wanted to rip it off her that instant.

"How did you get in?" he asked. His voice sounded like it felt, like he had a mouthful of burlap.

"Devora and I traded keys in case either of us ever got locked out. Do you mind?"

"What do you think?"

She waited until his gaze finished roaming over her body and returned to meet hers, then she did the same. The corners of her mouth curved appreciatively. "I think you're glad I'm here," she said.

"Very, very glad."

"And a little surprised."

"Maybe a little."

"And I'm sure you're probably wondering what in the world put the idea of coming here this way in my head in the first place, especially after you specifically asked me to wear something fancy tonight because you were planning something special for our first official date."

Watching and listening, Griff was reminded of a very nervous beauty pageant contestant racing through her prepared speech on how, if selected Miss Whatever, she planned to end poverty and cure kleptomania—all while wearing a bathing suit and spike heels. Clearly, Rose didn't have a lot of experience in the role of seductress. That pleased him on two counts, because she hadn't seduced a string of men before him, and because she was doing it now.

"What you're wearing is plenty fancy," he assured her. "In fact, it's perfect."

"Not for going out to dinner."

"So we'll order in."

"I didn't want to disappoint you, but…"

"Trust me, Rose, disappointed is not even close to what I'm feeling. *Impatient* is more like it," he added, moving toward her.

She held up one hand. "Wait. Don't you want to ask me?"

"Ask you what?" he countered, the need to touch her interfering with his concentration.

"Why I came in the first place," she replied.

"Not particularly. I'm just glad as hell you're here."

"I'll tell you, anyway," she said quickly. "I came because I knew that if that garland was ever going to get hung properly, I was going to have to do it myself." She tipped her head to direct his attention to the garland now hanging on the wall above his bed.

Griff forced himself to give it a fleeting glance. "Looks great."

The instant he turned back to her, Rose reached for the tie that held together the flimsy, robe-like thing she was wearing, and tugged it loose. "And I came for this."

As she spoke, her robe fell open. He sucked in air and still felt breathless. It didn't help when she moved her shoulders and let the robe slide to the floor.

She was standing close to the window. Outside, the sun was low in the sky, and it filled the room with the golden light of a late summer day.

Even now, she didn't look like a seductress. There was nothing blatant or erotic in the way she had captivated his senses. Her appeal was simple and straightforward, and far more potent. Again he had that enticing sense of both wanting to rush, and understanding that there was no need.

"I was beginning to worry you wouldn't get home before dark," she said quietly.

"Would that be so bad?" he murmured, much more focused at that moment on what he was seeing than what he was hearing.

"It would have been a disaster. It would have meant coming back tomorrow and doing this all over again, and, frankly, I don't think my nerves could take that."

"I don't get it," he said. "If this makes you uncomfortable, why are you doing it?"

"Because I want to make love to you in daylight. I *need* to."

"Why?" he countered, caught in the middle—his brain was telling him he ought to at least *try* to figure out what she was talking about, and his body was clamoring "Who the hell cares? Just toss her on the bed and sort it out later."

"Why?" She gave a small, self-effacing laugh. "I'm thirty-five, Griff. That's the age when they start filming Hollywood actresses through a filter, you know, to glaze over their flaws. I came here early because I knew that in daylight there'd be no glazing over mine."

What flaws? This time his brain and body were in full agreement. He didn't think he'd so much as blinked once since she dropped her robe, and he hadn't seen a single flaw yet.

He wasn't looking at details or body parts. He was looking at a whole woman, *this* woman, Rose, whose unique scent and laugh and eye color were encoded in him so deeply, it was as if they had always been there and he just hadn't known how to find them. Until now. Until she'd shown him where to look. She was in him so deeply, he could see her *without* looking. And when he did look at her, as he was now, he saw Rose, he saw woman—and everything in him that was man responded.

"I think I get it now," he ventured. "It's some weird sort of Mars-Venus thing, right?" he demanded. "Like…truth in lending between the sexes? This way I'll know exactly what I'm getting. Because if that's it, I have to tell you—"

She cut in before he could tell her that it had worked, that he was ready to sign wherever she wanted him to. Rose was not the youngest or firmest or sexiest woman he'd known, but there was not a doubt in his mind that she was the most beautiful.

"I'm not doing this for you," she explained. "I mean, not directly at least."

She bit her lip and gazed at the robe on the floor as if she'd like to snatch it and wrap herself up. Griff suppressed the urge to kick it out of reach.

"I'm doing it for me," she told him. "I didn't expect this…this *thing* with us to happen. I didn't want it to happen, not at first, anyway. But I don't seem to have as much control as I'd like to think I have. So if it is going to happen, whatever *it* turns out to be, I refuse to be doubting and second-guessing myself every step of the way.

"Last night was special for me," she revealed, looking more self-conscious than when she had dropped the robe. "It was the most intimacy I've ever felt…with anyone. It was the first time I realized that sex and intimacy are not synonymous. And it felt…good. Really good."

She moved a few steps closer, and Griff was seized by another, stronger yearning to touch her.

"I don't want to have to hide anything or tone it down. I want you to know everything there is about me, body and soul, and I want to know everything there is about you. And we'll take it from there."

He stood staring at her, until Rose's cheeks felt so flushed that she expected any second to combust and melt into the hooked rug beneath her feet. A fate that would not be unwelcome.

"I guess, now that I think about it, it might be a weird Mars-Venus thing, after all," she conceded. "Just the same, that's what I want. To be intimate with you…truly intimate…I just want to be myself. If that's not enough, I'd rather know it now, before…"

She had been about to say *before I fall in love with you.* But suddenly, being there so close to him, so close to being in his arms and in his bed, and wanting it as badly as she did, she realized it was already too late for that.

"Before we let it go any farther," she concluded.

Griff rubbed his jaw with the side of his thumb, his eyes narrowed, glittering with either desire or irritation, she couldn't be sure which.

"Was there a question in there somewhere?" he asked her.

"Yes. At least, there should have been. I just wanted to know—"

"Never mind," he told her.

There was nothing ambiguous about the look in his eyes as he reached out and ran his palm down her arm. It was desire. Definitely desire. He caressed her again, this time managing to brush her breast with his knuckles along the way.

It was desire at its most basic and unadorned. In fact, the way he was looking at her made her feel like a hot, juicy steak being eyed by a very hungry rottweiler, and her feminist side was duly appalled. It was also quickly overruled by the rest of her.

"It's not all that important what the question is, since whatever it is, this is my answer…"

He had been lightly stroking the inside of her wrist. Now his fingers tightened around it, and he pulled her close to him, his lips curving into a slow smile of anticipation as he lowered his mouth to kiss her.

His kiss was gentle and giving, moving from her lips to her face and her throat, never rushing, never demanding. A legion of pleasurable sensations came to life inside her, shifting and melting, one into the next like the colored patterns in a kaleidoscope.

He slipped his palms beneath her breasts and bent to kiss them, too.

Rose willed herself to be still…to be quiet…

"I have these scars," she whispered.

"Shh," he responded, his breath warm on the flesh he had made damp. "I know."

Rose closed her eyes and let her head fall back, shivering as his mouth meandered its way back to hers. When he eventually rested his forehead against hers, she was winded from being kissed.

"Good answer, Griffin," she murmured.

"That's not all of it."

Grinning recklessly, he moved her to the bed and nudged her down on her back. He stood over her, watching her watch him remove his clothes…shirt, belt, pants, the rest.

"I'd make you acquainted with each scar individually, but there're so many, even I've lost track. Rest assured I've got at least one of every kind there is."

He wasn't exaggerating. Last night's darkness had

shielded both of them. Naked, he looked even taller, his shoulders broader, his muscles more pronounced. His physique was close to perfect even for a much younger man. It was the flesh holding all that sinew and muscle in place that bore the marks of every one of his forty, rough, hard-lived years. Belatedly, it occurred to Rose that he might be as self-conscious about his body as she was about hers.

That worry passed quickly as he proceeded to take her on a whirlwind tour of his past mishaps, pointing out the result of each.

"The scars on my knees and the back of my thighs are all from surgery. I've got more surgical scars over here. This, on the other hand, is a souvenir from a different kind of knife." He shrugged off her look of dismay. "What can I tell you? I didn't spend the past twenty years in the suburbs."

"There are scars from burns, scars from falls—from various motorcycles, bridges, and balconies—your everyday punctures and lacerations, and somewhere around back of my right shoulder there's a dent that was once a bullet hole."

"Friendly fire," he explained before she could ask. "It happened on a hunting trip...and I don't even hunt. Take my advice," he continued as he lowered himself to the bed beside her. "Never go on a hunting expedition where there are more kegs of beer than hunters."

He propped his head on his hand and smiled at her, looking amused and irresistible. And not in the least self-conscious.

"Admit it, Rose, when it comes to matching *flaws*, you're going to have to go some to beat me."

"It's not the same," she countered.

He made a scoffing noise and regarded her reproachfully. "You are so wrong, and I would tell you why if I were in the mood for a discussion. Which I most definitely am not."

He covered her legs with one of his, bringing the lower half of her body closer, while smoothing his hand over her shoulder and breast, smiling with pleasure at her response.

"Is that a fact?" she drawled, lifting her foot and letting it glide up the back of his leg, then down. "What are you in the mood for?"

He snatched the bait with a grin. "You," he said, rolling on top of her, claiming the spot she made for him between her thighs.

"Then I guess this is your lucky day."

"Yeah. And just when I was beginning to believe I'd used them all up."

She moved against him, teasing them both, inviting the sweet ache of anticipation to take them higher. He responded by rocking his hips, slowly, maddeningly, coming against her in strokes that were sometimes almost unbearably gentle, and sometimes not. Excitement flowed through her, carrying her deeper and away.

With his palms flat on either side of her head, elbows bent, he lowered himself until his matted chest was grazing hers, letting her feel his heat and weight and the contrast between her softness and his strength. His movements were smooth, graceful. The only indication of the effort he was expending was in his biceps, which bordered her on both sides. They were flexed and enormous, glazed with a fine sheen, evidence of even greater power and strength than she had realized.

Rose smiled and arched her back, lifting herself into his caress even as she slid a few inches lower on the bed, adjusting the arrangement of their hips just a little…just enough…just right… And when they came together, him pressing against her belly, hard and hot and fully aroused, she made a breathy sound of delight.

And still he kept his hands off her and she did the same. By unspoken agreement, they made love to each other without using their hands or mouths or tongues. There was just his strong body caressing hers, and hers responding and giving back until something exploded, first in him, then in her, setting off a greedy rush toward fulfillment.

Now he claimed her, with his hands and mouth and tongue, marking her as his in the most primitive and elemental way there is, the way he was meant to, driving deep inside and surrendering everything to become one with her for a few seconds, for an eternity, for as long as heaven would allow.

Chapter Twelve

"You do realize, of course, that sooner or later you're going to have to admit it."

Rose responded to Maryann's declaration by pretending to study the map of New England open in her lap.

"You do, don't you?" her friend prodded, darting Rose a disgruntled look. "Will you please take your nose out of that map long enough to answer me?"

"Sure, as long as you don't blame me when we miss the exit for Route 104 and end up in Vermont."

"At least I'd have someone to talk to getting there. I came along to keep *you* company, and it's me who feels all alone."

"I'm sorry, Maryann. I should have mapped out our route before we left. I intended to, but I...got tied up."

Maryann perked up behind the wheel of the Volvo wagon. "Literally?"

Rose looked at her sternly. "No. Not literally."

"Shucks." She sighed. "Well. At least I managed to get

your attention. So, are you going to admit it and get it over with or not?''

"Admit what?''

"Admit that I was right…about Griff, about him being your Mr. Right, about *everything*.''

Rose nibbled her bottom lip, knowing her friend wouldn't be able to stand the silence for longer than a few seconds.

"Well?''

"I'm thinking,'' Rose told her.

"Thinking? *Thinking?*'' She slapped the steering wheel, ran her fingers through her hair, shook her head. "There's such a thing as over-thinking a thing. What if George Washington had wasted time *thinking* instead of crossing the Delaware? Or if Neil Armstrong had decided he was too busy *thinking* to take one giant leap for mankind? Thinking is highly overrated. For all we know, Nero was off somewhere *thinking* while Rome burned.''

"*Fiddling*. Nero fiddled while Rome burned,'' Rose paraphrased.

"Has that ever been documented?'' She tossed back her hair. "Never mind. Nero doesn't owe me and my gramma Viola anything.''

"And I do?''

"Well…'' She lifted one shoulder in a perfectly elegant shrug. "We did put you onto the scent—''

Rose cut her off with a gasp of mock indignation. "The scent? The scent of what? Insanity?''

"The scent of Mr. Right, that's what.'' Her palm came up in a preemptive gesture. "Don't deny it. You know it's true, I know it's true. Heck, I think just about everyone in town knows it's true. Even Ted,'' she added emphatically. "And he hardly noticed when *we* fell in love.''

"Are you saying everyone thinks I'm in love with Griff?''

Maryann slanted her a sardonic look and drawled, "And wherever would anyone get that idea? You two are not exactly discreet.''

"What does that mean?" demanded Rose, recalling that awkward night in the truck.

"It means, we're not all blind. Griff's been in Wickford for…what? Six weeks or so?"

"Six-and-a-half."

"But who's counting? And for six of those six-and-a-half weeks he's been mooning over you like a…teenager."

"Mooning?" She shook her head with disgust. "I'd hardly call going to dinner and—"

"Every night, *and* spending almost every other free moment together."

"You're the one who was always nagging me to date more," Rose reminded her. "And slow down…our exit is next."

"Yes, I did want you to date more and I'm not complaining, believe me. I'm just stating a fact. It's not bad to have a gorgeous man mooning over you. In fact, it's the sweetest thing I've ever seen—not counting Ted and Lisa, naturally."

"Naturally," she said with a grin. "Define 'mooning.'"

"The man *gazes* at you, for heaven's sake. *Gazes*. With those eyes…oh, his eyes." She patted in the general area of her lungs as if to restart her breathing. "And when he can't be with you, he wanders around town looking lost—at least, he did, until this week when he turned into Handyman Hank. What's that about?"

"The house needs work, lots of work, and Griff decided to try doing some of the small stuff himself."

"To pass the time when he can't be with you," Maryann pronounced. "And when he is with you, he finds reasons to touch you, and when he's not touching you, he looks like he wishes he was. It's your classic mooning."

"It's ridiculous is what it is."

"It's true. He's mooning over you and you know it, and that's why you get all fluttery like this."

"I am not getting fluttery. I never get fluttery," she insisted. "Is that really what people are saying? That he's mooning and I'm fluttering?"

''Of course not. At least, not the fluttering. Everyone knows you two are seeing each other, of course, but so far I'm the only one who's picked up on the fluttering. Probably because it's such subtle fluttering, on the inside.''

''And how do you know what I'm feeling on the inside?''

''Because I'm your best friend, remember?''

Rose shrugged. She was right about that, at least.

''And also because I have firsthand experience in this area.''

''You flutter around Ted?''

''Sometimes,'' she retorted with a touch of defiance. ''I have other things on my mind these days, but when we were first dating, I fluttered practically nonstop. Tell me this, when Griff is close to you, or goes to touch you, does your skin feel him even before he's made contact?''

''Yes,'' Rose admitted, understanding exactly the phenomenon her friend described.

''And sometimes right in the middle of talking to him do you forget what you were going to say?''

''God, yes.''

''And when you are just sitting quietly together, do you find yourself thinking that he has the most fascinating breathing pattern of any human being who has ever lived?''

''Oh, God, Maryann, I *am* fluttering.'' She closed her eyes briefly, then turned to look at her friend. ''I'm in love with him, aren't I?''

'''Fraid so.''

Their eyes met for only a second, but it was more than they needed to achieve total understanding.

Maryann grinned. ''I swear, Rose, if I weren't driving I would hug you. So, have you told him?''

''You mean in words?''

''Yes, Rose, in words.''

''No.''

''Well, exactly when—''

''When the time is right,'' Rose said firmly. ''As I've told you a zillion times, even a best friend doesn't get a full rundown of some things—no details, no specifics, no dimensions.''

"Spoilsport," she grumbled, then smiled again. "But I'll rise to the occasion and be gracious."

Before Rose could do more than turn to eye her warily, she added, "If you'll do the same. Come on, Rose, admit Gramma Viola and I were right, or, if you won't do that, at least admit you're happy."

"I'm happy," Rose told her without hesitation. "Very happy. Oh, hell, Maryann, I'm delirious."

"I know…and I'm delirious for you." She exhaled, squirming a little in her seat. "Thank God we got that settled. Now, will you please get back to that map and figure out how far it is to the next rest area? I'm rethinking the wisdom of having ordered that extra-large iced coffee for the ride."

"We're only about ten miles from Dana Edgerton's house. I'm sure she'll let you use her bathroom. She sounded very nice when I spoke to her on the phone."

"Ten miles? Don't you mean ten miles of winding, bumpy road?"

On cue they hit a bump, and Maryann winced. "Distract me," she ordered. "Tell me again how you found out this woman we're going to see has one of these special old birds."

Rose smiled at Maryann's description, and pointed ahead to where 104 forked to the right.

"Luck. I happened to see the small ad she placed in the *Treasure Chest*. That's a small paper for collectors," she explained. "She's collected this series of birds for as long as Devora, but she also collects several other pricey items and decided to concentrate all her time—and money—in a different direction. Because this is such a specialized item, she figured she'd try selling the pieces herself before going the auction route and paying a big commission."

"Makes sense," Maryann observed.

"We decided that because it is a private sale and we don't live too far apart, we would both feel more comfortable handling it face-to-face. This way I get to inspect the piece personally, and Dana gets cash.''

''And lots of it,'' countered her friend, her expression becoming wistful. ''Just think, with that much money you could buy those snakeskin boots I want, in every color.''

''Except, I don't think Griff is the type to wear high-heel snakeskin boots in any color, and Ted will end up buying you every color, anyway.''

She didn't deny it. ''Are you still planning for this to be a surprise?''

''Yes. I made an outrageous killing on that chintz I just sold, and Griff is always buying me flowers and dinner and frozen burritos, and I just want to do something for him.''

''Hey, I understand completely. It's that fluttery thing.''

''Probably,'' Rose conceded.

''So if this pans out, there will be only one bird still out there?''

''That's right. When I asked Dana if she had it, she gave this mysterious little laugh and said she didn't, but promised to tell me an interesting story about it when she saw me. That's another reason I was eager to meet her. I'm hoping to pick her brain for a clue where to look next. Everything I've tried lately has been a dead end.''

Rose had been watching the numbers on the mailboxes along the roadside. ''I think Dana's house is that next one on the right. She mentioned that her mailbox was a black-and-white cow and that there was a big stump in the front yard.''

''I see the stump,'' said Maryann, slowing. ''Which reminds me, John Lombardi said I should tell you that you ought to get rid of the stump in your yard ASAP, before you're inundated with carpenter ants.''

''How does John know I have a stump in my yard?''

''Evidently he was out there doing an appraisal of Fairfield House and he happened to see it.''

''I didn't know Griff was having the house appraised,'' Rose told her, puzzled.

"I thought it was a little strange myself. He hasn't changed his mind about selling, has he?"

"Of course he hasn't changed his mind," Rose assured her. "Fairfield House is part of his heritage. You don't sell part of your heritage…at least, Griff wouldn't. I do know the house is going to need a lot of work, which he won't be able to handle himself. Maybe he applied for a home equity loan."

If so, she thought, she was even happier that she'd decided to surprise him with the second bird.

"I made it," exclaimed Maryann, as they pulled into the driveway and parked. Without wasting any time, she reached for the door handle with one hand and her purse with the other.

"Hold on," said Rose, grinning, as Maryann turned back to look at her. "I know you're in a big hurry, but I just have to tell you this one thing… When your gramma Viola and you are right, you're right."

It had taken the better part of the afternoon to replace just two sections of the porch's rotted and broken balusters. But, thought Griff, it was worth it. He gripped one of the ornate wooden pieces and tugged, grinning when it failed to budge. It had been a slow, trial-and-error process at the start, but he was good with his hands and had a knack for knowing how things go together. Now that he'd mastered the task, the other dozen sections would go a lot faster.

But that would have to wait a while longer.

He was ready to knock off for today, and not for the reason he would have expected just a few weeks ago, because his leg or neck or back was acting up. Since he'd started working on the long list of repairs the house and grounds needed, he'd actually been bothered less by pain. Or else he just had less time to think about it. Whatever the reason, Fairfield House was in a helluva lot better shape than when he'd first arrived. And so was he.

It was, he mused, and not for the first time, as if he had

stepped into a movie version of his life. *It's A Wonderful Life,* starring Hollis Griffin. The plot and location and most of the action weren't even close to what he'd have written had he been consulted, but, of course, he hadn't been. Just the same, it felt right somehow, as if this *could* have been his life…if he had kept spending summers with Devora, or Gus had never taken him to watch planes take off or if he had upchucked his first time up instead of feeling like he was right where he had always belonged.

The day he stopped belonging in the cockpit of a combat jet was the day he started feeling as if he didn't belong anywhere. He had not expected that ever to change. He hadn't even *hoped* it would change. Because, he realized now, hoping would have been the first step toward acceptance, and he had no intention of accepting the lousy hand he'd been dealt, much less play it.

But somehow, change had happened. It had sneaked right past him. He wasn't sure of the precise day and time—only that one morning he woke up with the sweet smell of summer rain and roses filling his head and the most gentle and giving woman he had ever known by his side, and realized that the raw ache at the core of him that he had been sure would be there forever, was gone. Not that he had turned into a happy idiot overnight. But that hard nugget of pain, like a lead shot in his belly, wasn't there.

At first he'd tried to get it back. He *willed* himself to feel alone, to conjure that sharp sense of isolation that had been so acute that at times it had felt as if even the old wreck of a house didn't want him around. But it was no use. When Rose was around, it was beyond him to feel alone or isolated or anything other than lucky.

Thinking about how that particular rainy morning had played out kept him smiling to himself the entire time he was gathering his tools and grabbing a glass of iced tea to carry back to the porch. He could spare a few minutes before getting cleaned up, and this was one of his favorite times of the day. Mostly because Rose would be coming home soon, but also because it gave him a chance to sit by himself and look over the fruits of what was turning out to be a considerable amount of hard labor.

The truth was, he got a kick out of it. If anyone had told him he would one day be content to sit and contemplate a freshly mowed lawn or some wooden spindles that still needed painting, he would have been tempted to either shoot them or himself. But he liked seeing it come together, and was not at all daunted by how far there was to go.

The appraiser he'd hired made it clear that the place needed more than cosmetics to realize its full potential value. When Griff took a look at the figures John Lombardi had provided, he'd made up his mind on the spot to return Fairfield House to her former glory before doing anything else.

It was going to take time, and money. Money was not a consideration. In addition to the house, Devora had left him her small trust fund and some valuable stock, and he had arranged for that income to be used for the renovations. While cost wasn't a factor, quality was, and he was checking out firms as far away as Boston and Hartford because they were rated the best at what they did.

It was a pretty exciting venture...especially when compared to the past couple of years of his life. Which made it even more difficult to keep from talking it over with Rose. She knew he was doing some fixing up on his own, of course, and that he had plans for a new roof and paint job and to have the windows reglazed. It was Rose who mentioned that the house had its original "working" shutters and urged him to see if they could be made operational again. Listening to her talk about how his ancestors must have shut them as a buffer against the raging wind and sea during the worst hurricanes of the last century, made him, for the first time ever, feel a bond with those stodgy old relics whose photographs sat beside his on the piano. It made him feel as if he belonged.

Sometimes he longed to run an idea by her, to get her input on every detail. But he was afraid. Talking about the house would be like playing tag in a minefield. One slip and everything could blow up in his face.

Sometimes he longed to just come clean and tell her the truth about everything—the will and the house and the real reason he wanted to find the damn birds. But he was even more afraid of what might happen if he did tell her. Even worse than having things blow up in his face would be knowing he had only himself to blame.

Not that he could think who the hell else could possibly be to blame for any of it. He was the one who had let Rose believe he had no plans to sell Fairfield House, and who was continuing to let her believe it. At first it had seemed a harmless, expedient thing to do.

He couldn't recall his exact words from their first meeting, but someone with a flexible conscience could argue that *technically* he had not lied to her. You would have to be a lot more than *flexible,* however, to extend the same leeway to the all-out effort he'd made in the past few weeks to cover his tracks with attorneys and real estate agents and anyone else to whom he might have mentioned his intention—his firm, unwavering, impatient and pissed-as-all-hell intention—to sell. There was no way anyone could see that as anything other than what it was: the complete antithesis of the honest, open, intimate relationship Rose wanted, and believed they had.

Griff squeezed his eyes shut, but he still felt the heat from the late-day sun and the grinding of his own conscience. He hated having to keep something from Rose. But he couldn't risk telling her. Not yet, anyway. He was constantly reminding himself that there was no need to do anything rash. It would take a while to finish work on the house. Besides, his hands were tied until the other two birds turned up. After their initial good fortune, they'd had no luck and no leads. He almost smiled, thinking that at least there was that to be grateful for.

Sometimes he wondered what he would do if they *never* turned up. Legally, he wouldn't be able to sell the house, but

he could rent it out or sign it over to the town historical
society. Or he could just leave and forget about it, go back
to living his life the way he had been. There was an imme-
diate tightening around his heart which ruled out ever for-
getting anything about this summer in Wickford.

Maybe he could stay, he thought tentatively, testing the
possibility the way you'd test a frozen pond before skating
across it. He gazed again at the spindles, looking forward to
seeing them all freshly painted. He would use semigloss paint
on them, he decided. White, definitely, but nothing too stark.
The guy down at the hardware store had told him about a
place in Newport that specialized in mixing vintage paint
colors. Milk paint, it was called. Maybe he would drive over
there some day this week and check it out.

Maybe, while he was there, he would swing by the War
College and look into that consulting job. There was no way
he was going to be trapped behind a desk all day, but maybe
his former commanding officer had been telling the truth
when he said it wasn't that kind of job. It couldn't hurt to
check it out.

He told himself he ought to get up, go inside to get cleaned
up and see what there was in the kitchen to thaw, microwave
or grill, since it was his turn to make dinner. Reluctantly, he
got to his feet and stretched, aching, but not too badly. He
stayed a minute longer, standing on the porch and gazing out
at the ocean. He felt content with what he had accomplished
that day, and was already anticipating the evening and night
ahead. It was a good place to be.

Sometimes he didn't want to think about what lay farther
ahead. He didn't want to know how his movie would end.
Maybe because it was the kind you wished never would.

He'd showered and was pulling a navy-blue T-shirt over
his head, when he heard the sound of tires on gravel next
door, and smiled automatically. Rose was home. He glanced
at the clock in the hall on his way to the kitchen. She was
late. That was a lucky break for him. He'd sat on the porch
longer than he'd realized and still wasn't sure what he could

scrounge up and turn into something resembling dinner. And fast.

They'd fallen into the pattern of each cooking a night and then eating out on the third. Rose was constantly amazing him with grilled salmon marinated in lemon and dill, or incredible New England clam chowder. It was a while before he caught on that the reason she could turn out a genuine meal so quickly was that she started before leaving for work in the morning, either tossing stuff in her Crock-Pot or in some secret concoction to marinate all day.

Griff was willing to do his share on the food front, but he wasn't even close to the Crock-Pot or early-morning planning stage. Tonight he considered it a major feat to have the table set with chilled wine, a plate of cheese and an assortment of takeout menus by the time she appeared at the back door…bearing pizza.

"Don't tell me," he ordered, holding the screen door open for her and inhaling deeply. "Cheese, mushrooms, pepperoni and olives."

"Close. Artichoke hearts instead of olives this time. I just felt like artichoke."

"I'm very sorry to hear that," he responded, deadpan. "Have you considered therapy?"

"Ha-ha."

Grinning, he took the pizza box from her and put it on the table, then kissed her and kept on kissing her until she nudged him away, pointing out that, unlike him, the pizza was getting cold.

"You know, this is more proof that I lack sensitivity," he remarked when they were both pleasantly full and dallying over *just one more slice.* "If I were sensitive, as you accused me of being, it would really bother me that you outdo me with dinner even on *my* nights."

"I'm sorry," she said, not looking it. "What did you have planned for dinner tonight?"

"Something fantastic. And complicated. Real gourmet quality."

"Is that so?" She glanced around the spotless kitchen.

"It sure is. Something you would really love, too."

"Okay, Griffin, I know I'll regret it, but I'll bite. Tell me what it is."

"And ruin the surprise?" He shook his head. "No way, sweetheart. You'll just have to wait until it's my turn to cook again."

He made a mental note to himself to buy a gourmet cookbook first thing in the morning, scratched it and made a note to locate gourmet takeout.

"All right," she said, sighing. "But before my taste buds get their hopes up, at least tell me this much…is the main ingredient Cheez Whiz? Again?"

"Ha-ha. You'll have to wait and see." He carried their plates to the sink. "But just for the record, there is nothing wrong with Cheez Whiz. As a staple, it's right up there with Spam and marshmallow fluff."

"I rest my case. But as long as we're on the subject of surprises," she added, and stood to retrieve her canvas tote from where she had dropped it just inside the back door. She flashed him a mysterious smile. "I have one for you."

From her bag, she pulled a package about half the size of a shoe box. It was wrapped in black-and-white checkered paper and tied with shiny red ribbon. She placed it on the table in front of him.

"What's this?" he asked.

"It's a present," she replied, dragging her chair closer to his, her Mata Hari smile growing increasingly excited.

"It's not my birthday," he stated, eyeing it the way he would an explosive devise.

"It's not a birthday present," she shot back.

He glanced uncomfortably from the box to her. "I don't have a present for you."

"Sure you do." She ran her fingertip along his cheek and bottom lip, slowly, until he couldn't resist trying to suck it in deeper. She pulled away with a provocative smile. "And the sooner you open the package, the sooner I'm going to let you give it to me.''

Griff couldn't help smiling. Then he reached for the box and slid the ribbon off. He'd always rolled his eyes whenever someone received a wrapped present and declared it "too pretty to open." But this one was. Everything Rose did, she did with care; everything she touched she turned into something special and worth saving.

Inside the wrapping was a plain brown cardboard box, and inside the box were layers of tissue.

Deep inside, everyone has a catastrophe sensor, and Griff's was sounding a warning even before he peeled back the tissue and revealed the delicate porcelain bird. Somehow he managed to paste a smile on his face and appear normal on the outside, when inside he was cursing and pounding his fist and itching to throw the damn thing against the wall.

"Wow." It was the best he could do.

"Do you know what it is?"

"Sure. It's one of the birds." *One of those freakin', pain-in-the-ass birds that, one way or another, were destined to ruin his life.*

She laughed and gave him a quick hug around the neck. "Yes, but do you know which one?"

It looked to Griff pretty much like the one the guy from London had shipped to them, and all the others in the glass case in the parlor.

"At first glance, it looks to me like the..." He dragged the words out as his mind scrambled for the name of one of the missing birds. When it came to him, he nearly shouted it. "The Piping Plover."

Her smile was gentle. "Close. It's the Zebra Finch."

Griff actually looked at the bird for the first time and realized it had black-and-white stripes, like a zebra. "I guess I should have known that, huh?"

"I figured the paper would be a dead giveaway."

He glanced at the paper. Black-and-white stripes. He shrugged.

"This is…great," he said, then remembered to smile. "Really great. I had no idea you even had a line on another one. You haven't found the last one, have you?"

She shook her head, and his heart resumed beating.

"I'm afraid I may have some bad news on that score, but—"

"What kind of bad news?"

"First, let me tell you how I found this one, okay?"

Griff figured it was a rhetorical *okay,* so he listened, hiding his impatience, as Rose explained that she had seen an ad in a trade paper, made a phone call, and then, along with Maryann, driven to upstate Massachusetts to pick it up.

"That's…great," he said again. "So. What do I owe you?"

"Nothing. I said it was a gift, remember?"

"You can't do that. These damn things are expensive."

"I can do it if I want to," she retorted. Lowering her voice, she added, "And I want to. Really, Griff."

She laced her fingers through his and squeezed his hand. "I want to be part of this tribute to Devora," she told him. "It's little enough compared to all the help she gave me when I really needed her. I know this was your idea, but…" With a rueful smile, she continued, "That only makes me want to do it more. I want to be part of this *with* you. Please don't spoil it for me."

Griff's stomach felt weird. The rest of him didn't feel much better. Especially his tongue, which seemed to have doubled in size, making it impossible to say the words that wouldn't come, anyway. All he could do was sit here, and let her gaze at him as if he had invented sunshine, and feel every bit the lying, scheming bastard he was.

Chapter Thirteen

When he was sure he could speak in a reasonably normal tone, he said, "Hell, Rose, I don't know what to say."

"Say thank you."

"Thank you.

"You're welcome. And I have to admit, you were right," she added, her tone teasing, her smile so sweet and guileless that he wanted to cringe. She rested her palm against his cheek for just a few seconds. "It's obvious from your blasé reaction that you really are a totally insensitive lout, after all."

"I warned you."

"You did, and I refused to listen. I seem to have developed a latent penchant for living dangerously."

She didn't know how dangerously, Griff thought. She couldn't possibly. Her biggest fear going into this had been that he wouldn't like her breasts or the way she dressed, and that he would try to change her. Why would any man want to change her when she was perfect exactly as she was?

She'd been gutsy and honest with him about her ghosts, and he had banished them and watched her bloom as a lover, becoming secure and passionate and giving—never even suspecting he had a secret of his own. And that he wasn't nearly as gutsy or honest as she was.

Distracted by his own grim thoughts, he had to drag himself back to listening, as she said, "I guess now is as good a time as any to tell you the bad news about bird number three."

He wanted to groan. He'd forgotten they hadn't even gotten to the real bad news yet.

"You found that one, too, didn't you?"

She regarded him with long-suffering affection. "I said *bad* news, Griff. If I found it, I would have said I had good news, right?"

"Right. Of course." He nodded as if he weren't so caught in this web of his own weaving that he felt like he was strangling. "So you definitely have not found number three?"

"It's even worse than that, Griff. It might not be 'findable.' It's altogether possible the Boris Aureolis Piping Plover does not exist."

"You're kidding?"

She shook her head sadly. "It's true."

Griff let the news sink in, certain there had to be a catch somewhere. It couldn't possibly be this simple. He told himself to stay cool, thinking this must be how Moses felt when the Red Sea parted before him, presenting him with what appeared to be a clear path to a better place. He felt amazed, and grateful and blessed beyond belief, and at the same time a little uneasy about trusting those two giant walls of water enough to step between them.

There had to be a catch. There was always a catch. Wasn't there? He forced himself to refocus his attention on what Rose was saying.

"...and she's been collecting nearly as long as Devora."

"She's the woman who sold you the Zebra Finch?"

"Right. She was fiftyish, really nice—she even invited us to stay for dinner." As if sensing how badly he wanted her to get to the point, she sat up straight and continued. "Anyway, she's researched the subject extensively, even joined special Meissen Societies, and turned up lots of information about Aureolis and his work—both fact and rumor—that Devora didn't know. Which is surprising because Devora prided herself on being knowledgeable about the things she loved. Maybe she knew and just never mentioned it. Except, I tend to doubt that, since we were always discussing our collecting addictions."

"Rose, honey, the bad news you're about to tell me any second now, does it fall into the category of fact or rumor?"

She pursed her lips, her green eyes thoughtful. "Neither. It's in the category reserved for legends."

Legends. He was right, it wasn't going to be simple.

She regarded him pensively. "From your expression, I have the feeling you would prefer I save all the fascinating details about his mistress and the duel and the missing glaze formulas for another time and just stick to the facts. Am I right?"

"You're brilliant," Griff replied. "I'm sorry about rushing you, sweetheart, but this is really important to me."

Smiling that smile he'd been carrying around in his heart for weeks, she gave his forearm a squeeze. "Say no more. I understand completely what this means to you."

Want to bet? Griff thought, furious with himself for having allowed things to reach this point.

"The legend," began Rose, "is that Aureolis set out to make a series of twenty-four pieces—in other words, an even two dozen. But problems developed with one of his designs, something about the angle of the tail feather, and rather than take the easy way out and fudge a little to make the piece structurally sound, he insisted on scrapping the bird entirely and selecting another to replace it. Care to guess which bird didn't make the cut?"

"The Piping Plover," muttered Griff, sifting this new revelation through the dangerous maze of secrets and half-truths in his head.

"How nice! We're both brilliant. So, twenty-five original designs, but only twenty-four in the actual series. Maybe."

"Maybe?"

She nodded. "It's been a point of contention for over two centuries. Obviously, there was at least one original casting of the rejected model—more likely several. Supposedly the problem wasn't discovered until after the first painting and glazing was complete. And then more samples were probably made as Aureolis attempted to remedy it. It was only when he realized he couldn't fix it without compromising authenticity that he insisted on replacing it entirely."

"So what happened to the...what did you call them— samples?"

"Good question. Unfortunately, the answer depends on who you talk to. Factory records suggest that Aureolis ordered all of them destroyed. But here's where it gets really interesting. It seems the head honcho at the factory at the time suspected Boris was sleeping with his wife, which he wasn't—he was actually sleeping with the man's mistress..." She noted his expression and said, "But that's another story. Some collectors say that the boss-slash-iratehusband sold the samples privately, to strike out at the man he believed was cuckolding him and to cast a shadow on his reputation."

"Cuckolding?"

Rose shrugged. "I always wanted to use that word and never had the opportunity."

"The punch line, Rose," he prodded. "Get to the punch line. Is there a Piping Plover or isn't there?"

She lifted her hands in ambivalence. "There is and there isn't. The world of Aureolis fanatics is split just about down the middle, according to Dana. Some dismiss it outright, others consider it inferior work but wouldn't mind owning one of them if they do exist. Then there are those who believe the original samples still exist, but that one of them would be the quintessential piece for any Aureolis collector, because it represents the fragile nature of his art and his fierce drive for perfection.''

"Yeah, yeah," Griff countered, waving his hand impatiently. "But how many Piping Plovers are actually out there? And where? And can Devora's damn collection be considered complete without it?''

"Very few. Who knows? And technically, no. At least, I believe those are the answers, assuming I heard the questions correctly as you were barking them at me.''

He *had* barked at her. But only because he was anxious to know if this bizarre quirk of fate she'd uncovered was going to be his salvation or simply drag him in deeper.

He offered her an apologetic smile. "Sorry. I guess I'm just in a hurry to know where I stand. So if you wouldn't mind barking that last answer at me again, I'd be real grateful, ma'am.''

"How grateful?" she countered, matching his playful drawl with a seductive, heavy-lidded look that ordinarily would have him salivating.

"I'd rather show you," he told her. "Just as soon as we're finished here.''

"I'm going to hold you to that." Dropping the Mae West imitation, she continued. "I may have been exaggerating when I said it was *bad* news. It's closer to neutral news, sort of left up to your own interpretation. For instance…''

"Rose!''

"You're barking again.''

"Sorry. Just quit trying to cushion the blow and say it.''

"How do you know I was trying to—?''

"Because I know you," he said in a gentler tone.

She sighed. "Okay. According to Dana, who seems to know all there is to know on the subject, the answer to your question is no. Technically, the collection cannot be considered complete without the Piping Plover. Which we're about as likely to find as we are to drown in the Sahara.''

He sat silently, looking past her, as options and possibilities streamed through his head. Process data; take action. Everything in life was a simple two-step process for him. Always had been. There were no second passes in combat.

"That was a joke," Rose said, bringing his concentration to an end. "Drowning...the Sahara...?"

"I get it." He smiled, then laughed outright.

"Not *that* funny a joke."

He drew her closer. "I guess it was just the way you told it," he murmured as his lips settled on hers and lingered.

"Then you're not upset?" she whispered against his cheek, as he progressed to kissing her throat, nibbling her earlobe, making her eyelids flutter and her pulse race beneath her skin.

"Not at all."

"I worried you might be. Not that you should be. I mean, there's complete and then there's complete."

"And then there's real complete," he said, smiling, unbuttoning the top few buttons of her sleeveless dress and kissing her there, as well.

"I have an idea."

He grinned against the warm satin of her breast. "So do I."

"I thought you could..." She hesitated as he used his tongue on her sensitive flesh. Griff could feel the tremor that went through her, and it made him crazy. She continued in a rush, an edge to her tone as if she was determined to get it out.

Let her, thought Griff. He wanted her undivided attention tonight and he was willing to be patient. Especially in view of the weight she had just lifted off him.

"I think you should go ahead and donate Devora's collection to the Audubon Society according to plan, just the way she would have wanted. And I think you should also include a picture of the Piping Plover and a short explanation of the legend surrounding it."

"That still wouldn't make it complete." It sounded like an accusation even to his ears.

"Well, no," she agreed. "But I think it's the sort of thing Devora would have done, and since you're doing this in her honor…"

"You're right. I'll do it." At that moment he felt able to do anything, and wanted only to do this—make love to Rose without shadows and secrets hovering over him. The realization filled him with relief and a wired kind of energy.

The whole thing had been taken out of his hands. The collection could never be completed, at least not *technically,* and that was plenty good enough for him. He could never fulfill the terms of Devora's will. The house could not be sold. And he would never have to make a decision in that regard.

Best of all, however, now Rose never had to know about any of it.

Home free.

He straightened and started kissing her mouth all over again. He held her face in his hands and with featherlightness kissed her eyelids and the tip of her nose. Never had she seemed so fragile to him. In spite of her warmth and her eager response, he had the sensation of holding spun glass, and it made him more tender than he had ever been.

With one hand he undid a few more buttons and slipped his hand inside to wander over the soft curves of her belly and hips and bottom. His fingers skated along the lacy edge of her panties, and he smiled. One of his favorite things about undressing Rose was discovering what her panties looked like each day. Even when she was all denim and overalls on the outside, underneath she was pure silk and lace, pale colors, tiny satin flowers and ribbons; he could never make up his mind whether he wanted to rip them off her or kiss her right through them.

Right now, he wanted much more than he could manage to take standing in the middle of the kitchen. He reached for her hand and led her to big cushy old chair, which he knew from recent experience would accommodate them perfectly for what he had in mind.

He sat and pulled Rose on top of him. She moved easily, her muscles pliant, her expression dreamy. She smiled at him with lips that were red from his kisses and eyes heavy with desire.

When he cupped her breasts, she leaned into the caress, lowering her mouth to his for kisses that were long and lazy, drifting, open-mouth kisses that melted one into the next.

She drew back, her smile dazed now, and pulled his shirt over his head.

"I want to feel you against me," she whispered, moving to make that happen. "With nothing in between."

Griff skimmed his fingers down her back and along her thighs. When she trembled, it wasn't longing he felt, but tenderness, and when she opened his jeans, it wasn't an urge to take that reared up inside him, but an urge to give. He wanted to give Rose everything there was for a man to give a woman, more than he had known there *was* to give, more than he was sure he had in him.

"You're beautiful." His voice was husky. "So beautiful."

She looked at him as he said it, not flushing or averting her gaze as she had at first when he told her how amazingly perfect and astoundingly beautiful she was to him. She'd come to believe it. She'd come to believe *him*.

She touched him inside his jeans, and he groaned, the desire floating just beneath the surface becoming more insistent. Still looking into each other's eyes, they moved their hands, caressing, skimming, tantalizing. Desire became need and need became demand.

Griff worked his jeans lower. She pulled her skirt aside and lifted. He took her hips and drew her back down and onto him—a long, slow, sliding possession that made his head fall back and his eyes slam shut.

When he opened them, he was looking into a clear green lake, and through it, into the woman's heart beyond.

"I love you," she said.

It was not the first time she had said those words to him. She'd said them once before, blurted them, really, and immediately wished she could take them back. He'd seen it in her eyes.

That first time he hadn't said anything, either. He hadn't been sure what to say, or what he felt. So instead he'd kissed her to shut her up, and made love to her all over again so he wouldn't have to think.

This time he knew what he wanted to say. The words were everywhere inside him...everywhere but where he needed them to be—on his tongue.

He had never said *I love you* to a woman before. He wasn't sure he'd ever said it to *anyone* before. And he was sure he had never wanted to say it as badly as he wanted to at that moment.

Rose's gaze refused to waver, and still the words could not get past whatever had them locked at the back of his throat, making him feel as if he was about to choke on them.

Finally, she dropped a kiss on his mouth and moved her hips enticingly, drawing him back into the rhythm of mating. But those green lakes weren't as clear as they had been just seconds ago, and suddenly Griff realized she was moving without him.

"Damn." He moved her aside and got up, jerking on the zipper of his jeans and pacing a few feet away, keeping his back to her. His breath shuddered out of him. "Damn. I'm sorry, Rose."

"Don't be." He felt her hand on his back and then the warm pressure of her body as she snuggled against him. "These things happen. I—"

He exploded. "They don't happen to me. None of this has ever happened to me before." He pulled away and turned to face her, as she yanked her dress together and hugged herself to keep it that way.

"From the minute I met you things have been happening to me that never happened before...that I never *wanted* to happen before."

"Hold it right there," she said, looking less fragile and very angry. "If this has something to do with me saying I—

what I said, then let me make it clear that you don't have to say anything you don't want to say, or do anything you don't want to do. So if you're feeling some kind of pressure—''

He clasped her upper arms. ''That's just it…I do want to say it. For the first time in my life, I *want* to say it.''

Her expression didn't change.

He shut his eyes.

''Ouch,'' she said, and Griff realized he was squeezing his fists with her arms still inside.

''I'm sorry,'' he told her, rubbing the red marks gently before letting her go. ''Tell me again.''

It was an order, and Rose was about to tell him to go to hell, when she looked into his eyes and got a different message entirely. The look in his eyes was beseeching, and afraid. Typical. The man was great at barking orders and lousy at asking for what he needed.

''I love you,'' she said.

His eyes closed and slowly reopened, still full of longing. ''Again.''

She wanted to punch him, and hug him. She did neither.

''I love you, Griff,'' she said. ''You don't have to say you love me back. You don't even have to love me back. That's not the way it works.''

''That's the trouble. I don't know how it works, but I'm pretty sure I know a little about how it *doesn't work*. It doesn't work unless there's trust…and truth.''

Listening to him, watching his face, Rose's feelings shifted like the tide, from love and empathy, to confusion, and finally to dread. Her stomach muscles clenched so tightly they ached. It was the same feeling she always had in the House of Horrors, tensed and waiting for the next ghoul to spring at her from out of the darkness. This room wasn't quite as dark, but it suddenly seemed a lot darker than it had a few moments ago.

''There's something I have to tell you,'' he said. ''It's something I should have told you right at the start. I wish to hell I had, but back then it seemed simpler to…keep things to myself. I had no way of knowing it would come to matter so much. It never occurred to me that I…that you would come to mean everything to me.''

Ten minutes ago those words would have made her melt into a bigger puddle of mush than she already usually was around him. Now they only made her more anxious.

''What do you have to tell me?'' she asked.

''The truth, about why I was so desperate to get you to help me find the birds…and about why I came here in the first place.''

Rose watched his chest rise and fall, once, and again. She knew exactly how it felt to lay with her cheek there, to match her breathing to his.

She ran her tongue across her lips, but it didn't help. Her whole mouth was dry. She *felt* dry, like tinder waiting for the flames.

''You said you wanted to complete Devora's collection and donate it to the Audubon Society because that's what she always wanted—it was her dream. That's all true.''

''It's true that it was her dream, all right.'' His voice was taut, brittle. ''What I didn't tell you was that it was also an ironclad condition of her last will and testament.''

Her forehead wrinkled as she tried to understand.

Griff swallowed hard before spelling it out for her. ''Devora left me this house and everything in it, with the condition that I not sell as much as a box of matches until I completed her collection of birds.''

As she considered that, he continued. ''That's what I was alluding to whenever you'd pat me on the back for doing it and I'd say it wasn't my idea, or that I felt *compelled* to do it.''

''I thought you meant you were compelled out of a sense of loyalty…of love—and you knew that's what I thought.''

''Yeah, I knew it…and I felt like hell every time it came up.''

''You didn't do it for Devora at all,'' she stated, regarding him with disbelief and growing anger.

"Not entirely, not at first…"

"Not at all," she interrupted. "Otherwise, you would have done it sooner, instead of showing up out of the blue two years after the fact."

He didn't even attempt to explain, dashing Rose's small, stubborn, stupid hope that he would—that he *could.*

"So what made you come back now?"

He gave his head a weary shake, hooking his fingers inside the pockets of his jeans. "To get the lawyer handling her estate off my back once and for all. For two years he's been on me to do something about the house. An empty house is 'a liability and a potential hazard,' unquote. He was worried someone might break in or fall off the cliffs and get hurt."

"I see. So you decided that since you didn't have anything better to do, you'd get him off your back by coming here and…what, Griff? Why exactly did you come? Tell me your plan to eliminate this *potential hazard.* Did you come to stop the house from being empty? Or to sell it?"

"I never told you I was definite about staying," he reminded her.

"Yes, and you never said anything at all about selling. You just led me to *believe* you were staying…just like you led me to believe you were doing all this out of respect for Devora. You never *said* it, but you let me believe it… because you needed my help and you knew exactly what to say and do to get it." She lifted her hands to her face. "Oh, God, I can't believe I could be such a fool."

"Don't say that, Rose, please…" He moved toward her, and she backed away. "You can't believe that the only reason I—"

"Oh, but I do believe it. I believed all of it—hook, line and sinker. It's because I believed it…because I convinced myself it was proof that underneath all that *attitude,* you must be a decent guy…that's the only reason I agreed to help you in the first place…that's the only reason I—"

"Rose, give me a chance…"

"I did," she said, shuddering with the urge to get away. "I'm done."

Clutching her dress with one hand, she used the other to grab her sandals and bag. She could feel him following her, wanting to press his case, maybe to get one more night out of her before putting out the For Sale sign. Let him. She hoped he did sell it, and fast. She'd rather live next door to a...a strip mall than a liar and a user.

She pushed the screen door open and paused halfway out to glance back over her shoulder, wishing she had something sharper and more damaging to throw at him than the truth.

"You were wise to listen to that attorney, Griffin. He had the scenario dead right—someone *did* get hurt here."

Chapter Fourteen

Think. Griff knew there had to be a solution. He just had to think.

Unfortunately, all he was able to think about, as he sat in the glider on the porch, was how miserable he was without Rose, and how he had only himself to blame, and of all the things he could have said and should have said when he had the chance.

If ignoring his phone calls and his knocks on her door and the notes he'd tucked inside the flowers and pizza he attempted to have delivered to her, were any indication, she did not appear ready to give him another shot at explaining anytime soon. Appealing to her sense of humor, he'd even hung a white flag on her lamppost, where she was sure to see it when she left for work in the morning. She'd ignored it, and him.

He knew better than to corner her at work, but there had to be a way to get her to hear him out. He clung stubbornly to the hope that if he could get Rose to listen to what he had to say, she would forgive him. She might even understand, but being Rose, she would forgive him, anyway, and give him another chance. That's all he needed, one more chance. Because if he got it, he would never lie to Rose or hurt her again; he would take better care of her heart than he did his own.

He had messed things up from the moment they met, and it didn't lessen his self-disgust to note that his blunders had been predictable and could be chalked up to ignorance. He'd never been in love before.

He was now. He was in love with Rose Davenport and ready to tell her. If she would only stop pretending he was nonexistent and give him five minutes of her time. Ten minutes, tops. He had his speech all prepared, and he could deliver it without a single flub. He wasn't getting cocky, however. Rose was bound to be a tougher audience than a flock of seagulls. He had to allow for lapses in concentration and common sense when he was near her. Or worse.

What happened the other night had not been a mere lapse. It had been an outright debacle. Next time would be different. Next time he would start by telling her he loved her, and then explain the rest of it, along with all the things he'd figured out in four lonely days without her.

It didn't matter what he was ready to say, however, if the only person he wanted to say it to refused to hear.

He kept the glider moving with one foot. He did some of his best thinking sitting in that glider, on the front porch of a house he'd once held in contempt.

The methods of making someone listen that he was most familiar with—shouting and brute force—were not likely to work with Rose. Reasoning with her wouldn't be his first choice, either. She wasn't motivated by reason or practicality, but rather by her heart. All he had to do was to get her body to stand still long enough for her heart to hear him.

He halted the glider.

That was the answer. He had to come up with a way to

shock her into stopping and keeping still long enough for him to explain.

And if it didn't work... His mouth settled into a grim line as he pushed with his foot to get the glider going again. If it didn't work, he would just have to accept it. And come up with a Plan B.

"Your move."

"I know, Gus," replied Rose. "I'm thinking."

"Might help if you were thinking about dominoes."

"I *am* thinking about dominoes," she retorted, flashing him an indignant glance. She returned her attention to the tiles on the table before her and tried to recall the play she had been about to make. It was no use.

Lifting her head, her expression rueful this time, she shrugged. "Maybe I'm not thinking about dominoes entirely."

"That's a relief, because you're *playing* like it's not dominoes you're thinking of at all."

"Maybe we should call it a night."

"Maybe." Gus began picking up tiles. "Then again, maybe we ought to call it a night for dominoes and see if we can't put our heads together and hash out whatever it is that's got you looking as gloomy as a lost kitten."

"I am hardly a lost kitten," she informed him, hearing her own defensiveness. "Not exactly, anyway. I'm... I'm...oh, hell, Gus, I'm a mess."

His blue eyes regarded her with compassion, but not surprise. "Because of your spat with Griffin."

"Is that what he told you? That we had a spat?"

"No telling was necessary. I knew the moment I laid eyes on his sorry face what the trouble was."

"Well, I assure you it was not a *spat*," Rose responded. "At least, not to me. I was pretty sure you'd take his side, seeing as you two have become such great buddies lately. That's why I told myself I wouldn't even discuss it with you."

"We are buddies, Griffin and me, but you and I are buddies, too. Or so I thought."

"We are, Gus," she said, warmed by his reminder. "It's just hard for me to talk about this with anyone else when I'm not sure exactly what I feel myself."

"Does that include Griffin?"

"*Especially* Griff."

It hurt to just say his name. That was another reason she avoided discussing him; it was too pathetic to admit, even to Maryann. Especially to Maryann, she thought, though her friend was taking an uncharacteristic "wait and see" attitude toward Rose's plight. Her own attitude was to survive one moment at a time without reaching for a phone to call him...to hear his voice, to find out if maybe there was a good reason for what he had done, to ask him why. To give him another shot at breaking her heart.

She would not call. She would not crumble. She would not listen.

"I suppose that's the reason you've been playing deaf and blind around the fellow for the past week," Gus ventured.

"I suppose he told you that, too."

"That he did. Is that the truth of it?"

She shrugged. "It's true...which is more than I can say for most of what comes out of his mouth. Did he tell you he plans to sell Fairfield House?" she demanded, her voice rising. "And about Devora's will? That the only reason he had any interest in completing her collection of birds was because he had to in order to sell the house? And that he tricked me into helping him and into...being his friend," she concluded, her voice wavering at the end.

"He told me all of that, and more."

"I suppose he put a different spin on it, right?"

"Oh, I'd say the spin was the same—but that in his version you come out the loveliest saint who ever drew breath and him the devil himself."

"At least he got that right," she quipped. She wished

hearing it didn't make her go soft inside. ''Did he really tell it like that?''

''He did.''

''He didn't try to justify what he did?''

''Not a bit. He did what he did, and it's only sorry he feels for it.''

''Well, he should. It's not only me he tricked and lied to and used. He even had the folks here doing his bidding.''

Gus chuckled. ''And loving every minute of it—the ladies, anyway. I've a hunch they'd forgive him in a wink if you did.''

''It's not a matter of forgiving him or not forgiving him. I refuse to even get caught up in that nonsense. What happened, happened. It's over and done with, and I have no intention of giving that man another chance to disappoint me.''

''How about giving yourself another chance, Rosie? Are you against that, as well?''

''I'm not sure what you mean,'' replied Rose, placing the cover on the box of dominoes and getting up to put it away. She wasn't sure she wanted to know.

''A chance to be happy,'' Gus said, hitting her where she was most vulnerable. She *had* been happy with Griff... before she knew the truth about him.

''For a while, there,'' Gus was saying, ''you were happier than I've ever seen you. Maybe happier than you've ever been?''

''Maybe,'' she conceded, wishing the small room offered more to busy herself with. When minutes passed without another comment from Gus, she knew one wasn't coming.

''All right,'' she said, spinning to face him. ''Maybe I was happy, but it was all an illusion. And now I feel more miserable and alone than ever, and that's real.''

''He's hurt you badly. The man doesn't deny that, but he does regret it. As for miserable, I'm not sure which of the pair of you I'd give the prize for that.''

Rose dropped into her seat and leaned back, folding her

arms across her chest. "I told myself I would never be taken in by a man again, and I hate it. I hate myself for letting it happen and I hate Griff for doing it."

Tears filled her eyes and spilled out.

Gus pushed the tissue box toward her. "Mop your eyes."

As wretched as she felt, her mouth twisted into a smile and she made a sound halfway between a laugh and a sob.

"There," she said when she was done, "they're mopped." She sighed. "The truth is, I'm afraid, Gus."

"I know, Rosie, and you've a right to be. But you can't let fear take over so that you're afraid to even listen to what the man has to say."

"I did listen," she protested. "What more can he possibly say? Nothing that would change what he did."

"That's true enough. But you're missing the point, I think, and that's that he knows that he did hurt you, and if he had the chance to go back and do it over, he'd do it all differently."

"Is that supposed to make me feel better?"

"It can hardly hurt…if you think about what it means."

"Go ahead, tell me what it means," she said with feigned indifference.

"It means he's changed," Gus told her. "He's not the same man he was when he came here. Don't be rolling your eyes at me…. When you've lived as long as I have you'll see it's a fact. People change all the time. I've known the worst of men to change if they're given a reason to."

Her jaw lifted in a show of resistance. "It's easy to *say* you've changed. What guarantee do I have that he wouldn't do it again—or something like it—if I gave him the chance?

"None at all," replied Gus, calm and matter-of-fact as ever. "The same as you had the first day you met him, and the same as you would have sitting here now, if this spat had never happened."

It wasn't the first time she'd struggled to find the logic behind Gus's words. As she turned them over in her mind, he reached out to check the soil of the closest pot of dahlias.

"What guarantee do I have when I plant a seed that if I water the dirt and put it in the sun faithfully, something will sprout up? For that matter, what guarantee do I have that I'll grow a dahlia, and not a petunia or an onion?"

"All right, I get the point—there are no guarantees in life. But there are some things we can expect to happen based on knowledge and past experience and common sense...and maybe a little faith," she added. "*And* we can analyze a seed before planting it and be pretty sure whether we're going to get a flower or an onion."

"True enough. A pity, isn't it, that we can't saw open Hollis Griffin's chest and have a good long look at what's in his heart. We'd know for sure, then." His offhandedness didn't fool Rose one bit, and she found herself bracing to hear the follow-up. "At least we'd be sure unless he changed somehow, as folks have been known to do." His gaze was tender as it held hers.

"People are more complicated than seeds," she argued.

"That's just the reason I mostly prefer seeds. People change, Rosie. Griffin has changed. He says *you've* changed him."

"What if it's another lie?"

"What if it's not?"

"I don't know," she said, words that applied to more than what he'd just told her. They applied to her whole life at the moment. It was all this uncertainty and second-guessing that she wanted no part of. "And I'll never know...not for certain."

Gus didn't contradict her.

"The fact is, Griff only owned up to what he'd done when he realized he wouldn't be able to fulfill the terms of Devora's will and sell Fairfield House. When it no longer mattered." Her words were rapid and sharp, like gunfire. "For all we know, if he'd gotten his hands on the last bird, he'd have slapped a For Sale sign out front as fast as...as one of his stupid jets."

"Could be," said Gus with a half smile.

"And if I give in and he stays, and that bird happens to turn up a year from now, or ten, he could very well do the same thing." She sagged in her seat. "Maybe life *doesn't* hold any guarantees, but only a fool would step in front of a bus and *hope* it doesn't run over her. I'm through being a fool."

Gus nodded as if that was perfectly sensible on her part. He stood, pausing a moment to unbend his knees, then walked over to his closet. After rummaging inside for a minute, he returned holding a brown cardboard box tied with string. He blew a thin layer of dust off the top and placed it on the table.

"Open it," he instructed.

Curious, she did as he said, removing the string and lid. Beneath the dry, yellowed tissue paper was a Boris Aureolis Piping Plover in what looked to her to be perfect condition.

She gaped at it, then fired off a stream of questions. "My goodness, Gus, do you know what this is? Where did you get this? Do you have any idea how valuable—?"

"Whoa, ask me one at a time. I know it's one of those fancy birds Devora was so fond of. She brought that one here and left it…" He squinted into the distance. "Oh, I'd say not much more than a month before she passed."

"What for?"

He shrugged. "Safekeeping, I suppose. Devora did things her way and wasn't one to blab on about how or why. I suppose that's one reason we did so well for all those years."

Rose gave his hand a little squeeze. They had discussed his and Devora's "friendship" several times recently, and she knew it brought back bittersweet memories for Gus.

"She did warn me I should take good care of it, because it was worth more than my Buick. Back then, I thought she was pulling my leg," he explained, scratching his chin thoughtfully, "now I'm not so sure."

"Well, they're both antique collectibles in mint condition, so it might be a toss-up."

The diplomatic response made him smile. "It's a strange

world, Rosie. And it would seem our Devora is not through pulling strings in it. She told me I would figure out what to do with it sooner or later, and so I have.'' He nodded at the bird, which Rose had lifted from the box and set on the table in order to get a better look at the tail that had been causing problems for hundreds of years.

"It's yours now, Rosie. Take it and put him to the test. That way you *can* know for sure what he'll do." He patted her shoulder gently. "For today, at least."

Chapter Fifteen

Driving home, Rose considered her options carefully.

She could use the rare bird figurine safely tucked in her tote bag to—as Gus had put it—test Griff. Except, she hated just the thought of it. It made her feel…Machiavellian. Of course, the other obvious solution, thwarting Griff's plan to sell the house by keeping the bird herself, would make her feel like a thief, which she liked even less.

She was still grappling with the choice as she parked the truck and started down the brick walk. A stop sign was one thing; she would have to be more than preoccupied to miss the sign hanging on her back door. She would have to be blind.

In block letters, on the blank side of a four-foot piece of wrapping paper, she read, I HAVE GLADYS. COOPERATE AND NOTHING WILL HAPPEN TO HER. COME TO THE SHOP RIGHT AWAY. COME ALONE. Below that, on a line by itself, was the word PLEASE. It was signed Griff.

"I don't believe it," she muttered, hurrying inside to find that poor Gladys was indeed gone from her place on the hearth. Rose didn't bother looking anywhere else. Obviously, Griff had broken in and stolen…no, kidnapped…her flamingo. Her *cherished* flamingo.

She had a good mind to call the police, except that the way her luck was running, they'd send out Lyle Rancourt, who would remember Griff and her from the night he caught them necking in the truck, parked in front of the same shop where Gladys was being held captive, and fail to take the matter seriously. She sighed. She'd give a lot to see Griff being led away in handcuffs, charged with bird-napping and trifling with a woman's affections.

Rose's brows shot up. *Trifling with a woman's affections?* Where had that come from? The same place as the Piping Plover, she realized. *Devora.* That is precisely how Devora would regard the way her nephew had behaved toward Rose. She would consider him a devious, deceitful…scoundrel. And she would let him know about it in no uncertain terms.

And so would she, Rose decided.

Parking the truck behind the shop, she entered through the back door. Her first thought as she stepped inside was that the bowls of rose potpourri she'd scattered about were really doing their job. They smelled wonderful, almost like real roses.

Her second thought was the realization that the way her bones liquified and her tummy flip-flopped at her first sight of Griff in days was probably not a good sign.

He was sitting in a straight chair, tipped back on its rear legs, cradling Gladys in his arms.

Were *his* bones melting? she wondered. He smiled as soon as she walked in, and looked at her the way she'd seen couples look at each other when saying goodbye at an airport, as if soaking in enough of the other person to get them through the time they'd be apart.

Which signified nothing, she told herself firmly.

"Thank you for coming," he said.

"Did I have a choice?" Rose retorted, remaining by the door.

"Not really," he admitted without a smidgen of remorse. "I planned it that way."

"All right, I'm here. Hand her over," she ordered.

"Not until we've talked this out."

"I have nothing to say."

"Good, that will leave more time for what I have to say."

"You cannot possibly say anything I'm interested in hearing."

"In that case, close the door, have a seat and prepare to be bored."

She stared at him with all the disdain she could muster.

"Please, Rose."

Moving slowly, and only after a long, exasperated sigh, she did as he requested. "I want Gladys now."

He regarded her dubiously. "Forget it."

"Why? You wanted me to sit and listen, I'm sitting and listening."

"Why? Because I'd rather not have to chase you. Something tells me that even hauling a flamingo, you're faster than I am."

Rose leaned back, folded her arms and rolled her eyes. "I hope this isn't going to take long."

"That's up to you. I'm desperate enough to keep talking until you see things my way."

"We'll starve to death before that happens."

His mouth turned up at one corner in a manner so familiar and adorable, Rose had to struggle to maintain what she hoped was an aura of aloofness.

"Maybe that was a poor choice of words," he allowed. "I'm going to talk until you understand why I made all the mistakes I did, and agree to give me another chance."

"Heaven help us."

His smile deepened. "For my part, I'm counting heavily on exactly that."

Rose waited.

Griff gazed at her in silence.

Maryann's words wound through her head. *He moons at you…he moons and you flutter.*

She wasn't absolutely certain he was mooning at her now, but if mooning was made up of equal parts tenderness and raw hunger, he definitely was mooning. What's more, she was fluttering…her pulse, her muscles, the damn palms of her hands. Quickly clasping her hands together, she placed them on her knees and waited.

Nothing.

"Did you actually have something to say?" she asked finally. "Or can I go now?"

"I love you, Rose."

His voice was pitched low, like distant thunder, but the effect was more like a lightning bolt striking her heart, branding it with his words, whether she wanted them there or not.

"I love you, and I'm sorry for hurting you. It's funny, I thought I had a lot to say, but when I look at you, I realize that's all that matters. I love you more than I knew it was possible to love, and in ways I never knew existed. You're like…" He hesitated, a look of pain in his eyes. "Like part of me. The best part."

Rose's lungs ached from holding her breath; every muscle was taut. For the first time since she'd walked in, she allowed herself to really look at Griff, at his face, thinner than she remembered, lines etched around his mouth, dark shadows beneath his eyes. He looked both familiar and different. He looked, she realized, the way he had the first time he walked into her shop. Lost.

She felt shaky, inside and out.

"I should have told you I was in love with you that last night we were together. I *wanted* to. Badly. But I couldn't get the words out…just like I couldn't go on making love to you without telling you the truth, about everything. I knew if I didn't tell you then, it would be a repeat of my first mistake. It would be easier to let it go another day, and another, and then one day it would be too late to tell you and it would be between us forever." He shook his head, his grip on Gladys white-knuckled. "That's not the way I want it to be for us."

"We agree on one thing—you should have told me the truth a lot sooner," declared Rose, trying to hold on to the wrath and determination she'd walked in with. "You should have been honest with me from the start."

"If I had, would you have agreed to help me?"

She shrugged. "Probably not."

"Definitely not. You're nearly as attached to that house as Devora was. You'd have shot me down faster than the speed of sound."

"All right, I would have. That only proves that you intentionally set out to use me."

He whipped his fingers through his hair impatiently. "It wasn't like that...or maybe it was and I just didn't see it that way. Not at first, anyway."

"How did you see it?"

He thought it over, then shook his head resignedly. "The way I saw everything up until a few weeks ago...the way it suited me to see it, whatever way best served my purpose at the moment. I figured it was harmless since you were a stranger, it was none of your business what I did with the house, and I was paying you well." He gave her a small, quick, rueful smile. "I guess that pretty much describes using someone."

"I guess. And even if it was all right to use a *stranger,* I didn't stay a stranger for long."

"Exactly," Griff countered, becoming more animated. He placed Gladys carefully on the table beside him and leaned forward. "When you became a friend, it become harder to tell you. By the time you became my lover, it was impossible. I felt trapped...you know, the old tangled web routine."

Rose wanted to smile, but didn't.

"I woke up one day and realized I wasn't so sure I still wanted to sell. I wasn't sure of a lot of things. So, I simply didn't think about any of it. It was amazingly easy to do, because all I wanted to think about was you.''

He kept his eyes on her face, silently begging for a small sign of understanding, which Rose refused to give him.

"When you told me that bizarre story about the last bird, all I could think was…I'm off the hook, home free. It was out of my hands. I could never sell, so I never had to know what I would do if faced with that decision…and you would never have to know any of it.''

"That's true," she acknowledged, acutely aware of the weight of her tote bag against her leg, and the opportunity it held. Anytime she wanted, she could put Griff back on that hook. Then he would for sure know what he would do, and so would she.

"And I guess you figured that as long as you were forced to keep the house, you might as well get the summer out of it, and have some fun with the silly woman next door. I hope you weren't looking for a challenge, since I turned out to be so pitifully easy to seduce.''

"There's nothing pitiful about you," he declared. "And I never thought of you as silly, either. A little wacky now and then, but ironically, that's one of the first things about you that I fell in love with. There are at least a million others, most of which will sound pretty cliché and corny…like the way your smile lights up a room, and the way you can transform some worthless piece of junk into something beautiful and the way you manage to find magic in every moment of your life.''

Almost absently, he kneaded the spot just above his left knee with the heel of his hand.

"Why don't you stand up and stretch your leg if it's bothering you?" she ventured, trying to appear uninterested.

There was a hint of satisfaction in his smile, which Rose chose to ignore. "Thank you for caring.''

"I don't," she retorted. "I just hate it when you clench your teeth and get beads of sweat on your forehead, so I thought I'd head it off.''

He got to his feet without commenting, stretching his left leg before taking a few steps. In her direction, unfortunately. She was holding her own so far, but if he touched her, all bets were off.

"From the beginning, it seemed to me as if you lived in a different world than the one I lived in—a better world somehow—and when I was with you, I got to live there, too." He shrugged. "How was I to know I'd like driving senior citizens to auctions, and learning from Gus how to plant a garden, and hanging out at the hardware store on Saturday morning, discussing drill bits and pine bark mulch."

He moved closer, leaning against the wall beside her so that the only thing between them was her tote bag. Fitting, she thought.

"I've changed my mind about almost everything since I met you, Rose. Of course, I have no way to prove that."

I do, she thought, half wanting to pull the Piping Plover from her bag and let him prove it right that instant. Half of her not wanting to... What? Know the truth? Or put him to the test?

"I've worn out millions of brain cells trying to think of some way to make you believe I'm telling the truth," he continued. "This is the best I could come up with."

He reached behind him for a manila envelope and handed it to her.

Rose stared at it, her expression wary. "What is this?"

"Open it and find out."

She opened it as if it were one of those toy boxes containing a coiled wire snake, waiting to spring. No snake. Only a couple of papers—one new, one very old, yellowed and brittle.

"What...?" Her voice trailed off as she read the statement dated the day before, then glanced at the older document just long enough to realize that it was the deed to Fairfield House.

"It's yours," Griff told her. "Lock, stock and windowpane. All legal and notarized. You see, I can't sell the house, but I am free to give it away if I choose to. And I do.''

"What am I supposed to do with it?" she asked, utterly astounded.

Griff grinned and shrugged easily, as if he'd shaken off the weight of the world...or at least an acre or so of it. "Whatever you please...live in it, sell it—though the attorney suggests you hold off on that until he does some more checking into it—turn it into a museum if you like."

"This is absurd," she declared, carefully returning the documents to the envelope and standing to hand it back to him. "You can't *give* someone a house. I can't accept it. And even if I could, I wouldn't do any of those things. You still don't get it, do you? Devora wanted Fairfield House to stay in your family forever."

"I do get it...now." His smile was dauntless. "And I've got it covered. Marry me, Rose. Marry me and help add to the Fairfield ranks."

Rose was speechless, panicked, trembling, thrilled.

"I intended to do a better job of proposing," he told her, taking her hand, kissing it tenderly and pulling her toward the front room of the shop. "*The Guide for Grooms* recommended—"

She had to interrupt. "*Guide for Grooms?* Where in the world...?"

"The bookstore in North Kingston. Go ahead and laugh," he urged, as she did exactly that, the panic and trembling giving way to a feeling that was like fireworks going off all through her. "There's a lot of valuable information in that little book. Such as making sure to use both poetic language *and* the Grand Gesture if you want your proposal to be foolproof...and memorable."

They'd slowly made their way in the darkness to the center of the shop. Still holding her hand, Griff turned on a light, and Rose's shock at being handed the deed to Fairfield House was dwarfed by a new one.

"What is all this?" she asked, gazing around, wide-eyed.

She inhaled deeply, suddenly understanding why the scent of roses had been so strong, and so authentic, when she first walked in.

"This," Griff said, pointing to the bed where they had made love for the first time, now completely covered with long-stem red roses, "is a bed of roses." Waving his hand at more roses in what looked like every vase in the shop, he added, "the rest is because I wasn't sure how many roses you needed to make a bed of them. I didn't want to run short and ruin the Grand Gesture."

As Rose stared at the bed in amazement, he put his arm around her shoulders, lightly. When she didn't resist, he pulled her close to his side. "I can't promise you that living with me will always be a bed of roses, but I figured it couldn't hurt to start out in one."

That drew her attention from the blanket of lush, velvety crimson. Griff wrapped both arms around her as she looked up at him, laughing, tears running down her face, feeling so overwhelmed with happiness that it was an effort to speak.

"I have...one word...for you," she said, swiping the back of her hand across her eyes until he stopped her and kissed her tears, instead. *"Thorns."*

He flashed a grin worthy of the devil himself and held up his hands for her to see the dozens of tiny puncture wounds. "I swear to you, I didn't miss a single one."

Her gaze shifted to the bed of roses, her smile unfurling slowly. "In that case..."

They landed on the bed still holding each other. It felt decadent and smelled glorious.

Griff cradled her face in his hands and kissed her as if they'd been apart for years instead of a little more than a week. When he paused, Rose turned her head to rain kisses on his palms.

"Does this mean—?"

"Yes," she interjected. "Yes, yes, yes. Yes to adding to your family ranks and to Grand Gestures and to spending the rest of my life with you...in whatever bed is handy."

"Starting with this one."

"Starting with this one," she concurred. "I love you, Griff."

"I love you, Rose." He touched her cheek, a look of wonder on his face, then he turned out the light.

Only once, for a matter of seconds, did Rose give any thought to the contents of her tote bag. First chance she got, she would drive out to Willow Haven and return the bird to Gus—and invite him to the wedding. He could decide what to do with the Piping Plover, as Devora had intended. Maybe someday he would bequeath it to Griff or directly to the Audubon Society. It didn't really matter. It was beautiful and rare and the stuff of legends, but it couldn't tell her anything her heart didn't already know.

*   *   *   *   *

If you enjoyed this story by Patricia Coughlin look out for The Cupcake Queen *in October 2003. Only from Silhouette Special Edition.*

SILHOUETTE®
SPECIAL EDITION™

AVAILABLE FROM 15TH AUGUST 2003

THE HEART BENEATH Lindsay McKenna

Morgan's Mercenaries

As Lieutenant Wes James and Lieutenant Callie Evans raced to save victims in an earthquake-ravaged city, past pain kept Wes from surrendering his heart. But he ached to make Callie his...

MAC'S BEDSIDE MANNER Marie Ferrarella

Blair Memorial

Dr Harrison MacKenzie wasn't used to women resisting him—but feisty nurse Jolene DeLuca's flashing green eyes told him to keep away. He was captivated...but could he convince her to trust him?

HER BACHELOR CHALLENGE
Cathy Gillen Thacker

The Deveraux Legacy

Businesswoman Bridgett Owens wanted to settle down—but irresistible bachelor Chase Deveraux was not the sort of man she wanted to marry. Until a passionate encounter changed everything...

THE COYOTE'S CRY Jackie Merritt

The Coltons

Falling for off-limits beauty Jenna Elliot was Bram Colton's worst nightmare—and ultimate fantasy. But now that she was sharing his home, he couldn't ignore the intense passion between them...

THE BOSS'S BABY BARGAIN Karen Sandler

Lucas Taylor only married his secretary Allie so that he'd be able to adopt a child—but a night of passion resulted in pregnancy. Could he overcome his past and keep the love he'd always longed for?

HIS ARCH ENEMY'S DAUGHTER Crystal Green

Kane's Crossing

Rebellious Ashlyn Spencer was the daughter of Sam Reno's worst enemy...yet she melted Sam's defences. Could the brooding sheriff forget her family's crimes and think of a future with her?

Maitland Maternity

Where the luckiest babies are born!

For the Sake of a Child
by Stella Bagwell

A marriage on the brink... A little boy in need...
A family in the making?

Drake Logan was a risk-taker, but not when it came to his wife's life! He has never stopped missing Hope. But he is sure he is right, that they shouldn't have children. Even though she is just as sure he is wrong!

Hope Logan is delighted that Drake is coming home for his little nephew's short visit. The little boy adores him and she is hoping it might at least give them a chance to talk about the baby issue. But talking is not all they end up doing and their temporary reunion could have unexpected consequences...

AVAILABLE FROM 15TH AUGUST 2003

▲ SILHOUETTE®

Sensation™

Passionate, dramatic, thrilling romances

ALL THE WAY Beverly Bird
A ROYAL MURDER Lyn Stone
SERVING UP TROUBLE Jill Shalvis
ALL A MAN CAN ASK Virginia Kantra
FRIEND, LOVER, PROTECTOR Sharon Mignerey
THE TRUTH ABOUT ELYSSA Lorna Michaels

Intrigue™

Danger, deception and suspense

GYPSY MAGIC York, Voss Petersen & Rosemoor
PREMEDITATED MARRIAGE BJ Daniels
TOMMY'S MUM Linda O Johnston
DARE TO REMEMBER Debra Cowan

Superromance™

*Enjoy the drama, explore the emotions,
experience the relationship*

ZOEY PHILLIPS Judith Bowen
WHAT'S A MAN GOT TO DO Lynnette Kent
STRAIGHT FROM THE HEART Linda Warren
MATERNAL INSTINCT Janice Kay Johnson

Desire™ 2-in-1

Two intense, sensual love stories in one volume

SEARCHING FOR HER PRINCE Karen Rose Smith
THE ROYAL TREATMENT Maureen Child

ALL IN THE GAME Barbara Boswell
DO YOU TAKE THIS ENEMY? Sara Orwig

THE SHERIFF & THE AMNESIAC Ryanne Corey
COMANCHE VOW Sheri WhiteFeather